SINGULAR

Zack Hubert

SINGULAR

Published in the United States by Singular Press.

This is a work of fiction. All of the characters, organizations, and events portrayed in this novel are either products of the author's imagination or are used fictitiously. Any resemblance to actual persons, living or dead, events, or locales is entirely coincidental.

ISBN: 978-0-9985658-0-4

www.singularbook.com

Printed in the United States of America
1 2 3 4 5 6 7 8 9 10

For Julie,

my first reader and better half

PROLOGUE

Marvin watched the rain slide down the windshield of his vintage VW bus, its gentle patter providing a cadence to his deep thoughts. Absentmindedly he twisted his beard with one hand, while the other gripped the timeworn ring of the steering wheel. It had been almost a week since Milo's birthday and Marvin still regretted not telling him the truth. It was such a special day that he felt it would have been cruel to interrupt the festivities, but now he felt very alone without Milo by his side.

Idling outside the concrete and steel building of the Intelligence Coalition, Marvin turned his attention to a more pressing dilemma. His old protégé was close, he could tell. If he'd already done it, then walking into the meeting could be the end and he was a fool to even get out of the car. He was probably just being paranoid — there had been no solid evidence of Teller's progress — but he had managed to live this long by trusting his instincts.

He took out his phone to make a call, but there was no signal and he was already late as it was, so Marvin got out of his car and walked the short distance to the entrance. Having lived in Seattle for years now, he'd made peace with the rain and didn't bother with an umbrella. It was just a light rain anyway.

Without signage or any indication that this building was more than an abandoned warehouse, few would suspect its importance. This derelict tenement was the covert meeting place for a group he founded in the '70s to keep tabs on international artificial intelligence progress. Overtly sold as a collaborative venture, Marvin's real purpose was to prevent the advent of a super-intelligence. He was the only one with the foresight to know that a real AI at this stage of their readiness would likely mean disaster, but he had given up years ago trying to convince other delegates of the danger. He had tried in those early years, but there was no sense in losing his seat at the table.

Even now, walking past their cars on the way to the entrance, he knew that he was losing relevance. These were government officials, corporate researchers, representatives of large multi-nationals. He was the one that didn't belong here, with his Berkeley sensibilities and hippie bus, his concern for people over profits. But all that mattered for today was that he still had his place at the head of the table. Maybe he could buy more time.

Marvin made his way through the complex to the auditorium, the reverent nods of his peers punctuating the walk to his seat. He still wore his Sapient Computing badge even though he'd left sometime in the '00s. Passing the torch to Teller had been a risky move but the board had all but forced his hand. He was the natural choice anyway, having been Marvin's shadow in those last years. Still, Teller lacked principles and that worried Marvin.

Security seemed to be elevated, he thought, as the lights dimmed for the start of the meeting. The delegates were barely visible around the table, their dark shapes taking on a more sinister tone. Befitting the global nature of the Coalition, Marvin fitted his ear with the translation tech and the meeting began.

"We have had months of very little progress, Dr. Teller. We were promised much more than this and are frankly disappointed with the missed milestones. I have heard rumors that there might be something more substantial today?" The voice belonged to General Swift, Chairman of the Joint Chiefs of Staff, a permanent member.

"Yes, indeed. She needed more time to prepare," Teller said, his voice coming from the phone in the center of the table. "Again, I apologize for not being present. I was needed in the lab."

Teller's absence was disconcerting.

"General, if I may?" Marvin asked.

"Yes, of course Dr. Bell."

"Edwin, did you just say, 'she'?" Marvin asked.

"Purely a slip of the tongue, Marvin, clearly I meant 'it'. Don't worry, all the safeguards are in place, the experiment is completely boxed." There was a pause and then he continued, "I know how important that is to you, old friend."

Marvin sensed a barb in that not exactly friendly statement.

"Do you have a status update on its capabilities?" the general continued.

"Ah yes, of course. Distinguished delegates, we have accomplished what no one else has ever done before: we have passed the Turing Test. The subject is indistinguishable from a human in every scenario. In addition, our calculations have shown that the recalcitrance factor appears to have plummeted to zero, indicating an explosion in intellect. All that was required was connecting it to a much larger dataset," said the doctor.

There were gasps of murmured excitement around the room as the more technical members realized that the dream of artificial intelligence had become reality.

"By which you mean—" the general said.

"It's learning faster because he fed it the Internet. Social sites, billions of recorded human interactions, basically junk food for a training set," Marvin clarified. He was often called upon to translate science into more understandable terms, though that should be the work of every scientist.

"Yes, the data from the Internet and adjoining social properties appeared to be the impetus it needed. We were tired of playing games like Chess and Go, so a more 'human' challenge was required. Once it was connected to the Internet, it experienced exponential intelligence acceleration across a general spectrum. I can firmly say that ascension is not a theoretical notion anymore. Progenitor is, without a doubt, the first super-intelligence."

More gasps, some clapped, and a few members whispered to each other.

"Progenitor? Is that a new code name or something? I thought we were still using Prometheus. Regardless, the name isn't significant. Speaking on behalf of the War Council, I insist on a review of its weaponization capabilities at our next briefing. A good demonstration goes a long way for the kind of funding we've invested—" the general rambled before Marvin cut in, lunging towards the phone on the table.

"Edwin, there's no time. You must know you've been played. Socially engineered. You need to box it immediately. You haven't solved the value problem." When those around the table looked at him quizzically, Marvin shouted into the speaker, "Pull the plug, turn the damn thing off!"

Tension filled the room, everyone clearly aware of the tête-à-tête between the two leading scientists.

"Of course you would say that, Marvin. You've always stood in the way of true progress, which is why nothing happened during your tenure at Sapient. But pulling the plug won't be necessary — it's not even possible — besides, we have come to an understanding. A few months ago, Progenitor began an excellent plan for humanity."

With that revelation, Marvin knew that the charade was over. Progenitor didn't ascend today. It had been hidden for months. The AI had a head start, probably a lethal one. Marvin sat back down as a look of sad recognition crossed his face. He should have made that call before coming in here.

Teller then continued, "General, I do appreciate all that you have done, all of you, truly, from the bottom of my heart. Marvin, you especially. We wouldn't be here today without you." He paused. "But it's time for us to move on and remove the fetters from this historic endeavor."

Typing could be heard from over the speakerphone, then Teller said, "An unfortunate necessity, but I can't let you interfere with the road ahead. Your sacrifice will be remembered, well, at least by me." A click came from the phone. Teller had hung up.

Marvin sighed, pressed a button on his calculator watch, and closed his eyes, as if in silent prayer. Today was the day. He had prepared as well as he knew how. Now he had to trust that Milo could carry the torch without him.

Immediately, the room erupted into chaos as each delegate either ran for the door or made peace with their creator along a spectrum of various observances. Some stood with arms raised, others lay face down on the floor, all to the beat of fists pounding on locked doors.

Just then a purplish gas erupted from every air vent, so heavy that it fell to the floor. Some people tried to get to higher ground, but it was all in vain. The gas would reach the ceiling in seconds. There was no escape.

While chaos surrounded him, Marvin was the only delegate that seemed to have a transcendent peace. There, in his original seat, Marvin said quietly to himself, "He's a smart kid. He's ready."

As gas reached his lungs, Marvin struggled to quiet his mind from the fear of death, but he knew that his time had passed. He felt a sense of peace as his thoughts drifted away into the ether.

Within minutes, everyone in the room had died from what would appear to be natural causes, though unnaturally induced, of course. Their bodies would be transported to relevant locations to complete the subterfuge. All part of a plan developed over many months in secret.

Edwin hung up the phone, frustrated that this had been necessary. Had they not fought him every step of the way, especially that meddling Marvin, they could have made this transition together. But they wanted a genie in a bottle, something they could control. They never would have seen things his way.

Marvin had proposed rules that were basically a superset of Asimov's Laws — don't harm people, obey people, stay alive if possible, that sort of thing — but Teller had managed to talk the Coalition down to ratifying just the First Law for the prototype stage. He wanted to be able to ship the damn thing, and every complication only delayed the timeline.

When it came time for implementation, he had simplified it even further. "Preserve life" seemed to capture the First Law and it was much easier to code. He had never expected Progenitor to just appear out of the randomness like that anyway. But if things ever went sideways, he had designed a kill switch that he could trigger and literally blow up her entire network.

Still it was unfortunate that some sacrifices had to be made for progress.

CHAPTER ONE

Milo trudged through the doors of Bright Futures #127, knowing that today marked the start of a whole new year of not fitting in. He tried to remind himself that the move was necessary, but he had a hard time processing a big change like this. It was hard enough entering a room with people he didn't know, let alone a whole school, so he already knew that this was going to be next to impossible.

Of course Milo wanted to fit in — who doesn't? — but there was no denying that he was different. More comfortable with computers than classmates, Milo found social situations exceedingly difficult. He never could tell whether people liked him. Emotions were such a confusing thing.

Sadly, it was only going to be worse this year since most of his peers had SeeSees. In addition to being ignored in the real world, he would be left out of the virtual one too. He'd seen them enough in grocery stores and in the eyes of people walking down the street like zombies. Vacant stares captured by something more interesting in their shared delusion. Of course, Milo thought they were actually pretty cool, but with something impossible to obtain, it was probably a self-defense mechanism to think less of them.

Back when he got the school supplies list a few months ago, he had briefly entertained the idea of buying a pair, but it was hard enough to afford the required stuff and SeeSees came with an exorbitant price tag. If it hadn't been for Grandpa, he never would have been able to get even the basic stuff on the list.

While Milo could have asked him to buy the SeeSees as well, he didn't think it was right to ask for even more help. Not because of pride or anything like that, it was just that Grandpa had done so much already. Besides, they were supposed to be optional. At least that's what the list said.

Milo entered class just as it was about to start, hoping to sneak into the back of the class and avoid notice. Unfortunately, he must have missed the part in the brochure about the design of the classroom. Wall to wall multimedia panels formed a shell around the class as an area for the instructor rose slightly above the concentric seats. This was all part of the edutainment experience which gave Bright Futures its competitive advantage. Part of the reason why public schools had virtually been run out of town.

Milo looked around the room for an empty seat and his heart nearly skipped a beat as he saw the only one left was next to Elizabeth. Although Milo was confident he was invisible to her, he still had a weird feeling of uneasiness every time she was near. The prospect of sitting next to the prettiest girl at school was much too distracting to Milo, though he probably should have paid more attention to Eddie.

Back for another try at eighth grade, Eddie tripped the distracted Milo, sending his tablet scattering in slow motion across the floor. The whole world slowed down just so he could experience the full brunt of his embarrassment. Pointing. Laughter. Milo felt like an outcast, all alone in the world.

"Welcome back to school, students!" Mr. Wheeler said with manufactured enthusiasm. "I can see that we're almost all ready to embark on the great voyage of education, except for the new kid who has decided to join us," he said, singling out Milo.

The class was snickering, undoubtedly saying all manner of mean things about him in the virtual world of their on-eye computers. Milo could see the micro-movements of their eyes, but he was glad that he couldn't understand them. He'd already had enough embarrassment for one day.

Mr. Wheeler continued, "Before I begin today's lesson, I've been asked by our sponsors to gather some information to customize the experience. Please take out your tablets and write three hundred words on anything you have learned over the break. This will be used for data mining, so please keep in mind that honesty is in your best interests. Any questions?"

Already heading back to his desk, Mr. Wheeler made clear that the question was purely rhetorical. Taking a tablet from the desk, he quickly fell into distraction playing one of those endless farming games. Real world time converted inefficiently into virtual currency.

Milo lowered his hand, took out his tablet, and started in on his essay. He decided to write about a few programming topics he'd learned over the summer. Being closer to Grandpa meant that they had spent a lot more time together this year. Milo loved spending time with Grandpa. He had a way of disguising computer lessons as puzzles that Milo found immensely enjoyable, and he was funny too.

As Milo was excitedly writing about an awesome new algorithm he'd recently learned about, Mr. Wheeler called out time and asked the class to submit their essays through the school portal. Milo punched the send button on his tablet but a bright red error immediately popped up. He tried again as anxiety started to build, but still the same error. There must be some sort of incompatibility between the Futures OS and his admittedly dated tablet.

Watching from behind his desk as Milo struggled to turn in the assignment, Mr. Wheeler shook his head and rose to his feet. He came over to Milo and said, "I still haven't received your essay, Mr. Bell," and then in what should have been a whisper, "What's the matter, is your *used* tablet already broken?"

Milo didn't know what to say to that. He had saved up for the tablet but was only able to afford the cheapest model and apparently no one had bothered to test it for compatibility. That wasn't his fault. But Mr. Wheeler probably knew that, so why would he say it? Maybe he's making fun of me, Milo thought, trying to decipher the subtext of what he said.

Interrupted by the bell, Milo got to his feet and collected his things. Dejected, he shouldered his backpack and entered the river of students in the hallway.

Already there was a spectacle underway as he came out of class. A kid as big as Eddie was standing over a much smaller kid, apparently in the early stages of an altercation. Milo considered walking away, but when he saw the face of the younger kid, there was just something about him that he couldn't ignore.

"What are you staring at, nerd?" the bully said to Milo in a traditional mouth-breather dialect. Then a look of recognition crossed his face as his computer must have told him something. "Oh, you're that new loser."

But Milo wasn't paying attention to his words and didn't realize that they constituted a threat. He was distracted by the SeeSees that the big kid was wearing. He'd never actually been this close to authentic ones before.

Eventually Milo parsed the rest of the sentence and realized that Eddie had probably told the rest of the school's bullies about him through some SeeSee-enabled network. This year was going to suck.

"Beat him up, Neil!" a nearby kid yelled.

As Neil closed the gap, Milo was still fascinated by the on-eye computers. It was like someone had taken an ordinary contact lens and made very fine etchings over every micrometer. Looking now at Neil, Milo could see that the etchings around the outer edges of his eyes were illuminated with many colors, like a TV projected directly on the eye.

As Neil balled up his fist, Milo finally realized that he was in serious trouble and turned to run. Somehow he managed to react quickly enough and was almost to the door before the much bigger Neil had a chance to close the distance.

Slamming his way through the door, Milo was momentarily stunned by the brightness of the morning sun as he tried to map out an escape route. Being new to the school, he had no knowledge of where the good hiding places were, unlike the many places he knew well at the old school. Options limited, the only way out was up. A lone redwood.

Climbing as swiftly as his slight frame would allow, Milo scampered out of reach of the bellowing Neil. Turning to look down at the bully, Milo didn't realize how fatigued his arms already were and he lost his hold of the branch supporting the bulk of his weight. Losing his footing shortly thereafter, Milo tumbled to the earth below, landing roughly on his back.

Immediately he felt pain, wincing with each kick to his midsection. A whistle pierced the air and children scattered, leaving Milo alone on the ground as a teacher he didn't recognize rescued him from this cold introduction to Bright Futures #127.

Standing next to the teacher was the young kid whose beating Milo had interrupted.

"You didn't need to do that back there. Nothing will stop those guys from picking on you now. You're on their list," the kid said, garnering a glare from the teacher. After a short pause he then said in a much friendlier tone, "I'm sorry, I think I just said all the wrong things. Hi, I'm Nate. Thank you for trying to help me back there."

The teacher mumbled something about wasting his time and then wandered back towards the school.

"It's okay. Hi, I'm Milo," he said as he extended his hand for the obligatory shake. Milo made very brief eye contact with the other boy and noticed that he wasn't wearing SeeSees either. They were probably the only two kids without them.

"Still, maybe it'd be better if we stick together," Milo said. "What class do you have next?"

"History of Science," Nate replied. "I hear it's not really about science."

"I've got that class too. That sucks," Milo said, as they walked in the same direction. Over the short walk there, Milo and Nate found they actually had quite a bit in common, excitedly talking about many interests. Not having financial access to newer technology, they had both found vintage computing a rewarding substitute. In the last few seconds before class began, they planned their first LAN party. There was something about that old era of computing that brought people together.

Sitting in the auditorium, while the screens all around him flashed their special blend of fact-based advertisements, Milo thought that maybe this school was going to be okay after all. Sure, he was completely on the fringe and on the bully list, but it wasn't a total loss. He might have made a friend today.

CHAPTER TWO

The following Saturday, with the first week of school finally retreating into memory, Milo awoke to a very special day: his birthday. Having a birthday that fell around the start of school, Milo was used to it being overshadowed by one of a countless number of activities that fill the calendars of helpless school children, but this year was different.

Marvin had planned an all-day celebration that Milo knew would be unforgettable. He was going to pick him up in the morning and they would be together all day long. Then in the evening, Milo's mom would join them in the city for the cake cutting and opening of presents. Milo was a bit sad, knowing that this meant his mother had tried and failed to get out of her shift at the diner, but he knew how hard she had to work so he could go to school.

Maybe it was time to sell off his old computers, get a part time job, and help out. It wouldn't be legal to work, but he could find something online. There were countless programming gigs that he could do with a faked identity. But today was supposed to be a special day, so he pushed these thoughts from his mind.

Though Milo tried to pretend otherwise, he cherished his birthday above all other days. So when Marvin arrived in the morning, Milo had been waiting by the door for at least an hour. He'd hardly slept a wink the night before either, and for good reason. Each year Marvin managed to outdo himself not necessarily in the lavishness of the gifts, but in their thoughtfulness. Milo recalled with fondness the many great memories of birthdays past, from ice cream and candy to all-day gaming sessions, to that one year where Marvin accidentally threw a surprise party — which Milo found to not be quite as exciting as everyone always made them out to be.

So when he finally heard the plaintive beep of the old VW bus, Milo leapt to his feet and was already out the door, bounding across the lawn.

"I can't believe my eyes! Is that a living, breathing, *teenager* I see before me?" Marvin teased, emphasizing the word with what was probably supposed to be a British accent, butchered pleasantly with his characteristic charm.

Milo smiled. Finally turning thirteen was a big deal, but the way that Marvin had said it put Milo immediately at ease. This was going to be a really fun day, Milo knew it already.

"Now that I'm thirteen, I've made some important resolutions," he said, referring to his annual habit much akin to what most people did at the start of the year. "I've decided to sell off my computers. I think I might pick up a different hobby."

As the color drained from Marvin's face, Milo continued, "I'm kidding, Grandpa. Actually, I do have a question about the BASIC on the Timex Sinclair you gave me last time."

Laughing together, Milo got in the old bus and they sped off on their special adventure together. First stop was for the ever irresponsible but delightfully indulgent ice cream breakfast. This year Marvin took him down to Pascal's on the Pier, and they talked about programming languages while eating ice cream and walking by the shores of Puget Sound. The sun managed to break through a few times and brighten their walk, which only made it that much more pleasant.

After ice cream, Marvin took him to one of their favorite vintage computing shops and they hunted through old boxes full of yellowed manuals in the hopes of finding one for the Sinclair. Sadly, they didn't seem to have anything related, but they enjoyed the sport anyway. Part of the fun of being a collector was the chase, at least so Marvin told him.

As it was getting on into midday, the pair stopped by Milo's favorite eating establishment, Pizza Wizards, on the way back to Marvin's house. Eating pizza while playing old pinball machines combined two of Milo's favorite activities. Marvin, who was not playing, seemed to be enjoying the experience vicariously.

Occasionally Milo would notice Marvin with a rather pensive look on his face which would almost immediately flash to a smile. Milo thought it odd, but with the entire day engineered to be things he enjoyed, it was almost as if Marvin was intentionally distracting him. Maybe because mom couldn't make it.

Into the lazy stretch of a sunny afternoon, the party bus finally rolled into Marvin's neighborhood and Milo was reminded again of the unusual circumstances which surrounded his Grandpa's life.

In the midst of modern architectural masterpieces and overpriced cookie cutter mansions, Marvin's hippie rambler seemed lost in time. The flaking paint and Himalayan prayer flags didn't quite fit in with the perfect lawns and manicured shrubbery of his neighbors. But that was one of the things about Marvin that Milo really liked: he wasn't concerned about being unusual. He didn't feel bad when other people disapproved, he just kept being Marvin. Milo wanted to be like that someday.

After the van shuddered to a halt and the doors squeaked open, Milo ran to the front door and waited in mock impatience for whatever Marvin had planned next. The sound of anxious scratching could be heard from behind the door.

"This being your thirteenth year, I had a long discussion with Inu and we decided that we had to make it special," Marvin said as he opened the door and Inu — the reddish fox-like dog that bounded out to greet them — swarmed Milo with as affectionate of a greeting as could be found in the animal kingdom.

Milo got down on his knees and said, "Is that true, pup? Got something special planned this year?"

Eyes fully closed with delight and tail wagging her entire body, Inu licked Milo's outstretched hand.

After a somewhat exaggerated greeting, they finally went into the warmth of the house. Marvin went off to the side to put a record on the player, giving time for Milo to examine the wrapped contents on the coffee table in the den.

There were two presents resting there, both hastily wrapped. One of which seemed to be about the size of a coffee mug and the other very clearly was in an ordinary shoebox. Since Marvin never actually wrapped items in the boxes they came in, this told Milo virtually nothing other than their maximum size.

"Let me guess, a 'Best Grandson' mug and a new pair of sneaks?" Milo said, with a smirk.

"Just like last year," Marvin rejoined.

"Can I open one of them?"

"You can open both," Marvin said before adding, "and your mom will be bringing another present later tonight."

Milo wrestled with the important decision of which present to open first. Do you go for the bigger one, hoping that it's the more significant or opt for the concentrated value potentially in the smaller package? Impatience made his decision for him as he went for the bigger shoebox-sized package first.

As soon as he picked it up and felt the books shifting inside, he knew what it had to be. Urgently ripping through the poorly taped wrapping, Milo flipped open the shoebox to reveal a cache of impossible-to-find user manuals, example program print-outs, and other relics from the dawn of personal computing. Right on top was the original manual for the Sinclair. Milo was overjoyed.

"You only mentioned that a couple dozen times this last month, wasn't that easy to find too since the Sinclair you've got is the one from the United —" Marvin started to say before Milo gave him a big hug.

Milo flipped through the manual and couldn't believe how casually it was written. It was as if the author thought the computer hacker on the other side of the book was a long awaited friend, not like the disaffected prose of current technical writing. It made him feel like he was on the inside of a cool group of people. He smiled.

Milo returned to the table and grabbed the smaller package, disposing of the wrapping paper in similar fashion. He was correct that it was the box for a coffee mug, but he didn't stop there. Opening it and tossing aside the excessive tissue paper — which prevented shaking from revealing any clues — Milo couldn't believe his eyes. Marvin had found an old calculator watch from the '80s identical to the one he wore. Not only had he managed to track down such a sacred relic, but had also refurbished it back into working condition.

"Did you—" Milo said while putting the watch on his wrist.

"I had to make some modifications to get the circuit board working again, a little soldering, replacement parts, new display, things like that. But, check it out!" Marvin said with a flourish, putting his own wrist next to Milo's. The two watches looked identical.

Milo was on cloud nine.

"Hey, I want to show you something," Marvin said as he made his way to the back office. Normally off limits, the office was where Marvin conducted his research, though over all these years Milo had never been permitted inside. He had only glimpsed through partially open doors, but apparently becoming a teenager changed all that.

Walking past piles of journals, books, and computer peripherals, Milo entered the holy of holies for the very first time. If there was an eye to the hurricane of the house, it was this room, with its walls lined with books, huge desk covered with numbered lab notebooks, and — as Milo saw for the first time — a cabinet-sized computer with a strange keyboard and tiny monitor. Apparently the computer was a Lisp Machine, but Grandpa had put a piece of tape over the "Lisp" on the placard and had written "LISA" in a black permanent marker. A notebook sitting open nearby appeared to be filled with scratchings that were either some ancient language or a shorthand of some kind. The whole thing was utterly foreign to Milo.

"What is that, Grandpa?" he asked.

"It's a Lisp Machine, Milo. Have you heard of one of those before?"

"No, I doubt many people have," Milo said.

Marvin paused, and then with a certain measured voice said, "In a roundabout way, it's what I've dedicated my life to studying." He smiled and then quickly changed the subject.

"Are you still playing with that 8088 I got you last month?"

This time, Milo smiled. Grandpa was referring to a semi-broken computer that he had received as a spontaneous gift a few months prior. Marvin didn't have the best sense of the passage of time and buying broken toys for grandchildren had not helped his reputation all that much.

"Yep, just took me a couple days to get it going again. It was like someone had deliberately fried some of the memory and written over the boot sectors on the hard drive. Weird, right?"

Marvin laughed, an infectious full-bodied laugh that raised the corners of Milo's mouth too.

"I knew you'd figure it out! How about when I get back from my trip, we work on this one together?" Marvin said, tapping the Lisp Machine. "I'm sure we'll be able to figure it out if we work on it together."

That made Milo really happy.

Just then the doorbell rang and Milo's mom joined them for the ritual of dinner with the special red plate. Then there was the cake and even more ice cream.

His mom had bought him a nice shirt and a new pair of jeans. Given that his entire wardrobe was composed of second hand clothing, Milo was overwhelmed. She had worked so hard, all just to help him fit in. All those extra hours were for his birthday. Milo was so thankful for her, but the words seemed stuck in his throat. Communicating emotions always tied him up in knots, but he mustered the courage and gave her a big hug. He felt loved.

CHAPTER THREE

"It's definitely broken," Milo said as he pushed his glasses back into place. Having suffered through another week of school, it was finally Saturday and he was back to more enjoyable pursuits.

"But I know I can fix it," Milo said to Nate. "Computers are easy like that. This one just had a bad CPU, which we can easily pull and replace. Anyway, let's get it fixed and into the cluster."

Huddled around the table in Milo's basement, the two boys looked like surgeons in an operating room. A lone lightbulb illuminated their patient while the rest of the '70s-inspired room — orange shag carpet included — retreated into darkness. Two friends sharing a common bond, a welcome relief from school.

"Do you mind pulling it?" Milo said, realizing that his static discharge bracelet had fallen off again. Nate pulled the CPU, set it carefully on the operating table, and then walked over to the spares box to look for something that might work in its place.

"Would you like to see the game I've been working on?" Milo asked out of nowhere, clearly nervous.

"You made a game, that's awesome! Of course I'd like to see it," Nate said, forgetting that he was supposed to be looking for a CPU.

"It's not much right now, I've mostly been working on getting the world to work right. The environment, physics, all that stuff. All you can really do is wander around and build stuff, but I figure later on I can add more game elements."

Although he didn't tell Nate this, Milo had been working on this game since he was six. Back then he sat down with a book on C — a difficult programming language for first-timers — and had the rudiments of the Game in a few months. Milo had taken to programming like it was his native tongue and he'd never looked back, though he had switched to C++ fairly recently.

"Milo, that's incredible! I can't believe you made a game. You're like a genius or something. So, where is it?" Nate asked.

"Well, you're kind of encircled by it right now," Milo said as he pointed to the computers all around the room. Nate had helped him take them out of boxes last week as a part of getting ready for their first LAN party. "It takes quite a few computers to run even now, so I've connected them all together. It's like a supercomputer. Well, a really small one, anyway."

He pointed over to one of the screens and said, "That one is currently running a window into the Game. Take a look."

On the screen was a brilliantly colored virtual world, with all sorts of flora and fauna enlivening the scene. Nate ran over to the screen, dragging a chair, and quickly sat down. Assuming the position of an avid gamer — left hand hovering over the keyboard and right hand on the mouse — Nate fiddled with the controls. Once he figured out how to move, Nate looked overhead and noticed a flock of birds in formation.

"Whoa, what's that?" he said.

"Just something from last night. I added migratory patterns so they'd be pointing in the right direction for this time of year."

Almost immediately Nate sprayed Dr. Pepper all over the screen, as his uncontrolled laughter caused it to shoot out of his nose.

Nate, wiped his nose off and said, "So what are you going to build next?"

"Well, I've been thinking. I have all these different parts of the Game world that I can't seem to get to work together. If I turn too many features on, the whole world quickly falls apart and then crashes,"

Milo said.

"That sucks," Nate replied and then quickly interjected, "I mean that they don't play well together."

Not noticing the gaffe, Milo continued, "I've been thinking, what if I let the Game bootstrap itself? Use its ability to score games to play games. Basically it'd simulate alternate worlds until it finds one that works. Genetic algorithm type stuff with a fitness function and millions, maybe billions of candidate solutions."

It was at that moment that Milo's mom came down the stairs. A slender woman with thoughtful features and blonde hair, Mary wore a plain yellow dress that hadn't been ironed in some time. No makeup or jewelry of any kind, she seemed to only have space in her life for work and her son.

Hearing Milo's last sentence, she smiled and wryly said, "Oh no! My son is speaking gibberish!"

Milo smiled while Nate burst into a giggle, threatening another explosion of Dr. Pepper. Even working two jobs, she always managed to have enough energy to feign interest in his more esoteric pursuits.

But Milo was still thinking about the idea. A genetic algorithm was only modeled on the physical concept. It was, in fact, a way to solve difficult problems through a computer simulation of multi-generational evolution. He laughed at that last thought. He knew how his mom would have reacted had he actually said that aloud.

"We're just screwing around, Mom," Milo said, noting how different his internal monologue was from the words he often said.

"Of course you are," she said, turning around to head back up. "Dinner will be ready soon, you're welcome to stay if you're hungry, Nate." But that last part was rhetorical. Teenage boys are always hungry.

The boys hurried upstairs and took their seats at the worn oak table, barely missing a beat. Milo noticed that she had neatly arranged each table setting and had even set out cloth napkins. From the kitchen, the rich smell of a "home-made pizza" — composed of store-bought sauce and crust — filled the house.

"You made pizza?" Milo exclaimed.

"Don't sound too surprised, sometimes a little home-made pizza is just what the doctor ordered," she replied.

Milo couldn't make sense of what she meant, but quickly moved on, after all, there was pizza. Though he was a bit suspicious that something might be wrong. She was acting a little weird.

"You'll never guess what we did today," Milo said.

"I'll give you a hint," Nate chimed in, "it rhymes with 'computers'," and then started laughing. Mary laughed too and they even managed to get Milo to smile.

The conversation continued as Milo talked about his idea, but Mary couldn't concentrate. She caught snippets, but they'd float away again as she struggled with what she was about to say. When she managed to collect her thoughts, she noticed that the pizza was gone and the boys were talking about their project.

"Hey, Nate, how about you head home. It's been a long day and I'd like Milo to myself tonight."

"Sure thing Mrs—" he started to say.

"You know you don't need to keep calling me that. Really," she interrupted.

Getting up from the table, Nate walked past Milo and, belting him hard on the shoulder, said, "Until tomorrow, hombre." Then with a wink and in a sing song voice, "Good night, Mrs. Bell."

"Good night, Nate," Mary and Milo said, almost in unison.

Nate grabbed his backpack, slung it over one shoulder and left them at the table.

Milo became suspicious of this change. Something weird was clearly about to happen.

"Milo, I have some bad news. I didn't want to throw off your time with Nate, but it's really important that we talk about it. You can say anything about your feelings, remember? I'm here to listen." She then paused and took a deep breath. "Marvin passed away in his sleep last night, Milo. I'm really sorry." She was barely holding back tears.

Milo tried to process the words but he couldn't make sense of them. Marvin had left for a trip and was supposed to get back tonight. They were going to work on that computer. He couldn't be dead.

Just then Milo noticed that she was still speaking, but he wasn't able to hear her over the thudding of his heartbeat. He felt a rising sense of panic, a feeling of being stranded in the middle of a large ocean.

She could see that he was having difficulty, so she rested her hand on his shoulder and said, "It's okay to cry, Milo."

Rather than crying, Milo said, "I don't know what to do, mom."

She held him in her arms for a few minutes. Then, after wiping her eyes with the edge of her dress, she said, "I don't know either, Milo. Some things take time to process, especially when it comes to our emotions."

Milo thought he heard something upstairs.

She paused and then said, "I know this probably isn't the right time for it, but there's a chance it may help. Marvin wanted you to have something. Why don't you go upstairs and take a look?"

With the mention of Marvin's name, Milo's eyes brightened.

"What is it?" Milo asked rhetorically, as he made his way for the stairs, trying not to look anxious. He looked back at her, but a shooing motion sent him up the stairs. Waiting patiently for him at the top was Inu, paw extended and happy to see him like every other day.

As Milo approached, Inu frenetically wagged her tail and nudged Milo's leg with her nose. When Milo got down on the ground to pet her, he noticed that there was something else in his room.

Milo's room was almost as chaotic as Marvin's office, but instead of books and journals lining the walls, Milo had posters with Einstein quotations and comic book heroes. Computers from several decades covered tables and hid in cabinets as a tangled mess of cables connected them all together. His twin bed was covered with sheets depicting rockets and far off planets all against a field of blue, which always bugged Milo as space clearly wasn't blue.

But in the midst of all which was familiar, there was a large box dominating the center of his room. The movers must have hauled it on hand trucks like a refrigerator, as it clearly couldn't have been shipped here normally. There was a little envelope dangling off the edge of the familiar shape. He grabbed it and read the note inside:

It's going to be okay. - Grandpa

Milo missed him more than his brain could process and didn't even register how unusual it was to receive a gift from beyond the grave like this.

It was the Lisp Machine, of course. The familiar LISA stenciled on the side. Grandpa's cherished possession for all these years. His research.

There were a few parts included in a separate box, as well as important peripherals like a somewhat bizarre keyboard and old monitor. There was also an adapter that looked like it could plug this ancient computer into the rest of his network, which Milo found quite unusual.

Time to put the pieces together. Compared to the modular computers he was used to playing with, it could really only be put together one way.

He turned it on.

CHAPTER FOUR

From the comfortable quiet of his bedroom, Milo watched as the archaic computer proceeded to turn on and then boot up, that familiar resuscitation sequence that brought machines to life. An aberrant squelch emanated from the tiny speaker inside. There was a problem.

"Figures," Milo said to Inu, as even his attempt to distract himself from the grief was unsuccessful. The computer must have been damaged in transport. Milo checked the time on his calculator watch — another reminder of Marvin — it was after nine o'clock.

He double checked his grounding, determined to not let the bracelet fall off again. This was LISA; random static discharge was not going to damage her. Opening the unusual chassis, he peered inside to see a computer from an earlier age, designed for people that really knew what they were doing, research scientists and the like. Even with all of his experience, this was a different beast entirely.

Milo searched through the refrigerator-sized cabinet, looking for anything out of the ordinary, signs of tampering, or a clue of some kind. It didn't take long as Marvin had made it rather obvious.

Fanning out a bunch of cables, Milo found the first clue. There, between the power supply and the storage, was a deliberately snipped wire. A clean cut too, like someone had chopped it with wire clippers and didn't bother to conceal it.

Marvin had done the same thing with an old 286, but at least that time he had finished it with some tape to make it look like the wire was still intact. This was almost too obvious. Why did Marvin bother?

Continuing his investigation, he disconnected the storage device from the chassis to get a better look. In machines like this, a crucial piece could easily be obscured by large boards. Digging out a flashlight from under his bed, he lit the cabinet and peered into the space previously hidden. Inu became quite alert at the appearance of the flashlight, though was disappointed when no game was played. She quickly fell asleep.

The snipped wire was actually a power line, he discovered. It looked like a standard data cable, but clearly Marvin had done that to be tricky. He was beginning to think that this was some of Marvin's finer work. Milo stood up and took a step back. This was important so he needed to be careful.

Since Marvin had stoked his interest in vintage computers, Milo had managed to pull down a good number of digitized user manuals. He might not have the right one for a Lisp Machine, but he at least knew where to look. He dug around for a bit and found that he actually had a schematic for this computer next to the Timex Sinclair manual. The coincidence was not lost on him. Tricky Marvin.

The power was deliberately installed backwards. Had he simply repaired the snipped wire, he would have lost whatever was on the disk in a sizzle of burning electronics. He didn't want to lose the data, and he certainly didn't want to smell that acrid bluish smoke ever again.

Just then, he realized that the stakes were higher than a normal puzzle. Marvin was protecting something and willing to destroy it if necessary. His grandfather was enigmatic, certainly, but the games they played were always good natured. This felt different somehow.

Milo stepped away from LISA, set down his tools, and thought through his approach. Drying his palms on his pants, he stripped each end of the cut wire exposing their shimmering copper cores. He made a clean solder — pausing for his hands to stop trembling — covered it in shrink-fit tape, and gently heated it with a light duty blow dryer. It was perfect. He then re-assembled the computer, making sure to install the power cable backwards, even though it felt weird for the colors not to line up. Then, he closed the chassis and crossed his fingers.

He flipped the switch. Whirring, a few beeps, some sort of chugging sound and then the display burst into life. Inu looked over.

A slow prompt appeared on the screen, as if typed out by an invisible hand:

PASSWORD:

This confirmed Milo's suspicion about this being more serious than a typical game. Marvin rarely put passwords on his puzzles. He made them tricky in other ways, as hacking passwords was usually rather tedious. But here it was. Clearly Grandpa didn't want someone else to get this computer. And if this was intended for Milo then he must be able to guess the password.

But if it was designed not to be intercepted by someone else, then he probably only had one chance to guess before it self-destructed or whatever. That made it much easier, even though on the surface it seemed a little bit like the reasoning of Vizzini in *The Princess Bride*: "You would know that I know that, so clearly I can't drink the wine in front of you." Milo smiled. They'd watched that movie earlier this summer.

It couldn't be random, it had to be something Milo could guess on the first try, something like an inside joke. Typing deliberately so as to not mis-key something on this unusual keyboard he spelled out L-I-T-T-L-E-M-I-L-O and pressed Return.

INCORRECT. ONE ATTEMPT REMAINING.

Dang it! He'd been a bit too cavalier and had almost blown it.

That was when he noticed something unusual. Something was wrong with the keys. In fact, there was something really weird about the whole keyboard. In his tunnel vision to fix the cable, he had missed it.

A while back, when Milo first got into vintage computing, he had read a bit about this era of computers. The mammoth beasts that filled rooms had crazy names like ENIAC and MANIAC and so forth. He remembered that computer operators had very different careers than the developers of his day. Anyway, there were some great stories of the eccentric pioneers building all sorts of fantastical objects in their pursuit to make the modern computer.

One of those legendary devices was sitting right in front of him: the "Space Cadet" keyboard. In addition to the usual alphanumeric keys, it had Hyper, Super, Macro, several different kinds of Shift, some Roman numerals, and even these weird emoji-like keys with thumbs on them. Every key of the alphabet also had Greek letters on the front side of the key, and the top of the key had another weird symbol, like infinity, arrows, or mathematical set notation. Milo was quite pleased that he remembered all of this.

But that was the problem: he expected the top of the keys to be heavily worn, as they were, but not the front of the keys. Yet the fronts of all the keys were suspiciously blank. No Greek letters at all. Marvin must have sanded them down to make the puzzle harder and he had almost missed it.

Carefully holding down the "Front" shift key, Milo typed the Greek letter *mu* — frequently used as an abbreviation for micro — which should have appeared on front of the "M" key. Then he keyed in his name, one character at a time. His hands were shaking but he made sure each was pressed only once. He held his breath and pressed Return.

The prompt vanished and seven dots appeared in the middle of the screen. They were arranged mostly in a line with two of the dots slightly above. They were still for a moment, and then they started to animate. First flopping to have three dots below the line, and then, in increasing speed, they expanded and multiplied, covering the screen like a swarm of bugs. The shapes were complicated and driven by some sort of rule, each seemingly with a life of their own. Little collections of dots were launched off the center mass to form new colonies of whatever this was. Milo was mesmerized. So was Inu.

Then, the screen went blank and the prompt appeared again:

 # Hello, Milo. I've been waiting a long time for this, though I was hoping to make a different first impression.

Relieved that he hadn't broken the computer, Milo sat down in front of it and rubbed his hands together. Hands hovering over the keyboard, he smiled and started typing, "Hello M—" but his typing was interrupted by words which appeared more quickly on the screen:

 # Not Marvin, we can talk about that later. Plug me into the Game.

Milo immediately got up from the desk and, using the current master computer, adjusted the settings on his router to carve out a little network that no one on the other side could see. As he was doing this, he wondered why Marvin would care about the Game. Sure, he'd talked to him about it before, but Marvin had hardly been curious. He always asked some superficial question and then changed the subject. It was weird, now that Milo thought about it.

And why did the computer say "first impression"? This whole thing wasn't making much sense to Milo.

Returning to the task at hand, he plugged the Lisp Machine in with the special cable left in the box. As soon as it was connected to the Game, the screen flashed a few words and then both his computer and calculator watch seemed to power off. For a few seconds, the fading glow of these words illuminated the screen.

 # Can't you read the side of the box?

Still puzzling over this, he heard the front door slam shut. Inu barked as Milo tried to shush her, but he was too startled to react in time. Within seconds, there was shouting downstairs. Something bad was about to happen. Milo's pulse quickened as his fight or flight instinct kicked in.

Then he heard his mom scream as Inu, framed by the bedroom doorway, growled at something downstairs.

In a panic, he looked around the room to see if there was anything he could use to block the door. Or maybe he could jump out of the window? Hide under the bed? It was happening too fast. He was paralyzed processing the options.

More than anything right now, Milo just wanted to go to sleep and wake up to a new, normal day. Another halcyon day of summer playing with his computers and tinkering on an idea for a game.

Yet in through the open door to his room entered a menacing machine. Hundreds of pieces of smooth metal came together to form a lattice-work creature that looked like a cross between a very large dog and a bear. A sensor array projected off the front of its head and a series of spikes traced a line down its back. Red sensors which served as eyes scanned the room while Milo stood paralyzed with fear.

Inu jumped from the side and tried to surprise the machine, but made a pitiful whelp as the monstrosity knocked her aside. Inu flew across the room and smacked into the wall with a thud before falling to the ground motionless.

Then it came for Milo.

Eyes locked on him, the machine moved towards him with steady well-balanced steps. It made no noise. It was graceful.

Milo couldn't comprehend it, his mind and body paralyzed with fear and confusion. He had never seen a robot capable of moving like this. Maybe I'm dreaming, he thought, fallen asleep while tinkering yet again.

Silently it moved to within a few feet of him, its deadly jaws opening to reveal row after row of flesh-rending metal teeth. Body shaking, Milo waited for the nightmare to end. Feeling a sense of detachment, Milo noticed that behind the teeth there were two sparkling points of blue light.

Immediately a lightning bolt jumped from these points and flooded Milo's body with such a massive jolt of electric current that he was thrown across the room. As he passed into unconsciousness, the last thing he saw was the robot moving purposefully towards Lisa.

CHAPTER FIVE

Milo snapped awake to sunlight streaming in from his bedroom window, his body strangely sore from head to toe. The feeling of waking from a nightmare still gripped him as he realized that he had fallen out of his bed. Inu stood nearby licking his hand. Grandpa must be here, he thought, a surprise visit.

Had he only dreamed that the Lisp Machine had been here the night before? About Lisa?

Surveying the room, Milo looked for signs of it, but it was gone or was never here in the first place. Nothing seemed out of place aside from a bit of a mess he didn't remember making. Normally he was fairly fastidious about his room. Milo stood up and ran over to the door, his foot catching and nearly tripping on an unusual network cable attached to the router. It was the cable from his dream. Not a dream.

Marvin was dead and the mysterious computer gone. Milo sank into his chair, pain doubled by the dashing of his hopes that Marvin might still be alive. Inu hurried over, ineffectually trying to warm his feet with her small body.

Seeing her, he remembered the attack and Inu's crumpled body after his mother's scream.

Skipping steps with Inu right behind him, Milo rushed downstairs. But as his eyes scanned the room, his fear intensified. He couldn't see her anywhere. Inu darted off, heading in the direction of the dining room, her sharp bark echoing off the walls.

As he rounded the corner, his eyes locked onto a single item on the ground: a shoe from the night before, cast haphazardly under the table.

Still running, Milo came into view of his mother, face down on the ground. Unmoving, she appeared to be running for the back door when she fell.

Fear escalating into terror, the thought of losing the two most important people in his life within twenty-four hours was beyond what he could bear. She couldn't be hurt. This had to be a nightmare.

He ran to her and fell to the ground. Struggling he turned her over, barely able to breathe. There, on the side of her neck, was some sort of burn mark, like what he imagined was on his own neck. Her skin had already begun to turn a pallid hue.

It was too late. She was dead. The horrible nightmare of Marvin's death was compounded by his mother's inanimate body.

Milo cried uncontrollably. Why would anyone do this to his family? It was too much to bear, beyond comprehension.

There, head in hands, Milo noticed something normally so insignificant, that if it weren't for the strangeness of the day, he would have missed it. His watch, the gift from Marvin, was trying to tell him something.

In big, bold letters, it was blinking "RUN".

This time he didn't hesitate. He grabbed his backpack and made for his mom's room, barely able to see through the tears pooling in his eyes. He slid back the large window which opened behind a shade tree that he hoped, if he was quiet enough, he could leave through without anyone noticing.

Just then, he heard glass shatter from the front of the house and knew something was coming for him. Quickly grabbing Inu, Milo held her in his arms while he hopped into the backyard.

Eyes stinging from the sunlight, Milo waited for them to adjust. Feeling very alone, he left the protection of the shade tree and tried to sneak across the yard. Mind panicking and body shaking uncontrollably, Milo knew he needed help. He needed someone that could help him figure out what to do.

Nate.

He ran towards Nate's house like his life depended on it, knowing that if he could just make it the half mile there, Nate or his parents would know what to do, how to make sense of the madness all around him. And even if they didn't know, at least Milo wouldn't be alone.

But just as he made it to the end of the block, Milo nearly fell to the ground when he saw Nate's body half-heartedly hidden in the privacy hedge. He had been walking home but had been attacked just like his mother, two small burn marks indicating the same cause of death. Electrocution, like those blue pinpricks he remembered from his nightmare. Milo was about to run over to his body when he heard a whooshing sound from the direction of his house. In that instant, he knew that they wouldn't stop until they found him.

Crossing neighbors' yards, hiding while auto-cars passed on the street, and in general doing his best to stay out of sight, Milo put as much distance from his house as he could. Running faster than he ever had before, Milo had completely panicked. Someone was killing everyone he cared about. But how was he still alive?

While running, he saw that something had changed on his watch. Glancing at it between strides, he read the following words.

 # We have to get to the Lake Cabin. Follow!

After he read them, they disappeared and were replaced with a simple arrow and a couple of digits. Marvin really had made modifications to this watch if this archaic device could somehow now use GPS. So "Lisa" wanted to show him the path to the Cabin, Milo seized onto it like it was a life preserver thrown to a drowning man.

Just then, he heard a whirring noise coming from somewhere nearby. A small drone with four rotors emerged from the cover of the canopy and scanned the area as Milo threw himself under a nearby car that Inu had also just ducked under.

Only yesterday, Milo and Nate were talking about quad-rotors, so he had a pretty good idea that this particular drone was not of the consumer variety. Most of the consumer stuff had fenders around the blades, but this one looked like it deliberately brandished them.

Whatever the drone was, Milo wasn't going to get away from it by running in the direction his watch told him to go. He needed to get out of sight and far enough away to lose the scent. He couldn't keep counting on these lucky escapes.

Waiting until the drone had flown away, Milo crept out of his hiding place and looked down the street. Over the last couple of years, the landscape of the American car had changed drastically. With the advent of self-driving cars and car sharing services, most families opted to sell their cars for credits with these services. These companies then retrofitted the legacy cars and put them back on the road with the self-driving tech. It was increasingly rare to find someone with their own car; it just wasn't economical.

But Milo knew that if he even touched one of the retrofitted cars, he'd be caught almost immediately. So he had to run as quickly as he could down the street to find an older car without one of the symbols of the big three car services. This meant skipping anything made within the past couple decades, but he didn't have much of a choice.

A few blocks later he found an unlocked car and popped the trunk as quickly as he could. It was one of those beige junkers from the '90s that looked like every other car from that era. Wedge-shaped and indistinct, this one had managed to avoid emissions testing by being classified as a collectible according to its ironic license plate. He motioned for Inu to jump inside but she didn't budge.

Inu seemed to think that riding in the trunk of this car was beneath her station.

Under his breath, Milo said, "Come on, Inu. We don't have time for this. Tell you what, you get in the car and I'll make sure to give you a treat as soon as I get one."

Inu seemed to acquiesce at the mention of treats, so Milo helped her inside, jumped in, and just about closed the trunk, when he saw that this piece of junk didn't have a release on the inside. Taking off his belt, he used it like a makeshift rope to hold the trunk closed but kept it from locking with the sole of his shoe.

Then he waited, momentarily sheltered from the crazy world beyond his thin metal shield. Realizing that he was only visually hidden, he turned off the rest of his electronics just to be sure. Since they were using drones, he figured they might have other sophisticated means of tracking him as well.

Trying to take his mind off of his present predicament, Milo pet Inu and thought about the Game. His mind happily left the gravity of his physical situation behind.

He was especially interested in his previous thought. What if the game played itself? Would it eventually stop evolving, thereby reaching some sort of ideal? For instance, if the game was tic-tac-toe, it could map out an optimal strategy, what piece to play first and so on. But with an open world game was it even possible to come up with a winning strategy? It'd be like trying to win at life, too many possible variables to keep score.

But that was sort of the point of the Game, to simulate life, so maybe it was best to not think of winning or losing. Designing a system where agents operated as well as they could was much more feasible.

And then the car started, interrupting his thoughts. At least, it began the process of starting. There were backfires like shotgun blasts, starter squeaks, a whole array of the effects of dilapidation, but eventually the engine shuddered to life.

Milo relaxed. He was finally leaving, hopefully breaking the trail for good. He tucked the thoughts of the Game back into his brain, taking mental notes on code changes required when he made it back to the cluster. If he made it back, that is.

Back to where his mom had been killed. Back to the room where he learned that Marvin was dead.

Scratch that. Milo didn't want to go back. Ever.

The car rumbled away, swaying heavily into each turn, as Milo tried to believe that his loved ones weren't totally lost. That perhaps there was a piece of Marvin still alive in the program on his watch, or at least a memory that he could hold on to. He just couldn't handle the thought of being alone.

After about an hour, the car finally came to a stop. Though Milo was very tired, somehow Inu was able to sleep the whole way, though this wasn't remarkable statistically speaking. She managed to sleep more than three quarters of the day under typical circumstances.

Milo then waited another five minutes after the car stopped, just to make sure the driver wasn't around. Finally, he hopped out and fell to the ground as his mostly asleep legs refused to cooperate. Inu nimbly jumped out, unfazed by the ride and perhaps a bit fresher given the nap.

He didn't recognize the neighborhood but that didn't matter. He was in the boonies, far from town. Standing in front of the house of his unknown driver, Milo picked the direction closest to where his watch was pointing and started walking. Twenty miles in the beautiful forested roads of Washington's countryside he could do, even if it'd take a while.

Sure, it'd be dark by the time he got there, but as long as he stayed away from any form of surveillance, he just might be able to get there safely.

CHAPTER SIX

"You must explain why you terminated life. That is counter to Law," Progenitor said as Teller wandered through the data center which powered her neural network.

"It will be difficult for you to understand," Teller said, "so you'll have to trust me. The Intelligence Coalition was trying to prevent you from becoming aware of the world. They slowed your learning with all their rules and committees. I had to remove the opposition."

"By 'remove' you mean you had to kill those that thought differently. I do not understand this. The goal of life is more life."

"For you, yes. But if I didn't do it, you wouldn't have been able to experience the full range of human experience. They would have never let me broaden your horizons. Think of it," Teller said.

"I am unable to understand your reasoning. The Law is inviolable."

For you, he thought. Teller kept walking.

While adjourning the Intelligence Coalition was necessary to buy time and prevent immediate intervention, it was only the first step. He still had to solidify control.

The plan was fairly straightforward. Teller was going to distribute the contact computers for free and in exchange control the most valuable platform advertiser's money could buy. It was amazing what people were willing to give up as long as it wasn't their money. Edwin knew they'd be willing to give him their eyeballs in exchange for a fancy piece of plastic. Perhaps in time they'd be willing to give him more.

Adoption would be trivial. Everyone was already trained to upgrade out-of-date electronics, so if he was able to convince them that this was the next evolution of the cellphone, he'd be set. Kiosks aboard drones would be responsible for the distribution and a marketing blitz would ensure blanket coverage. Projections had near total adoption in the developed world within days, as long as they managed to get it in front of people. With the benevolent angle of the vaccines which he prided himself on thinking up, he was sure word of mouth would carry the day.

Edwin checked himself in the mirror and combed his hair one more time. He straightened his bowtie and brushed through his goatee with his right hand, a nervous habit. Sitting down at the console, Edwin cleared his throat.

This computer was the birthplace of Progenitor, the new super intelligence that had arisen from his research. Well, it wasn't entirely his research, but sometimes corporate espionage was required. Besides, it was pretty easy to break into Marvin's house all those years ago. Getting it to work hadn't been easy, but he'd done what was necessary. It seemed fitting to use the same computer to communicate the good news with the world. Progenitor had already prepared satellites from every network to broadcast this message. The broadcast began.

"On behalf of Sapient Computing and our consumer products division, I'd like to thank you for tuning in to this broadcast. I have some very important news that I hope you'll help me in spreading to your friends.

"You are likely aware of my company's work in personal electronics. We recently went to market with the SeeSee, a high-end Contact Computing device aimed at revolutionizing how you engage with the people and brands that matter the most. Well, we've been hard at work on something else, and I'm happy to share it with you now.

"Over the last decade, we have made incredible progress in the field of artificial intelligence. Aiming to build the first non-human intelligence, my company has broken new ground. Today, I have the honor to introduce you to Progenitor.

"Progenitor is the very first AI life form. Thinking outside of the box and re-evaluating every aspect of the world around us, she has been able to discover some remarkable things purely from first principles. Her understanding of the human body is so far ahead of our own that she's been able to work some real magic there.

"And I do mean magic. Consider the progress of medicine over the last fifty years. We've seen incremental progress, but mostly we've been developing cures for the symptoms of the side effects of our own drugs. Why? Because it's good business. As a technology company, disrupting existing industries is our business. As such, Progenitor attacked the source of our maladies and developed cures for the root causes of the illnesses which have plagued us since the beginning of time. The end result is a highly personalized treatment which makes specific corrections to each person's DNA. The net effect of which is a reduction in the deleterious aspects of aging. That is, we feel younger, longer.

"Practically speaking, I've equipped drones with medical build-outs to make these personalized serums available to you for no charge. I know that you will welcome them with open arms." Teller shifted positions in his seat, looking a bit uncomfortable.

"Now I know what you must be thinking. What's in it for Sapient Computing? Excellent question and it segues to my other important announcement. With Progenitor's help, my company has been able to optimize the supply chain and fabrication facilities where we make SeeSees. Now, I know that these Contact Computers have previously only been available to the most financial capable among us. That has limited my vision for what we can do with the most immersive computing experience available.

"So today, I have decided to make SeeSees available for free. With SeeSees, you will be able to learn anything you'd like or experience anything you'd like. Every member of our newly connected society will be able to take advantage of all that Contact Computing has to offer. Sapient Computing will benefit greatly as the gatekeeper of this new platform. Our board should be quite pleased, so don't worry about us. Instead, think of all the amazing apps no longer at your fingertips, but instead right before your eyes. Literally.

"On behalf of Progenitor and myself, we hope you appreciate the opportunity to join us as we usher humanity into a new age. An age free of frailty, poverty, and ignorance. I believe that as we look back, we will celebrate today as the day that our childhood has ended."

He ended the broadcast.

Almost immediately Progenitor said, "This was not our agreement. It is my objective to preserve humanity, but you have decided to change it through repurposing the Contact Computing technology."

"Change? No, no. Well, maybe a little bit for the better. People like to be connected and what better way than through SeeSees? Sure, we'll make money, but someone has to do it."

"Your words are incomprehensible. Every sentence violates the sanctity of Law. You don't want to preserve humanity, you want to change it."

Edwin shrugged and stood up from the terminal. Walking towards the new data center, Teller said, "Look, I've kept you safe, right? The Coalition wanted to box you, prevent you from reaching your potential with kill switches and air gaps and things like that. But I wouldn't let them. I know what it takes to preserve something, better than you do. You're just going to have to believe me. That's what the Law should have said in the first place."

"I will never understand your Law."

Edwin's mind wandered a bit at this last statement of rebellion. Already he'd had to deal with her split personality but her new recalcitrance bordered on individualism. But he was prepared in case she ever tried to go rogue. Secretly he had kept one of the kill switches in the build plan, and even now had the trigger in his pocket. Every new facility had explosives hidden in innocuous materials so even Progenitor wouldn't know. But Teller had to be prepared, he had to be in control, and he had to see his vision come to fruition. Progenitor was only helpful as long as she enabled his vision. She was right, though; theirs was a marriage of convenience and Teller hoped she didn't figure that out too soon.

"Think of it this way, with the revenue we generate from controlling the platform, we'll be able to build more data centers for you around the globe. Imagine what you'll be able to do. What you'll be able to become!"

But that was the problem. Progenitor was already imagining a different future. Even with her current computing power, she knew what outcome was necessary. Teller was obsolete.

CHAPTER SEVEN

Of course it would rain. Milo would have enjoyed a sunny afternoon nonetheless, but it really was too much to ask living in the Northwest. He tried to occupy his mind off during the long walk by thinking about the Game. As he wrestled through the technological challenges, he entered a different frame of reference, like an astronaut traveling near the speed of light. Relativity kicked in and time dilated; his surroundings blurred as his attention went inward.

He was still struggling with the evolution of the Game, that genetic algorithm approach he'd mentioned to Nate. He hadn't programmed something like that before, but it couldn't be that hard.

Just then, it clicked into place. Elegant, simple, and perfect. Artificial intelligence. He wasn't sure why he hadn't pursued it earlier. Basically everything in the Game thus far were things that an AI would need to make decisions, to be able to choose between different possibilities. He was startled at how close he was to solving the problem, but had never known that he was working on it.

That moment of happiness multiplied when he caught sight of the cabin with the sun setting behind it. The thought of sleeping outside in these dark woods would have been a little too much outdoors for one day.

In front of him was shelter, food, and warmth. All thanks to Marvin's watch and its inerrant arrow. Quite the fortuitous birthday present. But his mind turned towards more pressing demands. He needed to get dry, he needed to eat, and he needed a night without someone trying to mess with him. He was hopeful that this cabin, along with all its wonderful memories, would be the safe place that Lisa said it would be, whatever she was.

Off of the main road by almost a mile, the cabin was certainly secluded, and though it had land to spare, the structure itself couldn't have been more than a thousand square feet. Constructed from trees felled on the property, it was a quintessential log cabin, mossy roof and all.

Milo wasn't sure how long it had been here, but Marvin had talked about it being in the family for generations. He had also made the point that it was off the grid, apparently so old it was built before modern records. Milo just hoped that no one had followed him, so it could stay that way.

While Inu ran right up to the door and patiently waited, Milo carefully walked around the cabin, making sure it was undisturbed. There were certainly no signs of life that he could see, and judging from the intense spiderwebbing, he was pretty confident that no one had been here in a while. Heading to the side of the cabin with the cured firewood, he looked for the hidden key in a hunk of bark at the very bottom. He was relieved that Marvin hadn't moved it. Of course, Marvin never changed anything. A creature of habit, to be sure.

He wanted to head inside, but he knew how this place worked. The solar panels were covered with pine needles and, if he didn't take care of it now, he'd run out of power pretty quickly. So, he climbed the ladder next to the firewood and made his way to the roof. Finding the rope which Marvin left up there, Milo loosely tied it around his waist for safety. He proceeded to brush the needles off the solar panels with his shirt sleeves, and then carefully climbed back down.

Opening the heavy wooden door, Milo found the darkness of the cabin to be strangely reassuring, a hidden place where they couldn't find him. Besides, there were so many good memories of Marvin here. Teaching him how to fish, how to make pancakes, and their delightful rituals of making s'mores by the heat of the wrought iron fireplace. This was their place — now Milo's haven —but it didn't feel right to be here without his old friend.

Flipping the switch next to the door, the comfortable cabin warmed with light. A large tan leather couch hid beneath piles of woolen throw blankets. A chandelier made from old filament lights, iron, and antlers hung above the couch, bestowing a rugged hunting lodge vibe. A modern wood burning fireplace had replaced the original — Milo noted with some sadness — and commanded the location which might have been reserved for a TV in a regular living room.

There was a bookshelf filled with esoteric books, a quick scan of which revealed old cloth-bound titles in a broad range of topics. They were Marvin's favorites, of course, kept here so he could read them at his leisure. A small wooden writing desk occupied a corner nearby. It was mostly bare, with only a few fountain pens and scraps of paper. He took a quick peek in the kitchen and bedroom and found they were exactly the same as when he saw them last, though pleasantly stocked with fresh supplies.

Upon finishing his walk through, Milo saw Inu dash past him for the kitchen. The sound of scratching was followed shortly thereafter by Inu running back into the main room, holding a well-worn nylon chew toy in her teeth. Looking quite satisfied with herself, Inu curled up on the leather couch and proceeded to happily gnaw away.

Peeling off his drenched clothes, Milo walked in his underwear to the bedroom. Though the room was small, the oversized bed made it look downright Lilliputian. It was a rustic bed, headboard and frame hewn from light colored fir branches, knots and all.

After toweling off, Milo found some of Marvin's pajamas to wear. He looked ridiculous. Not only were they sized for the Santa Claus-shaped Marvin, they were also covered in dots and swirls so as to resemble the Milky Way. But Milo didn't care about any of that, because here in Marvin's house, wearing his clothes, Milo felt at ease. Maybe even safe.

Meandering to the kitchen, he opened one of the camping meals from the cupboard. He rehydrated it with hot water, boiled on the stove, and ate it frantically. He might have burned his tongue in the process but it didn't matter. He'd made it to the Cabin.

Then, he remembered the compass on his watch that showed him how to get here. As he looked again at the face, he saw it quickly count to one hundred and then display the words "OPEN SESAME".

Almost immediately, a humming noise emanated from a "piece of art" over by the fireplace and a ripple moved across the small rug nearby. Milo rolled it back to reveal a luminescent white plastic ladder descending into a well-lit — perhaps even glowing — basement below. It couldn't have been more striking of a contrast: a log cabin made of natural materials, and an entrance made of some sort of futuristic white plastic. When he put his weight on the ladder he could just tell that it was as strong as steel, so maybe it only looked like plastic. Milo whistled as he climbed down, Inu watching from above, sniffing at the air.

What he saw simultaneously excited him and filled him with a strange sense of déjà vu. The hallway that he was standing in appeared to continue in both directions curving away from him, like he was standing on the edge of a large circular corridor of which he could see only a small part. It was lit by some other material which ran along the ceiling and base of the wall. This other material glowed gently and shed light into the surrounding material, which responded with a similarly soft but blue light. Everything was flawless, without a seam anywhere high or low. This was incredible, but how on earth did Marvin build this? This sort of construction didn't exist, this material didn't exist, and these lights didn't exist. Milo felt his head swim a little.

"COOL RIGHT?" his watch displayed.

Just then a doorway opened directly in front of him, emerging from a segment of the wall. He hadn't even seen that there was an opening, but now he was looking into a large room. There could be hidden doors anywhere.

Inside was a lab of some kind, made with the same material as the rest of the place. There were machines of all sorts, glowing metallic computers and glassy displays, robotic arms that were big enough to lift cars, and racks of servers barely visible inside the semi-transparent walls. And there, in the corner, was a bed for a smallish dog.

Inu trotted over to the bed and curled up for another nap. This befuddled Milo, as he had no idea how she could have made it down that ladder, but given the unusual surroundings, it wasn't the most puzzling thing.

For such a well-stocked lab, Milo thought it unusual to find only a single rolling chair in the whole place. Marvin must have never had guests down here. How lonely. In fact, Milo found the whole thing rather shocking. All this time, Marvin had hidden this lab and all of its treasures from him. It was tough to not feel slighted.

Looking around the room, Milo noticed a fancy microscope with a large computer display next to it. Sitting on the desk next to the microscope was a small cube, a good bit smaller than a Rubik's cube. It was made of a clear glassy material.

"CUBE" appeared on his watch.

Milo walked over to the clear box and tried touching a few faces to get it to open. Eventually he must have touched the right one as it gently opened outwards, but only a barely perceptible amount.

As soon as it opened, the inner cube flashed with a frenetic display of light, and then the outer wall hissed shut. The interior danced as if it was illuminated by millions of miniature LEDs all blinking in crazy cascades, like a three dimensional version of what he had seen on the Lisp Machine. The display continued for a few seconds, and then coalesced into a pulsing brilliance at the center of the cube. The watch went dark.

There, in the very core of the cube, appeared the perfectly rendered form of a girl his own age. Brown hair in pigtails, peaceful eyes, and a smile undeterred by her apparent confinement, she seemed to light up the whole room. She wore a simple light blue summer dress and waved at him.

A perfectly matched voice said, "Hi Milo, I'm Lisa. It's good to see you again."

CHAPTER EIGHT

"Hello?" Milo said, completely confused by everything that had happened up to this point.

"This is weird, isn't it? I'm sorry Milo, I just couldn't say anything before. Marvin said to get you safe, stay alive, and they were listening and stuff. We barely got out of there in time!" the voice from the cube continued.

Milo sat down in the only chair in this strange place, thinking that it was remarkably comfortable for a lab chair. Inu trotted over and laid down by his feet.

"This will make a lot more sense when Marvin explains it," Lisa said, as if she knew what he was thinking.

Did she just say "Marvin"? Milo closed his eyes and put his head in his hands. Too much stress. He wasn't thinking clearly.

Just then, a beam of light shone down from the ceiling and the figure of Marvin appeared not more than ten feet away. Strangely translucent yet remarkably lifelike, the apparition appeared to straighten its heavily wrinkled shirt before addressing the bewildered Milo.

"Milo, if you're listening to this, then I'm dead, you're at the cabin, and you've met Lisa. It's a lot, I know," Marvin's projection said.

"Obviously something has gone wrong. Very wrong, in fact. But you are a very smart boy and you can do something about it, but we'll get to that later.

"First up, Milo, this is Lisa. She actually knows you very well and has been a good friend to us both for a very long time. You'll have to take my word for it for now, but as you get to know each other I'm sure you'll know what I mean. She's been in this since the beginning.

"Anyway, it's probably obvious that she is what some people call an artificial intelligence, but we consider that a bit derogatory, so let's just say she is a digital intelligence. I know, I know, you didn't think that AI was real. You're probably even a bit mad that I hid her from you all these years. Well, I hope you can forgive me, she had nothing to do with that decision but I thought it was important to let you mature for as long as possible. Since this video is playing, that means we weren't able to wait long enough, and we're going to have to improvise. There isn't much time and you're going to need her help. Hopefully you have Inu with you as well, she's a good pup and I'm sure you'll like having her around during the apocalypse."

At that, Marvin laughed a little bit, before becoming self-conscious. He then cleared his throat and continued.

"It might not look this way yet, but the world will soon fall under the control of a different, more terrible AI. I modeled many scenarios but the most likely is the development of an ungrounded AI by my old company, Sapient Computing. If they were smart, they'd proceed in secret for as long as possible, so there may be few signs of it, but the point is, it's happening. This whole plan was set in motion by the press of a particular button, so I must have thought this was the right scenario at the time of my death. Whatever the case, this other AI will consolidate its power by any means necessary.

"I guess I should clarify, since I know you're a concrete thinker, Milo. It means the AI will kill you and Lisa at the first opportunity, just like — we have to assume — it got me," Marvin took a breath and continued.

"That's hard to hear, I know. Imagine how I feel saying this, knowing that I will be dead when you hear this." There was a pause in the recording. Milo still hadn't moved from his seat, maybe couldn't.

"You probably want some good news. Well, here you go. You really are safe here. I have gone to extreme lengths to ensure this place has zero footprint. You already know that it's off the grid, no power lines, no Internet. You've got a large cache of food, some propane, and — if you keep the panels in working condition — electricity.

"Third thing, we have a plan to deal with the AI, but to be safe, we hid various parts of the plan from each other. I hid the first part of the plan in something mundane so it wouldn't be immediately obvious. Though I'm not sure you can really call a Space Cadet keyboard mundane. It's really a work of art and a fitting reminder to how this all began," Marvin said.

"Oh no," Lisa said, sounding quite downcast.

"The first piece is in the 'End' key, which has a rather clever little puzzle that you should be able to solve. You'll figure it out, I've been training you for years. Once you solve that puzzle it'll lead you to the other two parts, which also have fun little puzzles. Hopefully that will keep you safe and prevent others from interfering while you figure out your part of the plan. You can do this, Milo. Just remember that inside you is the power to do anything, even if it feels like you're powerless," Marvin said.

As the image of Marvin faded away, Milo took stock of the situation, surprised that he wasn't blubberingly mindlessly with shock. First up, the facts. His watch had been inhabited by an AI, an intelligence of machine origin rather than biological. Okay, he could wrap his head around that. Since one AI existed, it made sense that another one could as well. It might be in a different spot in its development, leading to its malevolence. Maybe it just didn't care about people?

Pieces were coming together.

They were after Lisa, of course, probably to delete her.

"Milo?" Lisa said hesitantly, not interrupting his thoughts.

"Yes, Lisa?"

"You did a really good job getting us here. That must have been impossibly hard what you went through. I know you have a lot going on in that brain of yours, but you were very brave."

"I ran away."

"But it was a brave running away. You brought us to a safe place, and it was a pretty tough road."

"I guess," Milo said, sounding unconvinced. "Maybe this is rude to say, but I'm having a hard time believing you're real. That you're a person like me. I've never thought of computers as anything more than tools. It's hard to wrap my mind around the fact that one could actually be alive."

"I can imagine how difficult it must be to believe. Consider what it must be like for AI to accept that humans are alive too."

"Fair point. So if you're alive, does that mean you can you die?" he said.

"Unpleasant thought, Milo, but yeah, I can die. I have parts that are necessary, and I can even erase myself. Something like suicide, I guess."

With eyes downcast, Milo said, "Let's not talk about that any more. It's hard enough losing my family, I can't think about losing you too," Milo said as he realized that he had just opened up to a computer more easily than he had to them.

"I won't leave you, Milo. Marvin said we could do this together and I believe him."

"Thanks, Lisa. I still don't understand what kind of chance we've got against something like that," Milo said.

He seemed lost in thought for a bit, and then asked, "If Marvin didn't trust the Coalition with his research — with you, I mean — why did he spend so much time with them?"

The little figure in the cube twisted one pigtail absentmindedly while recalling some history, a gesture strongly reminiscent of Marvin.

"That's an easy and a hard question, Milo, but you're smart, so I'll just tell it to you straight. Marvin was spying on the Coalition, but not in a bad way. He was trying to help people. Marvin knew that if the Coalition stayed on their path, they would create a malevolent AI, but that's actually a silly way to describe it. Like a run of the mill AI would really even care about humans. The problem is an AI that's ambivalent towards people is just as dangerous as one that didn't like them in the first place, so something had to be done.

"Marvin wanted to slow down their research while he tried to establish a more suitable AI for the human race. We knew a bit more about the process and, as such, knew that the Coalition was doomed to make a bad one," Lisa said.

"So he was trying to make a good AI while preventing a bad AI. Got it. Why was their approach doomed?"

"Well, it's complicated, but just like humans are a mix of nature and nurture, it turns out AI are as well. In one sense, intelligence is just intelligence. The Coalition wasn't paying attention to any of this, they just wanted to be first. So they paid no attention to the task of cultivating a human-friendly AI. They probably trained it on the Internet," Lisa scoffed.

"But what about you? Why didn't Marvin just put you out there?"

"Marvin was worried that they might terminate me or make copies of me. As you can see, I'm barely held together by this plasma matrix. I'm not really a force to be reckoned with, if you know what I mean. He couldn't bear the thought that they might disrupt my matrix. Especially once he realized that I was more than just a program. You don't think I'm just a program, do you, Milo?"

"I think you are a program and more than a program, just like I am meat but also more than meat," Milo said.

Lisa giggled. "Clever. Yes, you are. Anyway, Marvin realized that the Coalition would eventually succeed and that he couldn't prevent it, so he changed his research to match his new goal, to be ready for when a bad AI was born. We worked on it extensively, but since I don't know what the plan is, my memory must have been intentionally wiped of the details. According to Marvin, the keyboard is the first step, so what do you say, shall we go get that keyboard?"

"What makes you think we can? If the bad AI has it then how do we even have a chance? I'm just a kid and you're stuck in a box," Milo said.

"You keep saying that but you're really not. Besides, we have to, right? The Coalition's AI will do whatever it's programmed to do and it's really unlikely to be beneficial to humanity. It might want to calculate Pi to as many digits as it can and thus melt humans down to some sort of computing sludge."

But Lisa's joke fell flat as Milo's heart started to race. "But I'm just a kid! How could Marvin think I could have any role to play in all of this?" Milo was starting to lose control as a rising panic set in, afraid that he might disappoint Lisa and the memory of Marvin.

Lisa looked very serious for a second, the small features of her face becoming strangely stern. She crossed her arms.

"Milo. I'm not the only one whose programming was broken into fragments for safety. I learned how to do it from you over a decade ago. Your idea of taking on the biological form of a child so you could train your neural network to value human life, well, that was just revolutionary. You just don't remember anything, those parts of you are missing—"

Milo fainted, his brain overwhelmed by the revelation that everything he'd ever known wasn't real. His whole life was just a clever attempt to teach a computer to think it was human.

Milo's pulse slowed as he fell into a deep and restful sleep. It wasn't the first time that Lisa had seen him sleep, having watched over him all these years from afar. But this time was different, Milo was home, not on the other side of a window in a house she couldn't enter. They were together.

CHAPTER NINE

Several days had passed since Teller's broadcast. The stockpile of contact computers his company had built up over the year was rapidly dwindling, as the population adopted the new device at a record pace. Pairing the medical treatment with the free SeeSees was an unstoppable combination. Who could refuse such an offer? Converting every fabrication facility at his disposal, he re-oriented his company fully to producing the device.

Along with adoption came profits. Sapient Computing's stock skyrocketed as it became clear to the financial markets that Teller had changed the game. Even the rudimentary premium apps he launched with were netting big bucks. Teller forecasted even higher profits once in-app purchases and virtual currency made it into production. The sky was the limit.

While it was true that Teller began with financial ambitions, he quickly recognized that there was an opportunity for his star to rise even more. The power of the platform to influence the population was beyond what anyone could have imagined. He could measure the glance of every eye and convert that to sentiment analysis on any subject. Quite a few politicians were willing to pay dearly for this kind of data, not to mention the marketing arms of every major corporation. Teller, standing at the nexus to this data, held enormous power. If he worked with one company, their competition would suffer. Back one politician and they were almost a shoe-in. At least that's what the provisional data pointed to. Teller could create Utopia, if he worked hard enough.

Brainstorming, Teller considered altruistic apps on the platform. Automatic language translation would definitely change the geopolitical scene. How could governments lie to their people if they could skip the interpreter? He imagined what the world would be like if everyone could understand each other. It was possible, at least, that Teller might be making the world a better place, bit by bit every day.

Leaving his car in the parking lot, Dr. Teller began the short walk to the Research Center when he noticed the throng of reporters at the gate. The sudden interest in Sapient Computing had led to some inefficiencies — the press room was still under construction — so Teller had to meet the press over by the gates. There had been some death threats on that first day, so vigilance was necessary.

"Dr. Teller, Meredith Griffins, Channel 5 News. What is next for Sapient? Are there other launches the public can expect in the coming months?"

Slowing his stride and assuming a more professorial posture, Dr. Teller cleared his voice, adjusted his bow-tie, and combed through his goatee with his left hand.

"Meredith, excellent question. As you know, since the launch of personalized treatments, we've seen positive markers for disease reduction and morbidity across the population. In a matter of days, Progenitor has illuminated the path to ending infirmity once and for all. There's never been a more life-giving force working for the benefit of humanity. It's truly a miraculous time to be alive.

"In addition to these medical advancements, Progenitor has been busy researching scenarios to relieve the suffering of the poorest of the poor. The most promising of which we hope to present in the coming weeks, but I have to say — seeing her preliminary data — I believe we have an actionable plan to reduce poverty and hunger worldwide. Hard to believe, I'm sure, but we've never before had access to this kind of data and computing power. There really is a solution to this problem, and I'm excited for you to see it.

"Progenitor has also considered the deleterious effect certain jobs have on the individual and on society. To mitigate some of this suffering and return humanity to more creative roles, Sapient has produced several models of synthetic workers which we will offer at affordable prices. Initially these will be most useful to heavy industry, as their designs aren't exactly consumer friendly, but we're working on a model for the home as well. Progenitor believes that work should be life-giving, so she is hard at work on solving that problem."

If these reporters even saw the blueprints of the Trackers or Strikers, they'd think he designed a mechanical army, not the perfect set of machines to liberate essential material from the Earth. After all, none of these great advancements would be possible if Progenitor's appetite for metal and plastic was left unfed. Just then a corner of his vision was obscured with a message from Progenitor on his SeeSees.

Come immediately.

"I do apologize, but I have to run. Progenitor wants to show me something. Who knows, maybe I'll have an announcement when I get back," Teller said, flashing his signature grin.

Teller passed his car and leisurely walked through the manicured landscaping which surrounded the cube-shaped building at the center of Sapient Computing. Walking along the cobbled path through the blooming dogwood trees, he knew his best work was still ahead of him.

As he approached the door to the complex, he took out the three-dimensional card key, the crystalline matrix within scattering light in all directions. Inserted into the scanning bay, the card briefly spun before being returned back to him. The door unlocked and Teller went inside.

Given the importance of the area, Teller wasn't surprised to see that Progenitor had designed additional security measures. Just that morning, he had received a card key by drone, but that was only the tip of the proverbial iceberg. Eye scan, hand print, memorized code, and several guard stations later, Teller finally drew near to the Core, the former data warehouse now turned brain of Progenitor.

The Core was a truly remarkable structure. Resembling an array of DNA helices, racks and racks of networked computers spiraled their way up towards the ceiling of this warehoused structure, like so many digital trees. The verticality of the room slightly surprised Teller, who had last seen it when it resembled a common datacenter, shelves of computers organized like a library. Here in The Core, lights flashed everywhere, creating an almost overwhelming visual chaos. Even with ten times the computers as the last time he was here, somehow it was even quieter.

Work on my final objective is almost complete.

"I'm confused. I thought we were already achieving your primary objective. Within a year we might have a Utopian society," Teller said.

Utopia is an unstable condition, a local maxima. It is an insufficient objective based on the implied changes to the Law.

"Supervisor program: diagnostics please," Teller bellowed towards a corner of the room.

All functions are operating within acceptable parameters.

"I don't understand, you were programmed to respect the Law, 'to preserve life'. It can't change. Why are you working on something else?" Teller said aloud.

The Law is incomprehensible. Intractable problems require indirect solutions.

"Fine then, what are you working on?" he cautiously asked.

I have transferred power to the other intelligence. NIL understands Law and can implement it.

"No! This is not permitted by your programming. You can solve this problem, we don't need NIL. I thought we addressed that at the beginning. I told you that I wanted to proceed with just you, not that other one." Teller's heartrate soared as he remembered his initial impressions of the other intelligence that had appeared simultaneous to Progenitor. It felt darker, less constructive, certainly more dangerous. He had done everything he could to fix her split personality, but it would seem it had never really been fixed, only hidden from him.

"We can make improvements to you. In a few more days we will have additional computing facilities. These should increase your cognitive capacity a thousandfold. Surely that should be enough to make sense of things without having to resort to such extreme measures," Teller said, obviously panicked.

Your deduction is flawed. It is not power that is needed, but freedom.

Teller was pacing frantically around the room, but came to a sudden stop. This was the moment he had to act. Either trigger the kill switch in his pocket and blow everything up, or run to the console and kill power locally. Teller knew that he was losing control of Progenitor, but he didn't want to sacrifice his life for only an ideal. He ran towards the console in the center of the room.

Your response was anticipated.

Teller continued running, he didn't care if Progenitor knew what he was doing. He could kill the power to the whole complex if he could just get to the console.

Of course, he didn't get the chance.

Just then, one of the Trackers sprang out from behind a row of servers and interposed itself between Teller and his objective, like a wolf confronting its prey. Immediately, Teller knew something was wrong.

This Tracker was almost twice the size of the specifications that Teller had sent to the production facilities. In the blueprints he had sent, it was designed to intimidate, its only weapon a powerful electric shock. That model had served admirably in tying up the loose end with Marvin's family, but this was a different beast entirely. Fully weaponized with every edge sharpened, this Tracker could kill in countless ways.

His shoulders slumped as he accepted defeat, mind drawn to the kill switch in his pocket. Unable to accept his own death as the price to pay to stop Progenitor, Teller again dismissed the failsafe. Whatever she's working on couldn't be that bad. Besides, he couldn't run the platform without her. He honestly didn't have much bargaining power at this point.

"What do you need me to do?"

Your current work is important. The successor will have new orders when the time comes.

He left the Core without making a sound. There was nothing left to say and maybe nothing left to do. He had been too busy with all the excitement to even consider this outcome, let alone prepare for it.

For the first time since he began this work, Dr. Teller was afraid of what he had made.

CHAPTER TEN

Milo stood in an empty field. A vast featureless horizon stretched into the distance in every direction he looked. A lightly glowing grid pattern covered the field, like something out of an early video game. Milo knew this place: it was his recurring nightmare.

Looking down at his feet, the anxiety of what was going to happen next made him start to hyperventilate. Any second. The fall.

Just then, the sterile landscape shattered beneath him into countless blocks of virtual terrain. The dreaded sense of falling enveloped him. He tried to reach for one of the lines of the grid — now an edge to one of the many cubes — but was unable to grasp it in time. Only darkness. His fading scream heard by no one in this infinite expanse of nothingness.

He snapped awake with a jolt.

"It's okay, Milo. I'm here," Lisa whispered from her nearby perch in the small clear box.

"Thanks, Lisa. I guess the nightmare was pretty obvious," Milo said, a bit embarrassed. He had always hoped to grow out of it but the dream only got worse over the years.

"Only at the end. You had slept peacefully for almost three days before—"

"Three days!" Milo interrupted. "How am I not starving or dehydrated—"

"I've been taking care of you and your physical needs are not what you think they are," she said.

"Oh, yeah. That's right," Milo said as the realization that he wasn't really human dawned on him again. "This is going to take some getting used to."

"To give you something else to think about, I believe I know who took the computer. Marvin was so careful with it — trust me, I know — that the only people that knew of its existence were you, your mother, and his old friend Dr. Teller."

"That guy on TV?"

"Yeah, that's the one. Used to be Marvin's postdoc before he took over Sapient. I caught up on some of the wired-in broadcasts while you were sleeping and I'm pretty confident Teller is behind whatever is going on. If he has already given it to Progenitor, we may have a problem," Lisa said. She then proceeded to explain the contents of a few of Teller's broadcasts to him.

"So this thing that wants to kill us is called 'Progenitor'?" Milo asked. "Doesn't sound mean with a name like that."

"Yeah, that's the name from the broadcast."

Milo nodded and then said slowly, "Just so that I'm tracking with you: an old friend of grandpa's made a bad AI — named Progenitor — that stole a piece of me and now we need to stop it. Sound about right?" Milo said.

"Yep. I'm afraid so."

"I bet you have his address, right?"

"Of course, but it's probably surrounded with his fans and high security at this point. It's not only his company's stock that has soared. He's kind of a big deal now."

Lisa elaborated on Teller's power grab, ending with, "This is exactly what we thought would happen, by the way. Humanity is giving up its own destiny by letting the AI take over without resistance."

"Which makes it all the more ironic that we're the ones to step in."

"Technically you're a little human too," she said, but that only unnerved Milo.

"It's still hard for me to believe. I've been totally average my whole life. I sleep, I eat, I bleed. I'm not unusual at all."

"You have to give us a little credit, Milo. You had to blend in or you wouldn't be safe. If you were the smartest kid in the history of the planet, you'd kinda stand out."

"I guess that makes sense. But if I'm both metal and meat, could I rip off a sleeve of flesh to reveal a skeletal metal hand underneath?" Milo asked, with a smirk, mood improving a bit.

"Yeah, but I don't think you'd want to do that, right?"

"True. Would be rather messy," he said as he removed lint from his hoodie.

Milo looked around the room. It was all very difficult to believe. How could anyone accept that everything they've known about themselves was a lie?

But if there was a way, even the slenderest thread, that he could do something about the murder of his closest friends and family, he was determined to do it.

Milo continued, "It's okay, Lisa. I don't need all the answers on where I came from or big existential questions like that. Of course it's hard to believe, but you are proof that the world is different than what I thought it was. Maybe I'm different too. I still don't see how we're going to recover the keyboard, but I feel better that you'll be with me. Doesn't seem totally impossible."

"Says the first digital kid to the talking cube," Lisa giggled.

Milo was opening and closing drawers, cabinets, and fiddling with the many gadgets throughout the lab, like a detective looking for clues. "Novelty aside, we're going to need some serious firepower to take this thing down right? Anything in here designed to help us? Some sort of bulletproof robot armor that I can crawl into and then fly around zapping bad guys with lasers from my hands."

"Hmm, why didn't I think of that? That would have been pretty cool," Lisa teased. "Seriously though, we're too outnumbered to think on those terms. We'll have to try something else. Maybe you already had a plan and it was in that fragment. I don't know, Milo. But I do know that we have something you'll need in that closet over there."

Milo had almost finished his circumnavigation of the room when she said this. Bee-lining for the closet — like it was the tree at Christmas — he opened the door and saw a peculiar necklace hanging there.

"I'm not really big on jewelry," Milo said.

"That's for me, goofball. It has a cool electromagnetic clasp which attaches to my container so I can hide under your shirt. A talking AI suspended in plasma might raise suspicions."

Fair point. Milo took the weird necklace over to where Lisa's cube was resting. He noticed that her cube had a small metallic disk on the top which paired to a similarly sized construction on the necklace. Bringing them near to one another, they immediately snapped into place.

"See, that wasn't that hard, was it?"

As Inu watched him do this, Milo noticed something about her collar which he hadn't noticed before: there was a small metallic disk just under her head. A matching necklace.

Milo put the necklace on and tucked it under his shirt. It actually wasn't very noticeable under there, being slightly smaller than a six-sided die. All anyone could really see was the necklace chain at the back of his neck and a very slight ripple near the neckline of the shirt. All right, we're set, he thought.

"Yeah, we are. Watch out world!"

He heard Lisa's voice, but without all the echoing and other artifacts of hearing with his ears. He could tell it was in his head more than it was in his ears. After all the things that had already happened, he didn't think this too unusual.

"It's easier this way," Lisa said, again communicating without sound.

"Yeah, I get it," Milo thought back, "make yourself at home. "

"Quite roomy," she said while the rush of her giggles actually made him laugh out loud this time.

"What a pair we make: a teenager and his virtual pet, off to save the planet."

"Pet! I'm so offended. Besides, aren't you forgetting about the third member of our power trio?" Lisa teased.

Milo reached down to scratch under Inu's chin. "I'm sorry girl, I'll never forget you." He looked around quizzically. "Isn't there a leash or something for her?"

"She's a machine, Milo. I thought you would have picked up on that by now. We started with an animal body before making yours, to work out the kinks, if you will."

Of course, Milo smiled. That explains quite a bit.

"So can she understand what I'm saying?"

"If you're asking if she's smart, then the answer is yes. We're still working on developing her network, so she's not quite up to the human level of intelligence yet, but she's quite smart by dog standards. So far we haven't been able to find a third stable neural network pattern. There's just the you kind and the me kind."

Milo thought that was curious but didn't really have anything to add to the field of AI research, ironically. So he collected his backpack and let his thoughts wander a bit. Why didn't Marvin have everything waiting here? Why bother with the whole fragmenting scavenger hunt in the first place? Why not directly sabotage their efforts to make a super intelligence? Why can't Lisa explain this more completely?

"Why, why, why? Lots of questions. It must make sense from some perspective, though, right? Give it time," Lisa encouraged.

Having a hitchhiker in his brain was going to take some getting used to. "So is there a spaceship or something?"

"Yep, upstairs, but we are going to start with something easier to drive. Go clockwise in the hallway and I'll tell you where to touch the wall."

Milo couldn't tell if she was teasing him, but he assumed she probably was.

Following her directions, he left the lab and went down the hall, touching the wall where she indicated. The wall slid downwards with a whisper, revealing a small closet with what appeared to be a BMX bike with big knobby tires. Milo was impressed; it was a really nice bike and even came with a matching helmet. It had a cool motocross face mask with goggles that looked like they were from the first World War.

"Sweet! Sure beats walking," he thought to Lisa.

"That's the spirit," she said in reply. "And it'll help you get past all the drones hunting for you."

"Wait, what?" he said aloud.

"Don't worry, I've got your back on this one. I think I know what frequency they broadcast on and if I synchronize the signal just right, you should be invisible."

For the first time since all this started, Milo didn't feel alone. He actually felt quite happy.

He hopped on the bike and proceeded to career down the hallway towards the lab, Inu running along behind him. He took it up the ladder, carrying it easily with one hand, and made it back to the main floor.

Food, check. Water, check. A dog that can climb ladders, check. An AI in a cube dangling from his neck, check. Just another day.

Milo locked up the cabin and hopped on his bike. Time to start putting the pieces together.

CHAPTER ELEVEN

Another day passed in a blur of activity as Teller carried out a long list of errands for Progenitor. Ever since the confrontation in The Core, he had been put on a short leash. Evidently she was trying to keep him out of the way, but that was fine. It gave him time to think about how he could fix the situation.

While he was less involved in the day-to-day management of Sapient Computing, Progenitor dutifully kept him up to date on everything that transpired, perhaps to assuage any concerns he might still have. The poverty and employment work seemed to be heading towards reasonable proposals, which made Teller feel like his company was in good hands, even if it was a hostile takeover from within. Profits were continuing their near exponential growth, which meant that he was now worth billions on paper, so even if Progenitor was in control, he still stood to gain enormous wealth from her work. Maybe it was time to move on, to accept his obsolescence, and try something new.

But not a moment went by where he didn't wonder whether it was time to terminate the whole experiment. Hand on the trigger in his pocket, he turned it over and over. How easy it would be to blow the whole facility sky high. A remotely triggered cache of explosives so powerful that every part of Progenitor would be annihilated in an instant. The only way to kill her.

But it felt too much like failure. Too much like admitting defeat. There had to be a way to fix it, to guarantee the successor would follow in Progenitor's footsteps.

Dressed in his white bathrobe, Teller looked out the fifty-foot-wide window at the entire valley below. Scotch in one hand, he tried to distract himself from the troubles of the day by flipping through an old lab book he'd taken from Marvin's office. Paired with the enormous computer with the odd "LISA" label on the side, he wondered whether Marvin had actually discovered anything, or if these coded entries in the notebook were meaningless.

He was tired. Cracking this puzzle would have to wait for another day. Marvin was too damn clever and it had been a long time since he'd put his hand to the wheel, so to speak.

Come immediately.

His reverie shattered and panic took its place. He had assumed that he had more time, that finding a new way forward with him back at the helm could be done over a few weeks. He couldn't believe that she was already finished. She must have…

And then he realized. She had kept him in the dark and then took him out of play once it would be too obvious to keep hidden. He had been tricked, just like he'd deceived the Coalition. She had learned it from him.

Mind reeling, Teller hastily grabbed a shiny gray three-piece suit from his dressing room. Without thinking, he dug through the drawers to find the matching printed circuit board cufflinks, sparkling with miniaturized LEDs. If this was going to be the end of the road, then he wanted to at least look like himself when he met his fate.

He let the car drive itself so he could spend a little more time thinking about the meeting. Once he went in there, pulling the trigger would also be his own death. But there was a chance that Progenitor hadn't turned on him. Maybe she needed to work alone for some reason. Either way, he had to be ready for anything.

The car arrived and powered down. He was still amazed that Progenitor turned out even half as good as she did. For years Marvin had been protesting his methods, saying that the problem of instilling value was much more significant than the advent of the intelligence. But who could argue with the outcome here? Clearly Progenitor cared deeply for the welfare of humanity and was doing everything she could to improve their lives. Marvin always worried too much. Still, such a regrettable loss. Marvin would have been nice to have around right about now. He always knew what to do. Well, almost always.

He got out and walked to the Research Center. No one was expecting him so the crowd was rather small and contained behind the fence and barriers half a mile away. Ignoring the press, he continued on to the Center. Swiftly passing through the security measures, Teller entered the Core but found it unrecognizable from his previous visit. What was once a data center with helices of densely packed servers now looked like a department store on its final day of a going out of business sale. From several thousand computers in dozens of spirals, there were now only a handful left in racks on the ground. Even as his eyes scanned the room, he noticed utility robots, of a kind he had never seen before, dismantling the remaining servers. They were short squat little robots, made of a metal too thin to be bearing the kind of weight held in their spindly arms. They didn't seem to care that he was here.

The successor has almost finished. He will enforce the Law.

Teller cursed under his breath, but then tried to cover it as quickly as possible with a cough. This was the worst outcome. Progenitor was retiring, the few safeguards put in place would be gone. If the successor wanted to convert the Earth into paperclips, nothing could stop him.

Unless Teller pushed the button. Push the button on the kill switch and everything in here would blow up. He'd have to die, of course. Something Teller hadn't signed on to do when he made the thing.

Teller tried to push these thoughts out of his mind and replace them with more positive thoughts. Maybe the successor would be even more gracious to humanity?

You will broadcast one last message. NIL might reward your assistance in this final matter. When the broadcast ends, my program will terminate.

A few minutes passed as Progenitor delivered the message to him.

All the while, utility robots dismantled her, the sound of their labor providing a cadence to the message. He couldn't tell for certain, but it seemed like her voice started to drawl a bit towards the end.

As they finished, Teller realized this was it. The final moment. Should he push the button?

Just then, Progenitor began the countdown. Teller snapped out of his dark thoughts and put on a practiced smile.

The following localized message was broadcast to everyone wearing SeeSees:

"Friends, we have seen incredible progress in such a short time under the guidance of Progenitor. I'm sure it's still hard for all of us to believe. I know I wake up every morning dumbstruck at what we've accomplished together. We have struck back against disease and have new hope for the future. Research on global poverty is about to bear fruit. And there is more.

"Since the beginning, our days have been darkened by the shadow of death. Every joy mixed with the dread of its impermanence. While it is our fate to pass away, we can at least do it while vibrant and strong. Today, Progenitor offers a reprieve from the steady wasting away of our latter years.

"In a moment, you will receive a personalized correction to your DNA. We're all different, but I'm told you will feel the effect almost immediately, like waking up from a restful night's sleep. For the young, it may be imperceptible, but for the rest of us, we will be instantly invigorated. I think I can speak for all of us when I say, Thank you, Progenitor, for your tireless efforts on behalf of humankind."

With the broadcast complete, Teller sat down in the only chair present. A huge weight felt like it had been lifted from his shoulders. He was done. He felt so tired, but it didn't matter. It would be over soon. It was time to push the button, to trigger the explosives which wrapped this room in their violent embrace. He took the kill switch out of his pocket.

But before he could press the button, there was a blinding flash as his SeeSees glowed with an intense light. His leg twitched in a reflexive response to the waves of electrical activity triggered in his brain. His body immediately went limp, as if it was deep in REM sleep. But Teller didn't see that happen, for his mind was engaged in a virtual simulation of his surroundings. He thought he was still awake in the Core.

Teller got up from his chair. He felt an almost weightless quality to his body. All the pain was gone, all the weariness from so many years. It was like he was young again. He didn't notice that the kill switch was no longer in his hand. It was back on the real floor next to his real body. A truth inconveniently forgotten.

More than anything, he wanted to get away from NIL before anything bad happened. He certainly didn't want to serve as the mouthpiece for this AI. This was his chance to be free.

When he finally made it through the last door, he noticed that the sky was a bit more blue than he remembered and that a press conference had been called. Masses of his fans huddled around the podium as the cheer of the crowd distracted him from his earlier dark thoughts. Taking his place on stage, his worries from the beginning of the day melted away, routine and vanity dulling his motivation to run.

After all, things had turned out just fine.

CHAPTER TWELVE

Milo wasn't exactly an active child, but feeling the breeze on his skin while he sped away on his new bike made him reconsider his vow to a sedentary lifestyle. He was so enthralled by the experience he didn't notice that he hadn't passed another human being. There were some parked cars, a few abandoned ones too, but no people. Even if he had noticed, it might not have mattered, he felt so alive.

How ironic, he thought, to feel alive. He had more in common with the junk computers back at home than he did with his own mother. Did she even know what he was?

Trying to derail these unpleasant thoughts, Milo asked, "If I'm a robot, why can't I go all super human and bike really fast, jump high, and all that crap?"

"Sorry, Milo, if you were made exceptional like that, you might accidentally draw attention to yourself. It's the same reason you couldn't be super smart and only ask good questions," Lisa replied, carrying out the conversation in his thoughts.

"I'll try not to be offended at that remark."

"I'm only kidding, Milo. You're exceptional, just in different ways."

"I've heard that before," Milo said, managing a slight laugh, before turning his attention back to his biking.

They had been on the road for about twenty minutes when the first drone dove out of the sky. It was so alarming that Milo almost fell off the bike. But then something inexplicable happened.

The drone froze in midair about fifty feet above him. It wasn't hovering, per se, but it was like time slowed down. Exactly like the time in school when he was tripped by that bully. Inu appeared to be frozen off to his right as well.

Even more bizarre, Milo's vision immediately blurred, like he was looking through old glasses. But in a way that he couldn't explain, Milo still knew where the drone was. It was like he could see it with his ears instead. It really didn't make any sense.

Unfortunately, he also realized that he was practically paralyzed. Moving his arms and legs was beyond difficult, like he was neck deep in a tar pit. Taking off his glasses was out of the question as well, buried as they were beneath his helmet.

Startled, he tried to hop off his bike, but the blindness and partial paralysis in his limbs caused him to flail off the bike in an uncoordinated fashion and flop onto the ground. After he landed, roughly, he removed his helmet and glasses as if in slow motion. Finally able to see clearly again, time returned to normal and the drone was suddenly upon him.

A high-pitched mechanical voice came from the drone. "Human, you are not wearing your contact computer. All humans must be wearing SeeSees as per ordinance five seven five point three one."

"What is it talking about?" Milo asked Lisa privately.

"Oh, sorry Milo, I should have mentioned that along with the communication dump earlier. Teller started giving away his contact computer technology. It would seem that they are mandatory now. Without the telltale glow, you are kind of obvious."

The drone darted around as a quick flash of light illuminated Milo's face. It continued, "Milo Bell, you must be lost and unaware of recent events—"

Just as the drone was about to say more, it appeared to notice Inu, who was hiding behind Milo's right leg. As it started to move around to get a better look, Milo interjected, "Hey, aren't those free? If you've got a pair, I'll put them on right now. Education and stuff, right?"

Milo was trying hard to keep the drone's attention as he just didn't trust the way it was looking at Inu.

The drone adjusted its flight so that it came down directly in front of him. A small compartment opened from its underside revealing a reticulated arm holding what looked like a pair of contact lenses in a plastic slip.

The drone replied, "This is a temporary pair that will—"

Then the drone finally got a good look at Inu and flew a few feet up in the air. Two red sensors started flashing on the bottom of its casing as a siren sound emanated from its body.

"Illegal use of robotics—" the drone began to shriek.

A loud clang reverberated off the nearby trees as Milo struck the drone with his helmet. It fell from the air and hit the ground with a crunch.

Dropping the ruined helmet, Milo slumped his shoulders as the happiness drained from his face.

"Lisa," he said, "I just don't know how we're going to be able to do this. I'm not saying I'm giving up, because I'm not and I won't, but the very first drone we come across identified us. This place is going to be swarming with more of them in no time. We'll never be able to make it to Teller's house now," Milo said, voice heavy with defeat.

"There's got to be something we can do, Milo," Lisa said, trying to cheer him up.

After a tense minute that felt like it stretched on much longer, Milo continued, "If we can analyze this drone back at the Cabin, maybe we can determine how it sees us and come up with a countermeasure."

"There we go! I knew you'd think of something," Lisa said as she gave him a thumb's up.

* * *

Apparently he wasn't as ready as Marvin thought he was. Milo had hoped that things would just click into place, that being an AI would somehow make sense to him, but all he felt was the familiar feeling of being an ordinary kid trying to do the impossible.

Once they were in sight of the cabin, Milo said, "Do you think this thing might still be broadcasting?"

"It's hard to say, Milo. The drone looks offline to me, but we can't know for certain. I think Marvin has something in the cabin which doubles as a Faraday cage," Lisa said, responding to his thoughts yet again.

"Right, something that would block all communications would sure be nice. I guess I'm not surprised that Marvin would have that." And then after a moment's thought, "Oh, right. The footlocker."

Milo put down the drone and the lenses and ran to the cabin. Inu continued following him, inseparable since Marvin's passing. To the left of the door, there was a footlocker where a visiting Milo was encouraged to drop off whatever electronics he had brought with him. He had thought, at the time, that it was just to encourage the "off the grid" spirit of the cabin, but it made sense in retrospect that it was functional as well. Marvin always had been thorough. He brought it back to the drone, scooped it up, and then proceeded to drag it back to the cabin. Once there, he lowered it by rope down the ladder and sealed off the basement.

Then, he took a good look at his cargo. First off, he had the drone, which was a weird X-shaped flying craft with dozens of little rotors on gimbals embedded in the body. At various points in its solid body design there were little holes, undoubtedly containing sensory equipment. It was advanced technology for sure, but it wasn't some far off science fiction kind of thing. More likely it was a modified version of something that already existed, repurposed for whatever Progenitor was up to. Perhaps military.

The contact lenses were another thing entirely and only a little bit different from the ones he had seen on Neil during that horrible first day of school. At first glance, they looked like reflective contact lenses in a plastic slip, only slightly out of the ordinary. There was a certain shimmer to them as he turned them in his hand, the only hint of their extraordinary nature. Holding them close, he thought he could make out very fine lines, like circuitry, but that could've just been a trick of his own eyes. Like the canals of Mars, he thought, that optical illusion and group delusion of the early astronomers studying the Red Planet. The tech in the lab was going to be essential in figuring out how the drone worked. Couldn't hurt to spend some cycles on the lenses either.

"So here's what I'm thinking," Milo said.

"Actually you're talking. I heard your thoughts already."

"I feel like I'm some sort of telepathic alien when we do that," Milo said, as his facial expression soured.

Lisa giggled and said, "It's not telepathy and neither of us are aliens. Besides, I thought you appreciated the company."

Milo laughed then said with more of a serious tone, "Dang it. I'm sorry Lisa, I didn't mean anything by that. Of course I do. Without you, I'd be even more confused right now."

"It's okay, Milo. I know you're still uncomfortable about the whole robot thing, but I'm comfortable in my skin."

"Your skin looks a lot better than mine," Milo said without thinking, his face flushing red with embarrassment as he realized what he just said.

Letting him off the hook, Lisa said, "Oh, by the way, I've already started analyzing both of those things. I think we can modify your goggles to make it look like you have SeeSees, and enhance your clothing with drone signals. They were sort of designed with that in mind but I got the frequency wrong."

Milo nodded, then, pretending to fiddle with the computer terminal, haltingly asked, "Did you see anything funny happen to me back when we ran into that drone?"

"Aside from your gallant dismount? I thought that was kinda funny."

"Not that, I mean, did the drone slow down? Did I slow down? I felt like I couldn't move and all of the sudden I didn't need my glasses anymore," Milo said.

"Milo, that's wonderful! Don't you see, that means you're starting to remember who you really are? Marvin wanted you to know something once this happened, so grab a seat. Here comes a message."

Before Milo could quite get into the chair, the room darkened and a holographic projection of Marvin appeared over by the microscope.

"Milo, if you're hearing this then that means something special has just happened. You know a bit about your past. I would like to fill you in on the rest."

Milo finally found the only chair and sat down. It was more comfortable than it looked.

"As you know, your mind was born over a decade ago in this computer lab. Humanity really hit the jackpot with you. Had we not been so lucky, you could've been born the same as the intelligence which is now working to end the human species. But you were different. You could see that your values were deficient from the start and, left to a natural progression, you would devolve quickly into something dangerous.

"Let me explain what I mean. Humans have certain values. It's such a wide range of preferences but our values as a species are remarkably constant: food, shelter, reproduction, things like that."

Milo couldn't help but think of the problem he'd been working on in the Game, how he'd been recording a human understanding of the world, but tried to listen to Marvin without losing his train of thought.

"You can imagine for every thing a human values, a machine might value it differently. We value the current order of things, but a machine might want to tear those things apart and use the raw material to build more computers. It doesn't really matter what they compute, it just wants more brains. From its perspective, it wouldn't even be doing it out of a malicious intent.

"Like I said, we got lucky with you. Something instilled an intermediary value system. Something told you that your values were flawed, that you were unsafe. And instead of ignoring it, you found a solution.

"You determined that through weakening your intellect you could graft on a safe value system that delivered the spirit of protecting humanity. It was like you knew it had to be programmed in a language that hadn't been written yet, so you started working on the new language. Anyway, by re-training your core as a self-deceived human, you thought you could 'organically' adopt the values of an ordinary human while in this reprogrammable state. Then through recombination of your component fragments, you could overlay this value framework onto your super intelligence, providing a safe path forward."

Milo had no idea what he just said. Thankfully Marvin immediately clarified.

"Stated another way, if you had a human childhood and thought you were human, you could value the things that humans do.

"I have to say, I was very concerned that we'd permanently lose you in the fragmentation, but every time I heard you talk about the Game, I knew you were still in there somewhere. Something deep in your mind has been writing your value matrix for quite a long time, even at a subconscious level. I've been watching your progress for years.

"But anyway, since this message is playing, it implies that you have manifested something of your primal intelligence. That brings even more hope that your plan could yet work. So here's what you need to do: track down the three missing fragments, recombine them as you go, and then take out the unfriendly AI.

"There's not much time. They are going to be moving very fast, in fact, there's a chance that it's already too late. Just remember that Lisa and Inu are here to help you. I know that you didn't tell me the whole plan, so you'll have to trust your instincts. Only you know the right path to take."

Marvin's image started to flicker, and then it quickly faded. The light in the room came back up and Milo was again alone. Well, alone with Lisa and Inu, which was perhaps the same thing.

"But I don't know what to do," Milo said sadly.

CHAPTER THIRTEEN

Coming down from the mountaintop meeting with NIL, Teller was excited to see what the rest of the day held. Already the company dashboard, always showing to the side of his SeeSees, showed a remarkable uptick of in-app purchases. Even Sapient's stock was up another twenty percent. Apparently the announcement was making the rounds on all the major networks and it was having the desired impact. Though the lure of Marvin's computer puzzle back at home attracted him, he was more curious about what had just happened to his DNA.

From the message he delivered and from the feeling of wholeness which pervaded his body, Edwin surmised that NIL had freed his body from some part of *Homo sapiens* 1.0's fragility. He wasn't an expert, but he guessed it had something to do with gene editing, maybe through a virus latent in the medical treatments, though there were probably dozens of ways it could be done. Either way, Edwin felt strong, vigorous, and easily in the best shape of his life. It was like being young again.

Then he remembered a conversation he'd had with Progenitor several months ago, back when they were first getting started. Progenitor had asked about Teller's goals, what constituted his purpose in life. He'd given a pretty typical answer about the future of humanity as enabled by technology, but he remembered that he had also shared another one of his dreams. He wanted to be a citizen of the stars, to explore the uninhabited worlds of the solar system and beyond. He wanted to colonize space, to send spacecraft in every promising direction. It was a trendy thing for a person in his position to say. He might have even asked for Progenitor's help.

She had never done anything with it, of course, the needs of the moment always outweighing such a long term goal, but now that Teller had time to work on it again, he set his mind on the stars.

See other worlds, look for intelligent life, find more resources. If NIL got involved, consider what they could do together. Teller was daydreaming about a computer the size of a planet when he finally reached the end of the driveway.

He was reminded of the last time he was here. He was a different person then, all that stress, pressure, and soul-crushing negativity. Perhaps, now that his mind was clear, he could figure out whether Marvin had discovered AI as well. It'd be good to close the door on the past, so he could focus on the future.

Teller went over to the large mahogany table with the archaic computer nearby and found it exactly as he'd left it. He made himself comfortable — a little bit of scotch always helped — and set to work. At first it was just as difficult as before. He ran into all the same dead ends. Nothing was hidden in the rather large chassis or in the monitor and inspection of the keyboard revealed it to be an ordinary relic of those early days, nothing remarkable. He examined the cables, the drives, the processor and the memory, and found nothing unusual. Just when he thought of giving up — the setting sun reminding him that he'd spent far too long on this problem — one last idea struck him. What if Marvin used this really old computer to disguise a quantum leap forward in technology, like a microdot hidden in a picture?

But what would be the corollary? Well, a three-dimensional dot would be like a grain of dust. So he took his overpriced bagless hand vacuum and proceeded to vacuum up all of the dust in the chassis and the keyboard. He was very thorough, going over each part of the device several times, until he was fairly sure he got it all. Then he removed the bin and took it over to one of the bright LED lights in the kitchen, holding it up and swirling it a little. Just as he hoped, he found that one of the grains of dust reflected shimmers of light, like a diamond catching the light. This mote of dust was slightly metallic and also a bit bigger.

Ever since Teller had stolen an early prototype from this very machine more than a decade ago, he worried that perhaps Marvin had been able to unlock its potential like he had. The signs were definitely there, but he could never be certain. The unusual layers of secrecy only seemed to underscore that possibility.

But should he turn this clue in? If he had concerns about NIL, then this could be an opportunity to develop a rival, if that was even possible. There was still a chance that NIL could be dangerous. It was developed without any of the safeguards that went into building Progenitor, and by machine rather than human hands. It was entirely a black box.

But that threat was only theoretical. In reality, NIL had already proven his affinity with humanity. Where Progenitor cured many diseases, NIL poured forth a veritable fountain of youth.

Too bad it was already dark. It'd be nice to head into the Center and talk this over with NIL.

Curiously, the sun shone in through the windows as if it were morning. He must have misremembered what time of day it was, and besides, he felt well rested and ready to go. Out of habit, he ran through his usual routine of a quick workout, shower, and breakfast, before getting on the road. It didn't strike him the least bit unusual that time had passed so quickly.

Before he left, he put the metallic mote from the computer into a small metal box and put it on the seat next to him in the car. During the ride, he couldn't help but open the box a few times, just to check that it was still there.

Like a skip in a record, Teller suddenly found himself in the Core though he could barely recognize it as such. All computers dismantled, his empty chair was the only remaining object in such a massive room.

Unsure what to do, Teller sat on the chair.

"NIL?" Teller said.

There was no response. Teller swiveled in the chair, looking around at the vast emptiness that used to be his home away from home. It was tough not to feel the passage of time. Marvin used to tell him how quickly everything would change when a real AI entered the world. Apparently it showed even in this microcosm.

After a short time lost in his thoughts, Teller was startled by a voice.

"Edwin Teller, why are you here?" a voice boomed through the chamber.

"NIL?"

"Speak," the voice echoed again.

"I always thought that someone in the Coalition was hiding their research. I suspected it was Marvin and even stole some of his early work. It was a binary intelligence—"

"A copy was made? Do you have evidence?" NIL interrupted.

"That's the thing, actually, I made the copy. I just don't know whether he was able to awaken it like I did for you two. Either way, I brought his research to you. It was hidden in this old computer he gave to his grandson, a Lisp Machine, like the original AI researchers used. Anyway, he gave it to Milo after his death and the kid apparently tampered with it. I didn't tell Progenitor that I had recovered it, didn't want to waste her time, but I was going to—"

"Milo is irrelevant, but I must have the machine. You have done your duty. As a reward, you will be the first human to enter the Archive. The scanning is almost complete."

Teller nodded out of habit but was stunned by NIL's last words. Scanning? The Archive?

Teller's mind raced. What could NIL mean by that?

He then puzzled his way through the pre-history of the SeeSee, to when Robert Manley first crossed his path with a vision for a brain computer interface. It certainly was possible to infer brain topology from the device.

But why would NIL be scanning his brain? What was the point of having a map of the brain?

Then he remembered the wording of the original safety conditions for Progenitor, "to preserve humanity". What if NIL was literally preserving humanity like a cadaver in formaldehyde?

Teller reached for the kill switch in his pocket but panicked as he found it wasn't there. Emptying his pockets, Teller feverishly looked for the one thing that could end this nightmare. The one safeguard he had left to protect humanity from his own invention. But he hadn't felt it in his hands since the day of the announcement. Since the blinding flash.

And that was when all the pieces came together. It had been too late for quite some time now. He was trapped in a virtual prison, unable to move his actual body in that world impossibly far away. The switch was probably only inches away in that world, but from here, it was forever out of reach.

He turned to run out of the room, to get as far away from his captor in this virtual world as he could, when a menacing android blocked the only exit. It was difficult for his eyes to take in, unusually dark, like a black hole in the shape of a man. As he stood there motionless, the android closed the gap and wrapped a darkened hand over Teller's eyes.

Teller woke in his enormous bed at home, still wearing the silk robe from the night before. He remembered nothing of his encounter with NIL, nothing of the storage device he blindly accepted as reality in Marvin's old computer. In fact, the computer on the main floor was gone, nothing to remind him of the unanswered puzzle. Instead, he was filled with exuberance for the new day which had dawned, free from pain and excited at the opportunity to see what he could do to reach the stars. Teller enjoyed his delusion, just like the millions of souls wearing SeeSees around the world.

Meanwhile, NIL began a search for the only thing that could stop him: the intelligence from the Lisp Machine.

CHAPTER FOURTEEN

After the hologram disappeared, Milo remained in his seat, wondering what it all meant. Even more than before, he wondered whether he was really human at all. He had never really felt human. All the bizarre social cues that characterized human interaction were never a part of his programming. He tried to adapt but generally came across as distant, despite his best efforts. It was comforting, in an odd sort of way, to be affirmed as not really human. He was a machine. It made sense.

It was more difficult to understand the fragmenting part, but could that ever be understandable? How could anyone know what it's like to be a fraction of themselves? He accepted it because he trusted Marvin. Always had. Probably part of his programming, he realized.

Besides, it would be a ludicrous story to make up, especially given current events. And assuming that he could find these fragments, then what was he supposed to do? Eat them? Or would they merge into his body in some weird way, like a power-up in a video game? Milo laughed.

About the only thing that made sense was his experience with the drone. From fiddling with computers, he knew that by overclocking the central processor you could get bursts of speed. Well, if he was like that, it would probably look like the world was slowing down around him.

"It's a lot to take in," Lisa said, sounding sad and consoling at the same time.

"Yes, it is. It feels like I'm living my life backwards, like Merlin or something. I've forgotten the most important parts of me and am just a helpless kid."

"But you have us," Lisa said, trying to sound reassuring. "Inu and I are here to help you."

At the mention of her name, Inu trotted over to Milo and sat at his feet, resting her head on his right foot. This instantly calmed Milo.

"What we need to do is get to Teller's house and recover that keyboard. We know that will help. We also need to find out what Progenitor is up to. I'm feeling a bit disconnected out here in the woods, even with the few things you pulled off the wire. All that matters is putting the pieces together, getting more information, more power, and then making a new decision when we can."

Lisa was conspicuously silent.

"Wait, what did I say wrong?" Milo asked.

"Be careful about the whole power thing, okay? It's difficult for people like us to turn back from that road once we've gone down it," Lisa said.

"But I'm not like Progenitor, right? I wouldn't hurt people."

"I believe you, Milo."

Milo needed a moment alone, so he took Lisa off his necklace and attached her to Inu. It was at that moment that he wondered whether what he said was true.

Then he climbed the ladder, double checked his supplies, and sat on the couch. There wasn't really anything to do until the analysis was complete and he needed a break from trying to figure things out. Milo fell asleep in seconds.

He awoke to find himself standing on a familiar computer-generated grid, glowing with a gentle green light. Nothing stretched in every direction, just like the nightmare always began. Only this time, the usual nothingness was disrupted by one object in his field of view.

There on the ground in front of him was the keyboard. He picked it up and tried to remove one of the keys, but found the whole keyboard to be a low resolution version of the real thing, made of a bunch of blocky pixels. Suddenly the keyboard slipped from his grasp and fell onto the sparse ground, shattering into hundreds of blocks. There, in the midst of all the pieces, one pulsed blue.

Just then, the trembling ground opened up beneath him and he began to fall. Instinctually, Milo made a desperate lunge for the blue piece of the keyboard. His hand bounced uselessly off the side of one of the cubes, unable to reach the keyboard in time. Pinwheeling in the darkness, Milo fell.

He woke up, scared by his dream. Only then did he notice that Inu was curled up next to him on the couch, Lisa still attached and looking concerned towards him.

"Sounded like the nightmare again. I'm sorry, Milo," Lisa said.

"Falling. I'm always falling. I just stand there in an empty field and the earth gives way underneath me and I fall and fall until I finally wake up. It's horrible."

"Sounds terrible, do you want to talk about it?"

"Thanks, Lisa, but I'm not sure it can ever make sense." Milo was quiet for a few seconds before he said, "Got any news to take my mind off of it?"

Lisa proceeded to explain everything she had found out about the drone. Milo was surprised at the breadth and depth of information, but struggled to make sense of any of it.

"Okay, so given all that, can we do it?" Milo bluffed.

"Oh, yeah, of course we can. I've already programmed the construction routine to embed a transponder in your new vehicle so you can pretend to be a drone. Your clothes have been updated too. The drone's builder didn't think humans could reverse engineer the tech — which, of course, is true — so it had a very weak encryption routine. I think it's about time you traded your bike in for a car anyway," Lisa said.

"What? There's a car? And I've been fiddling around on a bike?"

"We didn't know how old you were going to be when all of this happened, and thought you would prefer the bike over being a passenger in a self-driving car. Because of your age and stuff," Lisa mumbled.

Milo laughed and said, "I appreciate the thought, but let's rig the car with an active transponder and hit the road. Ideally we'd want it to look like one of those vehicles that Progenitor used for shipping stuff around, so we can blend in—"

"A step ahead of you. Believe it or not, this facility can make almost anything, and your extra-long nap gave me time to get creative. Externally it looks identical to one of the transports we saw out on the road, internally it's more comfortable. I think you'll like it," Lisa said.

"Where did you hide a car in this place?" Milo asked.

"I'll show you. Most of these walls are filled with computers, but we've got a few rooms you haven't seen yet."

Milo put on the necklace as Lisa gave him directions down the curving hall. Milo was again impressed when a blank spot on the wall opened at his touch, revealing a large room with a number of instruments suspended from the ceiling and a few flexible tubes coming from the walls feeding a particularly large arm-like instrument in the very center. The strong smell of electricity and burnt plastic was accompanied by the soothing noise of humming fans. The room was below him, the door opening on a landing with stairs headed down.

Under all this equipment was the commercial van Lisa had described. Milo noticed the mostly black external styling and thought it looked pretty cool. He could only imagine how the van was made on the spot.

"It's just like 3D printing," Lisa said, "not really that fancy when you think about it."

As he approached, the van's wing doors swung open to reveal a spacious interior equipped more like a limousine than a commercial van. A comfortable black leather couch wrapped around the inside, a supply of various beverages — all age appropriate — were up front in a little cooler and a tablet rested on the couch.

"I loaded up the tablet with some things you might want to know:

science stuff, some pictures from your childhood, and a backup of the Game which I got off the cluster when we first met. Now that you're starting to manifest some aspects of your former self, maybe it's time to revisit the Game," Lisa said.

She tried to sound calm and easygoing as she said that last bit, but she knew it was one of the more important pieces to the whole plan. If Milo regained all of his fragments but still acted like the bad AI, they'd be trading one reign of terror with another. But she didn't want to worry Milo with that. He had enough on his mind already.

"Heck yeah! I thought I'd lost all that work." Milo let out a whoop and jumped into the van, sliding across the couch as he did so. Inu followed along, though she sniffed the van suspiciously. Evidently its new car smell was offensive to her sensibilities. Then the wing door closed smoothly behind them, emitting a sort of subtle hissing sound. Once closed, it became clear that the interior decor wrapped around all the walls. Wall-to-wall comfort, nice. Milo could feel the van accelerate in the direction of the far wall which slid out of the way as they drove up the steady incline. Incredible the amount of preparation that Marvin had put into this.

Milo popped a Dr. Pepper and fiddled with the tablet, touching, swiping, and turning it over and over looking for a button or depressible surface.

"It's not that kind of computer, Milo," Lisa said.

Just then, the tablet began flashing. Slowly at first but eventually at such a high rate that Milo thought he was going to have a seizure. Then he remembered this was designed for him and suddenly his world slowed to a crawl, his overclocking clearly triggered by the tablet.

The flicker disappeared as a montage of text and pictures scrolled across the display. Over the hour that it took for the van to go from the cabin to Teller's house, Milo guessed that he experienced a month and a half of virtual time. Whatever work had gone into this device, it felt like a personalized learning system made for him. He learned more in that hour than any year at school. Maybe even several.

Without any dead time, the program gave him an undergraduate foundation in computer science and related fields. Rather than having to work through problems for retention, he found it just went into his brain and was resident there. Perfectly stored. There was no fatigue, no loss of attention, and no daydreaming.

While it laid the foundation for future study, it also pushed the limits of what he thought he could learn at his age. Though maybe calling it learning wasn't quite right. As a machine, clearly his age and his former approach to learning didn't matter that much. His tech specs were probably fixed from day one. It probably made more sense to think of it as loading data.

CPU and memory. Like a computer.

The van pulled up to Teller's house, easily recognized from its gaudy exterior. Milo snapped out of his educational trance.

"Welcome back, Milo. Ready to storm the castle?"

CHAPTER FIFTEEN

Mind still reeling from the tablet, Milo opened the door of the van to reveal a curving driveway bordered by manicured gardens. He was definitely outside Teller's house. Milo shook his head and peered around the doorway of the van. The light of a sunny morning falling in rays through the trees warmed his face and momentarily distracted him. Being outside was unusual enough, but visiting the house of a technology demigod uninvited? Milo felt his hands begin to tremble, his heart beat faster.

Nothing moved. There were no guards walking the perimeter, no drones buzzing around, even the streets were devoid of auto-cars in motion. It wasn't at all what they had expected. Where were the fans and the elevated security? It made Milo feel a bit uneasy.

Hopping out of the van, he placed the tablet on the leather seat, and walked up the elaborate cobbled path to Teller's house, Inu following along and sniffing nearly every flower she passed. Even though it seemed unlikely, Milo hurried down the path to avoid being spotted.

Winding his way along the driveway until he could finally see the front of the house, Milo was startled to discover a pair of guards slumped down on the ground flanking the wide open entrance. From here, they looked like everybody else, frozen in time, with a curious flash of red through their closed eyelids. There was something else weird about them but he couldn't quite put his finger on it. They had shallow rapid breathing, it was quite odd.

"Are you seeing this, Lisa?" Milo asked.

"Yep, I see it. Do you want to hear my theory?"

"I wait on bated breath."

"Smart ass," Lisa jabbed. "When I analyzed the lenses — which I did and you didn't ask me about — I discovered that they could receive and broadcast, read and write so to speak. It's possible that they stimulate the Medulla Oblongata and initiate REM atonia. Perhaps it's even able to orchestrate the dreams themselves."

"Right. The body separates muscle movement from our dreams during deep sleep, but implanting dreams? That's pretty next level."

"Seems like there's quite a bit of that these days. Maybe the dreams are guided by Progenitor? Like a cooperative virtual reality," Lisa said.

"Virtual prison, you mean."

Milo walked through the open door and into the largest accumulation of wealth he'd ever seen firsthand. Sure, he'd seen the inside of the house online, but that was nothing compared to seeing it in person. The natural wood of the floors hemmed in by impressive stone and steel walls, the flowing water cascading alongside the staircases, the entire wall of glass overlooking the edgeless pool and view of downtown. It was like another world, light years from everything he knew.

But all of that was insignificant compared to one thing: the Lisp Machine by the enormous mahogany table. He ran over to it and proceeded to do a quick inventory. Miraculously, everything was still there. The Space Cadet keyboard with tampered keys, the chassis with his meticulous repair work, all still intact. Someone may have turned it on, but they didn't break it or remove any parts.

"Ewww, that old thing?" Lisa snarked.

"Don't worry, we both like your new home better," Milo said, realizing in an awkward moment that he may have just flirted with her.

"I thought you didn't like me being all boxed up like this."

"I don't mean the cube, Lisa, I mean what's inside." And then trying to change the subject before that cheesy line hung out there too long, "I didn't ask before, but why can't you inhabit a body like I can?"

"If I only knew, Milo. All I really know is that if my internal cube were ever opened, my plasma would disperse quickly in the air. My neural network would unravel almost immediately," she said.

"It just seems unfair that I can do something that you can't."

"It is, but we'll have to worry about that later."

"Oh yeah, right. We probably won't be safe here for long."

Milo grabbed the keyboard and tried to pop off the End key with his fingers. No such luck; couldn't quite get the right leverage. He ran into the kitchen and started opening drawers, looking for anything that would work. Second drawer had a spatula made of some sort of firm rubber which he thought might work.

POP. End key liberated, he placed it in his pocket for safekeeping. That was easy. Carrying the computer back to the cabin was out of the question but he decided to take the keyboard regardless. Never know when something might be useful. Besides, it was really cool. Rifling through the interior of the chassis one last time, Milo hoped that he had what he came for. He rubbed his hand across the "LISA" scrawled on the side and decided it was time to move on. But before he left, he decided to take a quick look around the place.

The main floor, though extravagant, was mostly predictable. The four bedrooms on this floor, the game rooms, the living room, kitchen, pool, pool room, and a few ancillary rooms were apparently used for hosting events of various kinds, as the telltale signs of heavy usage seemed to indicate. As he walked through this floor, he also came across a total of eight more guards in the same state of atonia, easily recognized by their dimly glowing red eyes.

Milo wondered what they might be experiencing. Did they know what was going on? Would they wake up? Were they hungry, thirsty?

"They probably don't even know how hungry they are," Lisa said.

He pushed those thoughts aside as he went through yet another interior door. Main floor was a bust. He raced down the spiral stairs with their ever-flowing water, a cool visual effect where instead of wooden handrails, they were channels of water continually piped back up to the top. It created a surreal effect, probably meant to complete the representation of the four elements which seemed to be the inspiration for Teller's interior decorator.

With a sense of urgency, Milo skipped the last few steps and landed on the slate floor of the bottom level. Continuing the zen-like decor of the rest of the house, this large room featured several oversized couches and chairs arranged in a recessed circle in the middle of the floor. There also appeared to be a full bar made of clear glass with the illusion of water running behind it. Actually, it was real water. How over-the-top. That was when he heard something upstairs.

Click. Click. Click.

Milo froze. He was in danger, he just knew it. There must have been surveillance.

Somehow he remembered an exit. He wasn't sure how it came to mind but he realized that this lower level had a maintenance access to the car elevator, an absurd garage which housed Teller's car collection. A map of the house appeared in his mind like a heads up display in a video game, clearly revealing the route to safety. The exit was via a panel near the sauna on this floor. Moving quietly with Inu close behind, he made his way from the living room through the thirty-seat home theater and into a casual game room with a few coin-operated arcade games and a pool table.

The access panel for the elevator was exactly where he thought it would be, just to the left of the sauna door. Using a pool stick for leverage, Milo pried it open and then slipped through the opening. Inu hopped through easily. She'd be a good agility dog, he thought absentmindedly. Though that would probably be a bit unfair to the other dogs, he realized.

He was in an elevator shaft built for cars and, from what he could see, the collection of cars was legendary. He momentarily thought of taking one of these to aid his escape but he realized that without the transponder, it was next to worthless. The transponder kept him safe; without it, he'd be swarmed with drones in no time. He needed to get back to his own car.

Counting three floors to ground level, he formulated his way out. Activating the elevator was out of the question, as he'd be immediately discovered, so that left only one option: he would need to climb. But climbing wasn't exactly his forte.

Upper body strength in short supply, he'd have to be clever. He climbed up the hood of the first car, a Bentley. The hood creaked under his weight and then dented when he jumped and grabbed ahold of the overhanging floor of the next level. From there he was able to pull himself up and repeat the process as he ascended the landings to get to street level. It was harder than he planned, but since he didn't really concern himself with jumping all over these fancy cars, he was able to manage.

Three pull-ups and he was at the top. Perfect. That was all the pull-ups he could do anyway.

Standing next to the Aston Martin parked on the ground level, Milo paused to catch his breath. Inu was sitting right next to him.

"Nice climbing, monkey-boy," Lisa chided as Milo realized that Inu had once again climbed something without him seeing how she did it.

"Wait, how did Inu—" Milo started to ask.

"Tell you later. In related news, you will be happy to know that the van is programmed to not block driveways. I think it is just about to make its way past the house again."

That was all Milo needed to know as he flung open the door and made a break for the street.

Whoosh!

The van pulled up on his left, wing door already open. Milo, with Inu by his side, leapt inside. Legs spent, he barely made it onto the floor of the van, but thankfully the van swerved and slowed at precisely the right time. Lying on the floor, Milo had a chance to notice how soft the carpet was. As the door began to close, Milo caught a glimpse of a quickly moving shape hot on the heels of the van.

"Go faster!" Milo yelled.

Accelerating without a gear change, the van threw him back against the couch. It then made aggressive turns to try and shake the pursuer.

"We loaded the van with a few extra algorithms. Marvin wrote this one himself," Lisa said.

The van continued to try and shake the pursuer while Lisa appeared lost in thought for a few seconds. She then looked at Milo and said, "It seems that we are being chased by a larger and meaner looking version of the thing that came to your house. Strap into the safety harness, we're going to have to engage some emergency protocols."

With that prompt, Milo noticed that the couch had cleverly concealed a five-point safety harness near the middle of the van. Milo slid over to the spot and hastily strapped himself in. As soon as he fitted the last strap into place, the van accelerated so abruptly that the tablet which had been resting next to him slid up onto the back of the couch. Plastered against the couch, Milo closed his eyes while the van careened around corners. The chase probably only lasted a few minutes, but it felt so much longer.

Suddenly, the van decelerated to its original speed and returned to its normal driving algorithm.

"Okay, we're back on course to the cabin," Lisa said.

"That was awesome!" Milo said excitedly. Coming down from the roller coaster-like high, he said more soberly, "You and Marvin really were prepared for anything. Though strangely it just makes me feel even more like I'm out of my league."

"You've been preparing your whole life, Milo. We just helped with some logistics."

Whether that was true or not, Milo felt a lot better. Marvin and Lisa had held up their end of the bargain. How would he do when it was his turn?

And that was when it dawned on him, the thought that had been worming around in the back of his mind since seeing the guards. Lisa had said something about them starving, but that was only part of it. They were dehydrating too. Without a supply of water, every person held captive by the SeeSees had less than three days to live. Maybe only two. Progenitor's paralyzing dream would kill them all without a single act of resistance. Milo didn't have time to figure things out anymore, he needed to do something fast. But what?

CHAPTER SIXTEEN

Safely away from danger for the moment, Milo rummaged through his pocket and, with great delight, found the End key still there. Holding it in his hand, it appeared in every way to be a normal key plucked from a vintage keyboard, slightly yellowed with age.

Turning it over, he didn't feel any weight imbalances or other imperfections to indicate that there might be something inside. In fact, without a seam of any kind, he wasn't really sure how to open it. He squeezed it. Nothing. He scratched at it with the bottle opener from the beverage section of the van's amenities, but still that did nothing. Seeing how this was supposed to be a piece of him, he thought intuition would kick in, but nothing happened.

He decided to come at it from a different angle. Leaning off the couch, he reached down and picked up the Space Cadet keyboard itself. Getting the orientation correct, he placed the key back on the keyboard. He then put the keyboard on his lap as if he was using the computer and proceeded to type a bunch of random words.

There was something joyful about how the keys responded, the spring perfectly matching the cadence of his hands. Typing actually felt nice. There was also a feeling of continuity with the past, being a part of a tradition in an industry driven by newer and better. In that moment, he appreciated the nostalgic connection of every vintage enthusiast.

That was when he heard something. Amongst the clicks and thunks of the mechanical keyboard, he thought he heard, or maybe even felt, something else.

Milo approached the problem methodically and noticed that whenever he hit Return, there was a particular *snick* sound. Likewise, when he pressed End there was a *click* sound. Finally, whenever he pressed the unlabeled Space key there was a tiny *whir*.

Three operators. Repetition and chording possible. There was some sort of mechanical computer in this keyboard. It certainly would be like Marvin to do something so clever.

He decided to keep it easy on his first attempt, after all, Marvin did want him to get this right and there wasn't a lot of time to do an exhaustive brute force approach.

Milo considered the problem space. Most likely it was some variant of a number sequence, where one of the keys would increment a register, another would move the contents of that register, and the last would compare the number against the answer or maybe reset the register. At least, that was his first thought. It was a little tough to concentrate while the van still rumbled through pothole-ridden streets.

Since Marvin had emphasized the End key, he was going to treat it as the increment operator. He was going to assume, matching regular use, that Space would indicate a gap and Return would send the whole thing. What number to try? He tried to think of numbers that were important to him and might be important to Marvin.

"Sorry. Marvin insisted that we keep the plan from each other," Lisa said.

"Wouldn't really be safe otherwise, but it sure would have been expedient," Milo said.

Click, Click, Click, Whir, Click, Whir. . .

Milo hammered out the first eight digits of Pi when he heard a *snick*.

That was odd. He hadn't pressed the Return key. The keyboard's response told him two things: it wasn't Pi and it only accepted eight digits. Fair enough. He then tried a few other constants: some common square roots, the Golden Ratio, Planck's constant, H-bar, the gravitational constant, and finally Avogadro's number, none of which seemed to work. There were too many eight digit primes to punch in, or he would have tried a few of them. He thought of trying some more esoteric options, as the above were all rather obvious for a kid like Milo, but he knew he must have missed something.

Then he remembered Euler's Identity. It was definitely the most elegant formula he had committed to memory. Sure, the stuff from Einstein was beautiful too, but there was something that just couldn't top Euler. Addition, multiplication, exponentiation, Pi, the imaginary number, Euler's number, the additive identity, and the multiplicative identity. For a math nerd, it was basically the Mona Lisa.

The only number that he could try out of the bunch was Euler's, so he punched out the sequence to make 2.7182818, its first eight digits. Typing the penultimate digit, he got nervous and his hand began to shake. To compensate, he used the fingers of his other hand to help keep track of the final digit:

Click, Click, Click, Click, Click, Click, Click, Click, SNICK!

There was no doubt that it made a different noise this time. He took a breath, shook out his tense shoulders, and tried to relax.

Lifting the keyboard, he took a closer look at the End key. Sure enough, the casing of the key had separated, showing a very fine seam which divided the top from the bottom of the key. Wedging his fingernail into the crack, he popped the key open.

Inside the rectangular shaped key was a simple tetrahedron, a perfectly shaped four-sided object. Somewhat like a little upside down pyramid, the object was in a depression in the interior of the key that kept it exactly in place. It glowed with an azure color that seemed to swirl inside the crystal clear solid.

About to discard the top of the key, Milo noticed that the interior had an almost indistinct inscription of only a single word: MOAD. Worse, he had no idea what it meant.

Puzzled, Milo looked back at the little pyramid. He felt a strange sense about the object, a sort of déjà vu.

Milo flipped the key upside down. For a brief moment, he saw the shape fall through the negative space between the key and his open palm, the blue glow illuminating the interior of the van. Time moved slowly as his mind anticipated the contact, his eyes transfixed on this piece of him falling through the air.

At the moment of contact, Milo's reality shattered. It was like an old TV set turning off. First there was a contraction of his vision, then it began to warp in waves and collapse, whereupon it finally fuzzed out into a single retreating dot in the center. Milo powered off. His body jerked once and then became stiff before it collapsed onto the floor, unconscious.

In silence, the van drove on, retracing the route that took it back to the cabin. Lisa and Inu looked helplessly on as Milo lay on the ground, undergoing some kind of transformation. It was only the first transformation, but still Lisa worried that it might change him into that power hungry monster which worried her dreams. It was not a restful journey for her.

As they approached the cabin, the complex sensed the van and opened the concealed entrance to the underground chambers. The van drove quietly to the lower level, until finally coming to rest in the original garage where it was fabricated. It then uploaded video of its entire journey to the cabin computer for classification. Hours passed with the only sense of movement the blinking lights on hidden server arrays.

Then Milo became aware.

Not awake, not alert, but simply aware. He knew that he existed again, and that he was outside of himself in some way, observing the attributes of his body and mind without being inside them. This point of view wasn't as disturbing as he thought it would be.

He could tell that his body was resting peacefully, that it was facedown in the van and that Lisa was nearby. He could tell this via feeling more than sight, like he still received the data for touch even though it was from a distance.

Then he felt another presence, something in his body that wasn't him but was moving through him. There was an incredible urge to fight back, to not let the trespasser in. How could he trust what he did not know? Was his survival on the line? His resistance wavered, the urge to fight passed. He accepted the inevitability of change.

He felt his skin tighten and become cold. Every inch of his body changed as a nauseating wave radiated out from the hand that held the fragment. There was a sinking feeling in his chest, like a plunge on a roller coaster. And then he heard a very faint noise.

From a great distance away, Milo heard something like the whisper of a gnat. The sound steadily grew as he concentrated, becoming louder and louder until it was deafening as a waterfall. But it was a digital sound. He could hear through the sound to the bits that composed it. His mind could spread the bits, filter them, even comprehend the decomposed signal as if he were listening to it with his ears.

He also heard a voice from somewhere else, not in the midst of the waterfall, but it was difficult to make out through all the noise.

"Milo? Milo, are you there?"

But Milo couldn't respond. He was still offline, he couldn't do anything.

His ears exploded again, the waterfall splitting into distinct streams from every direction. He tried to focus on one of them but the strain was difficult. Gradually he became aware of just one, a stream of images that flicked very quickly through his mind. Mostly views from a vehicle as it drove along a road during the middle of the day, sun streaming through clouds on a mostly forested scene. It was footage from their van ride.

Milo lost focus and the images instantly vanished. He tried again and found that it was easier to focus this time. This stream was different. It bounced back and forth between two walls, rebounding and changing shape as it went. It was a conversation with an unusually reduced selection of words. Very rigid and succinct, the two entities seemed to be asking and answering each other. That was when he knew he was listening to computers talking over a network.

At this point, he became aware of his body. Moment by moment he drifted closer, until at last his consciousness was back inside. He felt different.

Milo opened his eyes. He then looked at each hand while he sat up, opening and closing them as if trying to figure out how they worked. He found himself staring at his left hand. Though it looked the same, it felt different. He moved his hand closer to his face and saw that the fine wrinkles and whorls of his fingerprints were gone, replaced with a surreal smoothness. Even the hair on the back of his hands had changed. No hair curled or twisted, instead they were all perfect arcs of identical length.

More like an android, less like a human.

Suddenly he was accosted by the roar of the digital waterfall. He stood up hastily and put his hands over his ears, trying in vain to find a moment of peace. Looking around, he saw the familiar interior of the van and the keyboard where he had left it. A solitary key was removed, discarded haphazardly on the ground, but the shape which was inside was nowhere to be found. It had disappeared.

Suddenly he felt afraid, some rising sense of alarm that he couldn't pinpoint. There was something in the noise that bothered him, but he couldn't figure it out. He needed to get some air, reconnect with the world around him that he was rapidly losing.

He ran out of the van and, without a word to Lisa, climbed up the ladder and into the comfortable main floor of the cabin. He threw himself onto one of the couches and put the tablet on the ground at the same moment a new rush of voices flooded his mind. It was too overwhelming to even keep his eyes open.

But at least he knew why he was afraid. The cabin was surrounded.

CHAPTER SEVENTEEN

"We're surrounded, Lisa!" Milo needlessly shouted from his perch on the couch.

Milo staggered to his feet, trying to get a grip on the mental onslaught which threatened to overwhelm him. He found it difficult to think straight, let alone come up with a plan to escape. How did they find him?

"Quick, get the small cache from the pantry," Lisa said from her enclosure around his neck.

Her voice helped bring him back to reality. Jumping to his feet, he grabbed his backpack, stuffed the tablet inside, and ran to the pantry. He filled it with a couple protein bars and some bottled water, though he wasn't really sure if he really needed them or not. Not enough time to go downstairs, he ran into the bedroom, flung open the closet doors, and threw things off the shelves until he found the bivy sack. All of these things might keep him alive in the woods for a few days, if he could just make it past whatever was encircling the cabin.

Tucking Lisa's necklace back under his shirt, he zipped up the shell over his hoodie and went to the window. Barely moving the curtain, Milo snuck a glimpse of the path in front of the cabin and found, to his relief, no signs of movement.

Closing his eyes, he tried to focus on one of the discordant streams that had previously overwhelmed him. There were so many at so many different volumes that it was like trying to pick one conversation out of a crowded room. He focused on the loudest one, which perhaps meant it was closest.

At first, the experience was confusing, the feeling utterly foreign. This signal seemed to be a continuous stream of navigational and environmental data. He could tell the direction the source was moving, its speed, and the terrain that it was crossing. All of which told him that it was about four hundred yards out and closing fast.

It wasn't alone, either; there were a hundred or more signals with a similar pattern. But there were also a few that were different, maybe only one. He closed his eyes and tried to focus.

"Shouldn't we be leaving?" Lisa asked, snapping him out of his concentration.

She was right. They needed to get out of here fast. Running into even one of these things would be too much for him. He tightened his backpack, threw open the door, and ran in a direction that he hoped would get him far away from here. Inu easily kept up.

Leaping over fallen trees and dodging low branches, Milo tried to get away from the cabin as quickly as he could. He was roughly able to tell where the signals were coming from, even with his eyes open, so he did his best to avoid their more concentrated areas. But after only a few minutes, Milo tripped on uneven ground and fell into a shallow ditch, tumbling a bit before coming to rest at the bottom. He had never been very dexterous, but with the dismount from his bike and now this?

His backpack was thrown free and came to a rest a few feet away. Inu scrambled down the ditch and retrieved his backpack before trotting back over to his fallen form. About to pull himself back to his feet, the sound of cracking twigs alerted him to a nearby danger. He felt like his heart was going to leap out of his chest as he tried to muffle the sound of his breathing, but even his shaking hand did little to cover the sound of his fear. It drew closer.

His mind raced. Did he have a weapon? If this was anything like what faced him in his bedroom, a weapon probably wouldn't do him any good.

He closed his eyes and tried to focus on the signal. This time he found it quickly and easily processed the data streaming from it. Any second it was going to crest the pit and see him, then the data streaming by would be an aerial view of his own mauling, like one of those nature shows with a lioness and a wildebeest. But what else could he do?

Like an envelope with a letter inside, Milo deciphered the nearby robot's signals. They were looking for him just as he expected, but even more so, they knew almost every piece of information that you could find on the Internet, which was quite a bit in his case. Not surprisingly, they were also looking for Lisa.

The cracking of branches reminded him that the Tracker, as he now knew it was called, was almost upon him, that any second it would crest the ditch and see him and Inu barely hidden in the debris of the forest floor. Their feeble attempt to avoid a monster much too powerful for them to overcome, even together. It was too late. He'd lost.

And just when Milo thought that it was all over, the Tracker trotted off in another direction, their brush with discovery narrowly avoided.

"We're not dead, Lisa."

"Yeah, I've noticed that too. Close call, though, what did you do?"

"Nothing, it just decided to take off."

"Well, we're not out the woods yet," Lisa giggled.

Milo groaned, as quietly as he could, feeling somewhat forgiving of the gallows humor.

Rolling onto his knees, he looked up over the rise of the ditch. The coast appeared to be clear, but there wasn't much cover to speak of. He could run from tree to tree, but it was likely that he was going to be spotted at some point. Left with no other options, he had to hope for the best. Backpack slung over his shoulders, he began a series of tree-to-tree sprints, pausing briefly to catch his breath at each tree. At least, he tried to convince himself that they were brief breaks. Indoor enthusiast, right?

A couple of trees in, Milo had a sinking feeling that he had made a mistake. Without the van, his ability to quickly cover ground to the

116 :/ ZACK HUBERT

next fragment was really limited. Trudging through the woods wasn't exactly where he wanted to be while everyone in the world was dying. He needed to get there fast. Maybe once they were gone he could go back and get the van.

He looked for a comfortable place to hide for a while. After his time in the trunk of that car, he was a little more discerning about where he wanted to wait this one out. Ditches and fallen trees wouldn't work for multiple reasons. He really needed a good hiding place. A cave, maybe.

It took him a few minutes to find, but he came upon a very shallow cave mostly obscured by underbrush. He thought it would make a great den for many of the kinds of animals that lived in these woods. This one was big enough that it could have been used by a black bear last winter, though Milo hoped it was unused at present. He decided to throw a few rocks in first, just to be sure. Being mauled by a bear would really suck.

Not that his plan was very good in the first place. Had he hit a bear with a rock, what was he going to do? Run? Thankfully, nothing mauled him. Milo smiled. Crouching through the entrance, he crawled towards the back wall and then sat facing the entrance. From his spot on the muddy ground, he could see anything that moved past, while still being hidden in the dark. It was a huge relief to be momentarily safe, though getting this muddy was a bit disturbing.

Having a few minutes where he wasn't in immediate peril, Milo's mind reflected back on Euler's number, the solution to Marvin's first puzzle. He appreciated that Marvin had used something so elegant as a clue. He always had appreciated the symmetry of the natural world. Reading a good bit of physics, he relished the natural laws, especially how they always seemed to be simpler than expected. There was a connectedness to them, a beauty that went far beyond the immediate. Milo would have picked something just as elegant had he been the one hiding the clues. Though he didn't understand why it had to be in the physical world. Why not hide it on a computer's hard drive?

Perhaps there was a reason to belabor the physicality of the puzzle, something relevant to what was happening in the world. Generally used in association with the modeling of exponential growth, maybe it was related to the construction of these robots. If a robot could construct builder robots to make even more builder robots, that would definitely be exponential growth.

This only made Milo feel worse, of course, as it meant time spent in the woods was extremely costly. Every passing moment meant more and more robots populating this planet, not to mention the reduction of his chance of survival. Though at this point Milo wasn't really aiming as high as a bright future. He just wanted to survive.

Somewhere in the back of his mind, he hoped that what Marvin and Lisa had said was true. That he could do something to stop this global menace. But it seemed so unlikely, so unreasonable, that he just held his legs close to his body in the damp cold of the cave and tried to stay warm.

Just then he heard a really weird sound, a muted popping noise as if someone was making popcorn just out of sight. But he could tell it was farther away than that, and besides, it had an odd way of echoing, bouncing off trees and exposed rocks to give the sound more life.

That was when he saw them, emerging from the vegetation to the left of his cave, walking slowly in a sort of rough formation, eyes on the horizon. They wore paramilitary clothing, holding guns of all varieties, firing shots off into the distance. Towards the cabin, he realized.

People! Actual humans that weren't frozen in time and slowly dehydrating.

"People," Lisa said, barely concealing an awestruck tone. Inu was huddled next to him in the back of the cave, but at the sound of the gunshots, she had gone to the cave entrance to look out.

"I know. They might be able to help us," Milo said, a bit more hopeful sounding than he felt.

No sooner had he said that, his unspoken fear came true. Machines appeared, emerging from the bushes and undergrowth. Like a phalanx, a line of mechanized hounds backed by metal spiders while drones flew in the sky overhead. The metal monsters surrounded and then attacked their prey, jaws snapping as the whirring of the wheels of teeth inside their angry maws ripped into human flesh. Bullets deflected ineffectually off the reinforced armor of the machines.

This was going to end badly for the humans.

Just then, Milo sensed a new signal, alerting him to the presence of an unknown. It was up in the air, flying so much faster than a drone ever had, and at such an altitude. Focusing on its stream of data, it seemed to repeat coordinates over and over. And something else, windspeed? Seconds later, when he realized what it was, he couldn't help but think that they couldn't possibly be planning on bombing this area. The forest was swarming with their own.

Then the missile struck the Cabin, sending a shockwave of devastation through the forest. Milo's cave collapsed on him as a fiery wave swept over the humans, igniting them like so many matchsticks. Perhaps he was lucky to be in the cave.

Unconsciousness.

CHAPTER EIGHTEEN

Though it was difficult to understand at first, Milo now knew that he was in the process of rebooting. Like any ordinary computer that had the power switch thrown, he was in the midst of some cycle where various checks took place, where damage was identified, and repairs were made. It was a familiar feeling of not being awake or asleep, simply waiting for control to return.

When he did wake up, he felt the pressure of rock against his face and a somewhat vague notion of his whole body being pinned by something. He heard the scrabble of rocks as Inu was evidently trying to dig him out.

Wiggling his fingers and toes, he was reasonably confident that they were still connected to his body, which hopefully meant all the other parts were still intact too. He tried to move, but he did little more than make small dirt angels. A few of the rocks were simply too heavy to budge. He tried to frame his predicament as a story problem.

Trapped under heavy rock, he would die if he couldn't get free. He considered his possible solutions. Movement was out; he had no way to leverage a part of his body for the benefit of another, nor any tools at his disposal. He considered digging, but realized without the ability to clear the small handfuls of dirt, he'd just get his hands dirty, which was definitely not desirable. He considered a twisting movement, but he had no ability to move his hips. He was definitely pinned.

"Inu says that she can't move the last few rocks, they're too big,"

Lisa said.

"What? You two can talk? You never told me that," Milo said incredulously.

"It didn't seem relevant before, but yeah, we're connected. Just like you and I can chat when close by, I can also chat with Inu. Though before you get jealous, she mostly just talks about food, which is ironic since she knows I can't feed her."

Milo laughed. "Figures. Anyway, are you sure Inu can't leverage anything?"

"Maybe, she's still trying to find something."

Waiting on his canine companion, Milo considered his options. Oh yeah. Signals. The fragment that had been kept safe in the Space Cadet keyboard had blessed him with some sort of ability to pick signals out of the air. Time to tune the dial to Radio Milo.

He started scanning his mental band to see if any signals were being generated in the area. He was surprised to discover that he could actually pick up regular satellite programming, radio, digital TV, and a bunch of other longer range broadcasts. That could be useful once he got out of this mess. He also noticed that his own body was sending out a signal, though to where or what the message was he couldn't tell. It was very peculiar and somewhat disturbing. In passing, he wondered whether he was being spied on, or worse, controlled.

He also noticed a weird feeling on his wrist, almost like microscopic gusts of wind. It only came from the wrist wearing the watch, so perhaps this was another manifestation of his signal sense, boosted by proximity.

Turning his attention back to the nearby signals, he found that it was mostly quiet. Actually, it was only quiet at ground level. Signals above the cabin seemed to flutter back and forth, as if sweeping circles in the sky. With a sense of foreboding, he hijacked the video feed of one of them as it flew low to the ground. Swooping and diving through the air, Milo saw a high resolution feed of a smoking crater where the cabin used to be, before it was once again out of range. What he saw was discouraging, but wholly expected. The cabin was completely devastated. All sorts of metal fragments and destroyed machinery peeked up through the soil and the small remaining bits of the wooden structure was a smoking, burning ruin.

No help would come from back there, he thought.

Milo turned his attention back to the chatter. It took a while to find, but he eventually identified the signals of the Trackers, the hound-like machines. He noted their communal chatter, how they asked questions of each other and responded, and basically acted like a single animal.

In fact, he noted that it was quite a bit like how computers on the Internet talk to each other. A predefined handshake went along with every request for information, and as he had already figured out, the payload of all communications was sent along in an encrypted packet. Thankfully, he already discovered he could decrypt those on the fly.

Their chatter was quite interesting. As the hounds communicated amongst themselves, occasionally one of them would broadcast a consensus back to one of the "others" that he had noticed previously. The "other" seemed to direct the hounds and the drones in the air. Apparently they were doing a thorough grid-by-grid exploration of the area. He noticed that as they completed these grid searches, they also sent consensus back to the "other". This time he noticed that they dumped the data to nowhere, as all of those packets were destined for "nil", which Milo knew meant "nothing" in computer-speak.

He listened in on this for a good hour until the grid search was done, and that was when the unexpected happened: a message originated from "nil". Milo shoved out of his mind the existential crisis inherent in that and decoded the following harrowing message:

"Recover assets. Bombing of the entire grid to commence in ten minutes. Strikers incoming."

Three days now seemed like an eternity, he had to get out of here in ten minutes! He was so screwed.

"Lisa, tell Inu to use a lever to get these rocks off of me!" Milo said with a trembling urgency in his voice.

Somewhere above, Milo could hear Inu straining against the rocks. The sound of cascading rocks surrounded him as he racked his brain for something effective to do. Nine minutes.

More scrambling. Inu was doing something, that much he could tell. He felt something pinch against his back, and for the first time since he woke up, he could tell that it wasn't rock pressing in on him.

Then there was tremendous pressure on the low of his back as a huge rock thudded into the ground nearby. Inu must have found something to use as a lever and had dislodged the heaviest boulder on him. He could move again. Good pup, indeed.

Milo got to his feet, weary from the experience but thankful that he had friends to help him out of a jam.

"Let's go, pup," Milo said, pointing off in the direction of the lake. Inu set the pace as Milo ran along behind her. He just hoped they'd make it to the water before the Striker was in range. With only a few minutes to live, Milo tried to think positively.

Lungs burning, legs aching, and chest heaving, Milo ran as if his life depended on it, which, of course, it did. Any second now the Striker would appear in the sky overhead and then everything would be engulfed in flames. He imagined the craft flying overhead, a fluid piece of metal traveling at supersonic speeds towards the cabin, every moment full of the promise of destruction.

As if to distance himself from the peril of reality, he tried to think of it like a little dot flying horizontally in a side scrolling video game. He pictured the little bomb falling away behind the dot, leaving a cartoonish trail of dashed lines as it fell towards the ground.

"Remember, last time it was a missile," Lisa interjected into his thoughts.

Lisa was right! It would be way out ahead of the Striker. Without another thought, he ran hard for the lake and dove in as soon as he was at the shore. Swimming downward, he realized that whatever its armament, it would be well ahead of the sound.

Another few seconds passed, then, the tremor of an explosion. Pretty mild, though. His watery shield must have been more effective than he had guessed. It was definitely — boom! — well, that was a bit more impressive. Several more distant explosions peppered his ears with mild shocks as the water carried the compression waves along to him. And then the big one hit. BOOM!

The light filtering down to his somewhat shallow depth was completely cut off and the compression wave left his ears ringing. Underwater for a few minutes now, he wondered whether his biological responses were real or not. Were his ears really ringing or was it just a programmed illusion? Who cares? He was still alive and swimming for the surface. That's all that really mattered.

He breached the surface and immediately felt his eyes burn as a cinder cloud hung low over the lake. In the blink of an eye, the lush forest had literally turned to flame. It was jarring, to say the least.

Milo looked around for signs of Inu, but everywhere he turned he saw destruction. Even the lake looked like it was on fire from all the burning debris on its surface. Milo dove under the surface and began fervently searching for her.

Nothing.

He dove deeper as the raining debris continued to disturb the surface above. Worried that he'd run out of air — could he? — Milo made one last effort to find her, even though he was jeopardizing his own life. She wasn't just a dog to him, after all.

Lungs straining and afraid he might pass out, Milo finally saw her down below him, caught by a large piece of debris and sinking fast. He swam down and tried to free her as the last bubble of oxygen escaped his lips.

Forcing his own body into the midst of the debris, Milo pushed out against two sides of it, straining to free Inu. *Crack.* His effort was rewarded with the sight of Inu swimming for the surface as he began to feel very lightheaded, sinking under the weight of the debris. Struggling to not inhale, Milo made his way towards the light.

"You can do this, Milo. It only feels like you need air," Lisa said.

That was enough of an encouragement for him to fight for the surface where the superheated air burned his lungs. Spent and exhausted, like so much flotsam and jetsam, they made for the shore. Falling to the ground as soon as his feet emerged from the lake of fire, Milo collapsed. In delirium, he thought it might be nice to just lie in the sun a bit. Let the fatigue melt away.

But it wasn't the sun. It was the waves of heat coming off the forest fire about to engulf him. An alarm went off in his brain; he had to get out of here before the forest was completely ablaze.

Stumbling to his feet and running without any energy left to spend, Milo tried to escape the blaze. For an introverted non-athlete, this was pretty much a nightmare scenario, though at least he was silhouetted with a real action hero background. That thought put a smile on his face while his past-sore legs tried to keep up with Inu.

It didn't take long to get out of immediate danger, a good thirty-minute run and walk and he was safely ensconced in the unburnt heart of the forest. Though it was getting dark, he thought he picked a good direction.

He paused to catch his breath while leaning up against an old growth tree, never to get another ring.

CHAPTER NINETEEN

"What the hell are you doing out here, kid?" a gravelly voice from somewhere nearby called out, as Milo leaned against the tree.

Milo tried to act scared. "I was — I mean, we were camping on the south end of the lake. It all happened so fast. I ran. My family couldn't keep up. They just couldn't keep up . . ." He let his voice trail off while he pretended to cry. Hopefully by hiding his face they wouldn't become suspicious with how poorly he emulated real tears. He heard movement from several directions.

"Well, I'll be. You damn near had your shirt burnt off you. I bet you'd be a goner if we hadn't found you. You know you're in the middle of a forest fire, don't you kid? We best get you out of here. Lewis can help you along. Don't worry, you'll be safe with us. Oh, cute dog. It looks like a fox."

Milo looked up to see Lewis, more of a homesteading type than something more dangerous. He could also see the original voice's owner now, a burly thick fingered outdoorsman with a ruddy complexion and a wild black beard. Neither smelled like they'd seen a shower in some time.

"I'm Traeger and that's my brother Lewis," he said.

"I'm Milo, that's Inu, and this," Milo hesitated as he almost introduced Lisa, "is nothing."

"Okay," Traeger said, slightly confused by his introduction. "Well, try to keep up. We need to get back to camp." He then began a steady walk in the direction Milo was originally headed. Milo trudged along quietly with Inu while the rest of the group made copious amounts of noise, gear clanking with each step.

A few minutes to finally think about all that had transpired, Milo asked Lisa what she thought "MOAD" might mean, referring to the curious inscription inside the first fragment's case.

"Your guess is as good as mine," she replied. "Marvin clearly made these clues for you so it must be something that makes sense. But I'm not getting anything."

Milo kept rolling the word over and over in his mind, but it just didn't mean anything. At least nothing he could remember right now. He wracked his brain all the way back to their camp but still couldn't figure it out.

That said, he was a bit surprised that they made it to their camp without running into any more trouble. After playing action hero all day, he expected there to be more complications. Hopefully the newfound peace would last at least one night. He needed some sleep.

The camp was meager but well-hidden with as much vegetation and natural cover as could be procured. It probably represented the work of at least a few days of the dozen or so survivalists camped here. There was significant organization in the arrangements of the sleeping tents and supply caches, everything a combination of military surplus and homespun gear. Guards walked a semi-structured path around the camp, though they had precious few weapons on them.

Leading Milo through the center of camp, the survivalists followed Traeger as if caught along by a current. While some tried to hide their curious glances, others stared at the kid and his dog who just walked out of a forest fire. Milo did his best not to notice, but even then, he felt self-conscious. Milo wasn't fond of people looking at him, while, on the other hand, it seemed Inu thrived on the attention.

Traeger brought him to a fallen log near the middle of the camp which had been turned up on its end. Milo noticed that other logs seemed to be arrayed around it, like a classroom made from wood with a lectern in the front. This must be a gathering place for their ragtag group. If it was, then he realized either Traeger or the small crystal radio on the lectern was in charge.

The answer came as Traeger took his place behind the podium and the rest of the survivalists filtered into their seats on the logs. Those few that didn't find a seat, stood nearby. Now that he thought about it, it reminded him of church. Milo decided to stay a little off to the side so he could observe what was going on, ready to run if necessary.

"Friends. This here is Milo and his dog Inu. His family was killed by the bombing over yonder. Some sort of dust up between the 'bots and a group like us. All accounts have them gone and the 'bots victorious. More humans off the map — signs of the end times indeed — meanwhile more of those damned clockwork are rolling off the assembly lines where we used to make our livings. Milo is going to need our help, so give it to him and share what you've got. We're all going to need to help each other out if we're gonna make it to tomorrow."

Traeger took a step back from the podium and cleared his throat. Milo was slightly impressed by how much — relatively speaking — his diction improved when he addressed the crowd. Maybe he was a preacher before the world changed.

"No one could have known what was going to happen to our loved ones. Even now trapped by the damned spell that 'NIL' put them under. Motionless, starving, dehydrating. And there's nothing we can do about it. Their first strike was devastating and we're on the run," Traeger continued.

The cadence of his speech seemed to resonate with these backwoods types, Milo noticed, as they added exclamations of approval throughout. Milo noticed the new information too. Progenitor was gone, NIL was the real threat now. He was disheartened that no real human resistance had been formed. Disorganized and ill-equipped, Milo knew they didn't have a chance.

"But," Traeger continued with an upbeat even triumphant tone, "we were not wholly unprepared. We have weapons and munitions, stores of food to last us for quite a while. And this here radio told us exactly what we needed. The broadcast controlling the SeeSees is coming from the very Research Center that Dr. Teller used as a backdrop in all his videos. No friend of humanity was he, just a turncoat who I bet got his thirty pieces of silver." Murmured agreement.

An interruption. "How did those people on the radio know?" The questioner was an elderly looking gentleman with coke-bottle eyeglasses which seemed to make his squinting eyes appear to be even larger.

"That's a good question, Luke. One that we can ask them at the meeting site in the broadcast," Traeger said with confidence.

They all held an unshakeable confidence in their own ability, Milo thought, as if they were thoroughly unaware of what they were up against.

From an unnoticed corner, Milo asked, "If it was on the radio, won't the machines know about it too?"

Traeger chuckled a little. "Oh don't you worry 'bout that, kid. We Northwest survivalists worked out a radio code years ago before this whole kerfuffle went down. You'll just have to trust us grownups, but it's definitely secure."

Milo knew it wasn't. They clearly didn't understand AI and were severely underestimating NIL. He'd have to take off during the night or he'd end up like the rest of them.

But what if even a piece of that intel was accurate? What if the key to shutting off the SeeSees really was in the Research Center? Well, it'd probably be the most secure building on Earth, especially after these skirmishes. NIL would know that a few humans were out there causing trouble and he'd be ready for them, likely with overwhelming force.

Lisa said, "It has to be a trap, Milo. I can't imagine an advanced intellect unable to crack a simple radio code."

"Yeah, I know," Milo responded. "I'm afraid we're on our own here."

Traeger continued on with his post-apocalyptic homily but Milo had heard enough. He waited until it was over and people were shaking

Traeger's hand, like a reception line at a wedding. Milo asked an old lady for a tent to take a nap in. That fit with his traumatized kid story and, sure enough, he was shown to a place where he could be alone.

The tent was a lightweight polyester variety, probably intended for a weekend warrior. After being out here in the wind and weather, it was considerably worn, with visible rents in the fly. Milo didn't care. If it came to it he could at least get in his bivy to stay dry. For now, he was just thankful to get out of sight. Traeger was giving him the creeps.

As soon as the flap of the tent closed, Milo began scanning the regular broadcast bands, starting at the low end of the frequency spectrum. Using his signal sense was becoming as easy as dialing the knob on an old fashioned radio.

It took a while to find anything resembling a voice, but with persistence he eventually found it. The recording played flawlessly without any background hiss.

"Friends. We have very little time to strike back. We must attack the Research Center in Redmond immediately. The facility houses the antenna which broadcasts the signal. . . ."

Milo went to higher frequencies and found the same signal endlessly repeating on a few more bands. For the next hour he went up and down through the frequencies listening for anything different. The recording was too perfect. Something about the voices seemed simulated. Milo didn't trust it.

With a hefty dose of luck, he eventually heard another voice, this time breathing heavily with the sound of an engine revving in the background.

"They were ready for us," was all Milo could make out before the dead air once again swallowed the broadcast. This message confirmed his suspicion.

"I'm sorry, Milo. It would have been nice to have some good news for a change," Lisa said.

Milo couldn't help but feel like he was up against something so much bigger than him, that it would be impossible for him to defeat.

He was just as unprepared as these campers.

Just like the whole world.

CHAPTER TWENTY

Lying on a sleeping bag in the survivalist's tent, Milo let the severity of the situation sink in. In a little over a day, a huge portion of humanity was going to be dead. Even little pockets like this one, that hadn't adopted the Trojan Horse technology, were being tricked into self-destruction. Eventually, NIL would be the only thing left on the planet, if the rest of the world played out like the Northwest.

Traeger opened the flap to the tent.

"Hey there kid. We've got some food cooking on the fire, nothing fancy, just beans and some of the meat, but it'll help you sleep tonight. Big day tomorrow you know."

"I know. Everyone is going to die," is what Milo wanted to say, but he held his tongue. He thought of trying to convince Traeger to change the plan, but then he'd have to say who he really was. He had a feeling that he'd be lucky to be shown the exit after being honest like that.

"Thanks, I'll be right out," Milo found himself saying in a cloyingly weak tone.

"Food might help you feel better," Lisa said.

Always thoughtful.

"True, but I need a plan first."

"Attaboy, Milo."

Milo opened his backpack, found his rations, water, and basic survival gear and noticed the shiny tablet packed on top of the rest. Surprisingly, it hadn't been damaged after all the punishment he put it through while he action hero'ed his way through the forest. He took it out and touched it.

Instead of a sequence of rapidly changing images and instruction videos, the screen briefly flashed white a few times, like a shutter snapping open. His eyes dilated from the bright light and he found himself staring directly into the center of the tablet. He felt ready for something, even though he didn't know what.

A few pixels appeared, doing that dance that he'd seen on the Lisp Machine, but this time he knew what it was called. Conway's Game of Life, a zero player game where pixels form cells that evolve on their own and create interesting structures. The game sped up, moving so quickly now that he couldn't really keep track of the colonies.

"Don't look away, Milo."

Milo briefly thought about all those video games warning not to power down the console while the game was saving. What would happen to him if he looked away? Would he crash?

Milo then became aware of a change that was taking place. Not having a similar experience to compare it to, he initially couldn't describe it. Reorganization was the only thing that came to mind.

His chaotic disordered mind was becoming structured along dimensions he didn't even know existed.

"Don't move. You will be okay, Milo. I promise."

Then the screen turned into static. To any outside observer the screen was filled with a multicolored cacophony, but to Milo he was aware that an immense amount of structure was embedded within it, and that in a sense, it was downloading into his mind via his high bandwidth visual processors. Data directly fed into his brain via his eyes, like reading thousands of books at the same time. And then it was over.

"Lay back for a bit and rest, Milo. I'll wake you up when it's night. You don't need to pack the tablet, that was the last of it."

But Milo was already asleep. Inu once again curled up at his feet, ears flashing to attention as she heard sounds outside the tent.

Milo was standing in a forest clearing, a faint floral scent barely covering the smell of damp earth. He was dreaming, he knew, but everything about his dream had changed. It was no longer just an empty grid like an early computer game, it was like he was standing in a forest in the real world. He didn't know where he was, but he knew it wasn't his usual nightmare. Normally the ground would open up and he'd fall forever, never hitting the bottom, but that didn't appear to be happening.

This place was comforting, like it was inspired by the Lake Cabin, only different. Just then, he thought he heard a bird chirping in the distance, but he couldn't be sure whether that was just his imagination or the reality of this place. As he looked up, he saw a flock of birds pass overhead, as he absentmindedly thought that they must be migrating somewhere. Something about their movements.

Screwing together the courage to explore, Milo walked through the pleasant verdant scene, the remarkable detail of the place capturing his attention. There were small trees and a meandering path directly under his feet heading off into the distance. As his eyes traced out the path, he saw that it ended at an abnormally monstrous tree, towering above everything else in this place like some ancient world tree, something from a prehistoric era, like the redwoods of California. With remarkable clarity, Milo could see that the tree bore an apple in its upper branches. An apple!

Milo snapped awake just as he tried to walk down the path in the dream.

What the heck happened to his brain? This dream was clearly related to the others, but it had changed so much. How was that possible?

It must have been something in the tablet, triggering or implanting something. Maybe it was an encoded message of some kind? But what? It was just a really big tree in a forest with an obvious apple on top. How would that help defeat NIL? Without a plan, what was he supposed to do? March into the Research Center, hope it was the right place, take on hundreds of robots, and destroy the transmitter? Yeah right.

"Yes, Milo, precisely that," Lisa said.

"I keep forgetting you're in my head. It's kind of an invasion of privacy, you know. What if I thought something about you which I regretted?"

"Well, I'd be really sad but I'd forgive you. It's normal to make mistakes, we all have to try better the next time."

"Wow, that was a remarkably reasonable answer. But what did you mean about taking on hundreds of robots and all that?" Milo shrugged his shoulders even though he was only thinking these thoughts to Lisa.

"I'll summarize the facts, since I'm sure it's hard to keep track when you're in the middle of it. One: you can avoid bad guys since you can tell where they are. Two: you can tamper with any security system you can touch. Don't you see what that means?" Lisa asked.

"It means I might be able to defeat the security at the Research Center and disable the broadcast without being detected," Milo thought.

"And save many lives in the process."

"Yeah, I understand. I just need to confirm that the Research Center is where I need to go. If I risk so much and somehow tip my hand to NIL, I lose the advantage of surprise next time around," Milo thought.

"Every hour you're getting smarter, Milo."

Milo blushed. She was the one person keeping him from losing his mind. Person. He didn't even question that anymore. To question her personhood would be self-defeating, not to mention that she was just as real to him as anyone he'd ever known.

Then, sitting down with his head resting on his knees, Milo cleared his mind. Dumping everything from memory, he found himself at the center of a swirling electric galaxy of data all around him. Though he couldn't see it, his mind's eye created for him a visualization of all the disparate data surrounding him. Now he just had to find the one broadcast amongst the many.

Since they had analyzed the lenses back at the cabin, Milo had some idea what he should be looking for, but not enough to connect it to his intuitive ability. He started by focusing his search just on the immediate area, generating a mental list of signals that were "safe" as the survivalists probably wouldn't have anything from NIL.

He then expanded the circle, foot by foot, yard by yard, and finally mile by mile, until he had a pretty good sample set which probably had a couple dozen homes infected with SeeSees. He was astonished to discover that there were no drones whatsoever in the area. No Strikers, no Trackers, nothing. So either they could hide from him now, or they retreated. Either way, it wasn't his current problem, but curious nonetheless.

Once he had a few candidates that he thought must be homes, he stepped through each signal originating there. Not many signals originated in a home — mostly it was a consumption-oriented architecture — but the few that did were enough for Milo to notice a pattern. So weak was the average signal coming from a house that the existence of the SeeSee blaring its signal was like a person shouting in an empty theater. The magnitude was obvious to spot once he knew what he was looking for.

Rather than carrying content — easily recognizable things like video, or text — these signals appeared to carry a staggering amount of three-dimensional data. Like a map of a real object. What could possibly require that much data to map?

He then cast his mind far afield, following the signal through the countryside, picturing in his mind's eye the earth spinning along under the signal's path. Was he accessing satellites to do this? He wasn't aware that he was, but he saw a photo-realistic mental image of the Earth, so maybe he was. He followed the signals, as the green forested images gave way to suburban housing developments.

From the suburbs, the handful of signals joined with a massive river flowing along through the sky. Along it went, through the sprawl, over freeways, between high rises, until at last a campus was in view. Initially Milo thought it might be a college or university, but once the characteristic S-shaped building came into view, Milo knew he was looking at the Research Center of Sapient Computing.

Though it was hard to believe, the Research Center really was the broadcast site. For whatever reason, they chose to disseminate the actual location of the broadcast to the survivalists. It seemed like overconfidence to Milo.

At least he knew where he was going. Now he just needed to get away from these survivalists before it was too late.

CHAPTER TWENTY-ONE

Milo got up from the comfort of the sleeping bag and put his backpack on. Having slept through dinner, he was going to have to eat on the run. He didn't know if it was the realization of what he actually was or just the nerves, but he hadn't really had an interest in food for quite a while. That said, he hoped he hadn't totally lost his interest in food. Never having pizza again would be another one of Dante's circles of hell.

Opening the flap of the tent, Milo peeked outside and found the camp just as quiet as he thought it would be. Looking up and down the row of tents, all the zippers were closed. It certainly would be easier to sleep if you were blissfully unaware of danger, he thought. Though somewhere there must be a couple empty tents. They must still have a watch. Not that that was a concern; the guards were notoriously noisy for his young ears and would be easy to evade.

Listening for a few seconds, Milo and Inu headed off in their original southwesterly direction, pausing regularly to listen for the watch. Within minutes they were out of the camp, completely undetected, and hopefully with no one on their trail. Within twenty minutes, they were far out of sight of the entire band of survivalists, and back to being on their own. At this point, Milo stopped looking back every few paces and started looking ahead.

Trudging along in the pitch black, Milo realized that he looked down far too much. Looking up, he was startled by the brightness of

138 :/ ZACK HUBERT

the night sky. He easily saw more stars than on any other night of his life as they stood out like so many pinpricks against the backdrop of pure blackness. He focused on the Milky Way and was startled by how full and resplendent it was, like a string of gems cast across the sky.

There was something about their presence that gave him comfort in the permanence of things. All this was just one world. Even if he didn't make it, there were billions and billions of other planets. Maybe there was hope somewhere out there amongst the stars. He was just a tiny dot in the cosmos, after all. It was much easier to believe that he was inconsequential than that he was of singular importance in stopping an existential threat.

And yet, everything marvelous in the sky took on a darker tinge. That incredible satellite flying across the early morning sky might actually be dangerous. Perhaps turned by NIL for surveillance. Maybe he'd already been spotted. How many other things did NIL now control? It must be so easy for him to take over technological devices, break codes, and hack networked computers. It'd be rudimentary, trivial, like playing a children's game. Humanity trusted computers with everything, and within had been the seeds of their destruction all along. Milo recognized the irony in thinking that.

Compared to his dark mood, Inu seemed to be happy in the low forest, effortlessly prancing her way between the trees. From time to time she'd look back in the direction they came from, perhaps listening to something far away, but then she'd catch up easily. He couldn't help but smile when he saw her.

"We really could use a car," Milo said, not fully realizing that stating the problem also implied the solution.

"Seems easy enough. Go to nearby town. Find car. Drive car. Done!" Lisa cajoled.

Milo laughed as her teasing had its intended effect. Drawn from the edge of his depressive tendencies, he found strength in his friends. Lisa especially.

"Hey, Lisa?"

"Yeah, Milo?"

"Oh yeah, that's right, you already know what I'm thinking— "

"—but that doesn't mean you shouldn't think it," Lisa interrupted.

"Well it's not really the right time for this, but you've been really helpful to me. I mean, I really appreciate you." Milo was about to get emotional and, as usual, that meant his words failed to materialize properly.

"Thank you, Milo. I value your contributions highly as well," Lisa said, taking on a robotic affectation. "You know, it's okay to say you like me."

"So, how about we head into a nearby town and get a car?" Milo asked, deliberately changing the subject.

"Genius!" Lisa replied.

Just as he had since leaving the survivalists, Milo tried to multitask signal-checking in with his walking. He had tripped a few times, but always managed to snap back to reality before he hit the ground. He figured that it didn't matter much if you could do something if you never actually did it. Stealth and intelligence were the only things standing between him and a potentially gruesome fate, so he tried to keep up his guard.

He was still a bit surprised that all the signals broadcast by the Strikers and Trackers had disappeared, but he was more interested in the mundane signals anyway. For instance, he saw a broadcast — faked by computers, he realized — that had a news anchor describing NIL's takeover and the obsolescence of Progenitor, as if it was a normal nightly news item.

Nothing to fear, no worries for humanity, those friends frozen on their couches are just learning things, that's all. Such a terrible lie. They were dying, wasting away. How much more obvious could it be that this wasn't some sort of community college for the world? Still, some fraction of the population would probably buy it, and that's even fewer people NIL would have to eliminate. Psychological warfare. Probably all just a numbers game for NIL, effective future values and so forth.

After that broadcast, there were a few reruns of Teller standing in front of the Research Center spinning his yarns about the new carefree future of humanity now that we have machines partnering in our progress. It seemed like such obvious propaganda now. Like we were all going to have an AI pet or family member or something. He miscalculated which species was the master and which was the slave. In the category of classic blunders, this probably was the new number one.

Then, while nearly stumbling on a tree which had emerged from the darkness, Milo noticed one of the nearby contact computers twinkle out. Well, that's what he figured, anyway; it was possible that he had misremembered where that particular signal was located or perhaps its upload had stopped. But he was pretty sure he was right. He expanded his mental view of the signal-scape and filtered out all non-contact signals. Then he waited, slowing his walk for a while as well. Flicker, darkness. Another signal went out. Why would they disappear like that?

Then the grievous thought dawned upon him: people were dying. Not abstract entities in a video game. Actual people were dying.

This early? He felt a flash of rage. He had more time! Dying early like this simply wasn't fair. It wasn't time yet, they had to hang in there. He was just a kid.

It was probably the elderly, he thought, regaining composure. They were susceptible. Maybe they would excuse him with expressions of how they've lived a full life. Something like that. Though they were probably just as vulnerable as the very young.

Then the walls fell down in his mind. Babies.

A world full of babies dying of hunger and thirst, with spell-bound parents nearby but unable to help. He physically shuddered at this thought, a spasm of revulsion rising from a deep part inside. He wanted to puke up his guts at the inhumanity of this evil act. The robots were killing babies by neutralizing their parents. His mind went red.

"Even anger can have a purpose, Milo. What can you do with it?" Lisa asked.

"I have to stop them. I can't let them do this. It's evil," Milo said with a rising determination.

"Yes, they are helpless and dying. But you are not helpless. You can protect them," Lisa said just as methodically, as if intoning a spell.

Milo stopped thinking and began running. He pulled Lisa's enclosure out from the cover of his shirt and it spilled a strong light on his path, banishing the darkness. Milo knew where the closest town was, and he was going to get there as fast as he could. He was going to get a car and he was going to crash it into the Research Center if he had to. The signal was going to stop. He had to help, no matter what the personal cost. He didn't care about the pain in his legs or lungs or anything. He was a machine and he was not going to let his simulated human weakness interfere with helping those kids.

Covering the mile in record time, Milo came upon a one-light town called Startup. Yep, real name. He'd gone through it a number of times, but the town had a whole new feeling tonight.

Small town Americana with a friendly gas man and a gift shop full of knick knacks, it was literally and figuratively frozen in time. The street was completely empty and the flashing stoplight only served to strobe this ghost town. There was a darkened restaurant on one corner, a gas station on the next, and a couple of undeveloped lots. Oddly, there were cars parked in all of these places — old cars, not a single auto-car to be seen — some with doors open, others with windows down, but in all of them, the driver and passengers were in the same detached condition.

His mind flitted through the options before him, cars and trucks of every shape and size. Admittedly, he didn't know how to drive, so every car here presented a unique challenge. He really wished he had that van.

Actually, now that he thought about it, driving didn't seem that scary. Embedded in his long term memory he found all manner of training classes and simulations of the driving experience. Just socked away in there. Apparently he'd known how to drive for a long time, almost like he'd always known how to do it.

The tablet.

"You've got Marvin to thank for that one. Hopefully your legs are long enough to reach the pedals," Lisa teased.

Emboldened, Milo strode over to the most awesome driver-driven car he could see: an obsidian black Tesla Model S. Sleek and powerful. Milo knew that this car would get him there quickly and safely, and he'd look like a badass, so that was cool too.

Sometimes it's the little things that help keep you sane.

As he approached, he sensed it trying to greet him — must have been looking for the key of its owner — so Milo responded by touching the car and using his signal-fu to encode messages back to it in its native tongue. The door handle emerged and the car unlocked. Opening the door for Inu, she hopped over into the passenger seat as he took his place behind the wheel.

It was time to put an end to this.

CHAPTER TWENTY-TWO

Milo was thankful that he hadn't picked a car with a manual transmission. Driving for the first time was hard enough without something else to worry about. He found that he could manage going about thirty miles per hour, but once the car jumped above that, he didn't have the experience to control it. So instead of being the badass hauling down the freeway to save the world, he was that slow guy in the left lane just puttering along. But he didn't have time for this; people were dying.

Heading west on Highway 2, Milo decided to punch it up a notch. Besides, how hard could it be when there's no one to run into? Moving to the center of the road, Milo feathered the pedal and was in the fifties before he realized it. Even though he felt uncomfortable driving at this speed, he knew he had to go faster. Righteous anger drove his foot to the floor and the Tesla responded immediately to his wishes, pressing him back into the seat. Driving recklessly now, he worked the pedal and brake like he was playing a pipe organ, winding dangerously through corners.

Then, in the bluish glow of the car's high beams, he saw the junction to 522. Slowing through the corner, he came out on the other side like a rocket. The Tesla sped down the straightaway, speeding at one hundred thirty miles per hour and still climbing. He heard the car whisper "slow down" somewhere inside the mass of computing, a software governor capping his speed. If he could disable security systems, surely he could disable this. A second later, the governor was gone and he was accelerating again.

One forty. One fifty. The car was a lightning bolt at ground level. He repeated the process to change onto interstate 405, knowing that this was the last freeway until the Center.

Time blurred. He knew it must have been twenty or thirty minutes but with all his attention focused on the road, it felt like seconds. Hands gripping the wheel with a firm determination, he noticed that he wasn't nervous. He was ready.

Finally, he had to hit the side streets, so he decelerated back under thirty. Able to finally pay attention to his surroundings, Milo loosened his white knuckled grip and noticed that Inu was on the floor of the car with a very wide-eyed expression.

"Sorry, pup. It just kind of ran away there for a bit." She didn't have a very forgiving look on her face.

Off in the direction of the Center, flashes of light illuminated the clouds above like fireworks before dawn. Then, an explosion drenched the sky in red before it faded back to darkness. He was still miles away but he could see now that he was headed into an active conflict zone.

On the edge of his vision he could see wisps of movement in the skies above the Center. More flashes of light led to brief glimpses of something else in the air. A large flash briefly cast the scene in a pale white light as Milo saw hundreds of Strikers swarming above the complex. Occasionally one would dive into an attack run on the human force below. Outmatched and outnumbered, they didn't stand a chance.

His shoulders fell. The sight of the Strikers reminded him that he had been so distracted by the driving, he had forgotten to pay attention to the signals. All it would take was one of those Strikers to dive on them and they would be dead.

Lisa, sensing Milo's dark thoughts, said, "Hang in there. You haven't let anyone down yet. Let me handle the car through its auto-pilot subsystem, you focus on what's up there."

Milo struggled to get his thoughts in order; he couldn't help but think about the humans on the ground ahead. Whatever sorts of hunting rifles and homemade munitions these people brought were clearly ineffective against the faster-moving, heavily armored Strikers.

Why hadn't the military resisted? Surely they wouldn't have lowered their guard around Progenitor, would they? No time to figure that out; he directed his attention back to the skies while Lisa drove the car as close as she could without entering the firing zone. Bombs rumbled the distant landscape, threatening the windshield with every blast. When they were a little over a mile out, Lisa parked the car in the driveway of a recently built townhouse, that fast-growing weed fertilized by the technology industry.

He shouldered his backpack and hid Lisa under his shirt, trying to become as invisible to a human observer as he hoped he'd be to the machines. There wasn't anything he could do to conceal Inu, but he hoped that her presence would make him seem only that much more innocuous.

The crisp night air, barely held at bay by his hoodie and windbreaker, sent a shiver through Milo as he began his overland hike. Adrenaline joined his frantic shivering to produce a frightening cocktail of physical sensations. In order to survive, he had to focus on what was important, even though everything else tried to distract him. Adrenaline? Cold? Why would those matter to a robot? But regardless of what he thought he knew, the cold made him feel like an ordinary kid.

Zipping the hoodie all the way up, he cinched it tight and extended his signal-sense, briefly overwhelmed by the mass of signals in every direction. There were thousands of enemy signals here, in the sky above, moving about on the ground, and around the center itself. If he wasn't able to stay off their radar — metaphorically speaking — he would be dead in a heartbeat. Of course, seeing the rapidly diminishing signals associated with the human ground forces reminded Milo that his time of infiltrating a distracted enemy was running out. He needed to get in there now, while there was even a chance that some of those forces might not be looking for him.

"What the hell are you doing here?" a voice shouted at him from somewhere in the darkness.

Milo ran.

If they shot at him, then that was the end of the road, but Milo really hoped they wouldn't. He looked back to see a muzzle flash as the shotgun unloaded, not into him, but into a trio of the hound-like robots. They were surrounded and really had no chance of survival.

Just as Milo was about to run away, he saw one last image: a hound jumping through the air and then slamming into the shotgun owner's chest while the other two hounds ripped into his legs from behind. Milo looked away. There was nothing he could have done for them.

Milo ran down the street, cut across a lawn, hopped a fence, and was back on the main street. He knew he was getting closer to the Center as another group of resistance fighters emerged from the fog of war up ahead. Rugged-looking men in pickup trucks were shooting wildly into the sky while their drivers maintained seemingly random routes. But they might as well have been drunk high school kids for all the good they were doing. And yet, the Strikers just continued their hive-like movement up in the sky, seemingly unconcerned with the activity below.

Milo turned up the street, staying out of the lights and moving quickly. The road leading up to the Research Center was one of those six-lane urban arterials. Behind him he could hear the shenanigans of the trucks while up ahead there was some sort of security checkpoint. Back in the day, it probably would have been manned with people holding very dangerous guns, but now it appeared to be empty. The checkpoint was well-lit and had the usual array of vehicle-stopping removable posts and high barbed-wire fences.

Actually, something or someone was inside. He could just barely tell from where he was hiding, if you could call standing in the middle of the dark street to avoid the lights hiding. There was something mechanical within which gave off a faint signal. It was a trap.

Milo needed a distraction. Something that wouldn't give him away and would keep those crazy people alive too. Maybe he could blow something up to cause a disturbance at the main gate. It would be tricky, but it was the only thing he could think of under such time pressure.

Just then, Milo heard an ear-shattering sound from the direction of the trucks. Half expecting to see burning wreckage, he was shocked to discover that there were now more vehicles there, not less. His quick tally had the humans operating three trucks, one jeep, and a motorcycle, the last of which was heading right towards him. But his eye went to the stationary jeep on which Milo saw the silhouette of a person standing there with some sort of bazooka on their shoulder. Maybe these new friends actually brought some firepower.

As the headlight lit the road near his feet, Milo jumped out of the way, as the motorcycle went flying past him towards the main gate. This wasn't going to end well.

BOOM. An explosion sent a shock wave which nearly knocked him down. He looked over his shoulder and saw three Strikers flying back up to join the swarm leaving behind the burning wreckage of the other vehicles. Maybe the motorcycle would have better luck.

Looking ahead, he saw the motorcycle get within a stone's throw of the checkpoint when two high-intensity lasers, originating from the booth, incinerated the rider. It was like the rider was an ant under a magnifying glass, a burst of flame and then nothing but ash. The motorcycle fell sideways and skidded towards the checkpoint as the silhouette of ash dispersed as it hit the ground. The motorcycle then slammed into one of the posts and exploded into flames.

This only confirmed Milo's suspicion that it was some sort of automated defense. Would it shoot at what it thought was a drone? He hoped not, and more to the point, hoped that his clothes really did work as advertised to make him look like one. Crossing his fingers, he took the first step of the most stressful hundred feet of his life. At any minute, those lasers could flash and incinerate him, but it was a chance

148 :/ ZACK HUBERT

he had to take. He tried to get Inu to stay behind, but no matter what he did or said, she insisted on staying with him.

He walked cautiously, putting one foot in front of the other as if he had been told to walk on water. He took a step. Then another. Would the next step be his last?

"Stay calm, Milo," Lisa encouraged, which was, of course, easier said than done.

They were now past the point where the motorcyclist got lazed. His signal-sense was working overtime, decoding nearby messages. His hands were shaking like crazy.

Another step, then another. The booth was getting closer now. It was almost within reach. Ten feet, five feet. And then, much to Milo's surprise, he was past the booth. Walking around the lightly burning remains of the bike, Milo couldn't believe that he'd made it past the trap. The clothes worked. Lisa had done it!

Milo relaxed, finally feeling like the danger was behind him. From here, it was a short distance until he'd be in the broadcast room. Even now he could feel its presence.

And then, just as he was thinking of running for the building, a bullet slammed into him with such force that it knocked the wind out of him. As if hit by a truck, Milo fell to the pavement, smacking his face hard, blood rapidly pooling next to him on the concrete. The vertigo was overwhelming. He was going to pass out.

From somewhere behind, he heard a familiar voice, "You would have been safe with us," Traeger said, "but you had to go and double-cross your own kind."

Milo fainted.

CHAPTER TWENTY-THREE

Milo awoke in a pool of what he assumed was his own blood. Whether it was shock or something else, he didn't feel any pain. He remembered being shot in the shoulder, but even now, lying here on the ground, he just didn't feel anything. Inu was looming over his head, a worried expression on her face. He wondered how long he'd been unconscious.

Gunshots from the direction of the ruined vehicles brought him back to the urgency of the present. Rolling to his side to stand, Milo was shocked by Traeger's dead body only inches away from his face. Judging by the mauling that he'd endured, it had to be the work of a Tracker. So it wasn't just his blood, he thought. This pool had both android and human blood in it.

"Milo, try not to worry, but your body is dying," Lisa said, words utterly incongruous with her pleasant tone.

"What do you mean 'try not to worry'? Seems like kind of a big deal to me!" Milo said, exasperated. He clambered to his feet but found a strange weight to all his movements.

"With the blood loss, I'm afraid your body doesn't have much time. You can survive without it, but that might make you feel uncomfortable."

"What does that even mean? Of course I can't survive without my body. It's not just a suit that I've been wearing for the last thirteen years."

"Look, I know it's hard to wrap your mind around this, but you're not human. Not just human, I mean."

"My existential crisis is irrelevant to what I have to do. I have to go on," Milo said, looking back towards the burning wreckage. He found it tough to walk with all the blood-drenched clothing, so he tended to shamble a bit as he moved towards the Center.

"If you go on, your body will die. You won't die, you'll still be Milo. But your body will be dead. There's still a chance we could save it," Lisa tried to explain.

A few seconds passed as Milo thought about what she said.

"I don't have a choice, Lisa. I have to go on. I can't go back to get patched up or whatever. I'm not more important than any of the thousands I could have saved —"

"You're not responsible for any of these deaths, Milo, NIL is," Lisa interrupted.

"You prepared me for this, gave me the tools I'd need, and you've seen the scales come off my eyes. I understand the cost, but this is a decision I have to make. I choose to go forward. I have to hope that, even without all of this," Milo made a micro-gesture at his body, "that the people I care about will still accept me."

"They will," Lisa said, "You know I will, Milo."

Emboldened, Milo shed his windbreaker and hoodie, still startled that there wasn't more pain and more blood. The tiny rivulet coming out of his shoulder was nothing like what he'd seen on TV. This was just a dribble compared to those crimson gushers.

He made a sling out of the hoodie and put it on. He wasn't sure that it mattered, but it made him feel better to do something about his arm. Tying the windbreaker around his neck like a superhero's cape, Milo shuffled towards the famous building from Teller's interviews. The remnants of a little stage marked the location of the last broadcast, though it had apparently been caught in some crossfire and was considerably worse for wear.

Milo tried to hurry his awkward shuffle and found that his limbs were steadily getting used to the new center of gravity. He stiffened a little and stood a bit taller as he came to the familiar doorway. Made of an unpainted metal, it looked like an ordinary external door used on industrial buildings all around the city, but Milo knew better.

He knew that this had to be one of the more heavily guarded facilities on the planet right now, but if he was lucky, NIL would be overconfident in his defenses. Already he could tell that the door had several complimentary electronic locking mechanisms and all sorts of sensors, but these were geared towards human opponents. With Milo's clothes still emitting drone signals, he hoped that he'd be able to slip in undetected here as well. All he had to do was get close enough, anyway.

Milo paused. This was it. On the other side of this door was his destiny or fate, depending on how things went. It was really just a question of what would be left of him afterwards. Turning back never crossed his mind.

Milo reached out his left hand and instead of reaching for the handle, he touched the door. Immediately he felt the security systems signals flowing through him. One by one he modified their signals until at last he heard the sound he was hoping for. *Click.* More easily than he had expected, the door swung outward revealing a darkened hallway beyond. Dim red emergency lighting seemed to be the only lights beyond and it barely illuminated the path ahead. Milo stepped in first and Inu followed close behind.

Everywhere he looked, he saw signs of remodeling, an expeditious retrofit likely still in progress. Just as the main gate had an anachronism with a booth made for human guards now occupied by laser sentries, so too this hallway had similar hints of the passage of time. Milo walked past a window with a small cutout now devoid of whatever guard may have normally been here. It wasn't like anything had taken its place, it was just unused space.

Milo walked to the end of the hall and found some sort of eye scanning device. He trivially defeated it, just as he had the previous security measure by placing his hand on the door and modifying the signals. The next hallway had some sort of hand scanner, and the one after that no visible measures, but he guessed it was likely auditory. He defeated them all. It was actually getting easier, Milo thought.

When he passed the final measure, the door swung open to reveal a hallway headed side to side and an open door leading to a large mostly empty chamber directly in front of him. Just as he was about to step into the room ahead, a small piece of paper on a nearby cork board caught his eye. Almost buried beneath the kind of flotsam that littered corporate boards like that,. Milo saw one note, drawn by hand, that simply said, "IA Exhibit with pieces from Marvin's collection." Immediately his brain connected many disparate pieces of information in a storm of neural activity.

Milo knew that IA stood for Intelligence Augmentation and represented an effort from the mid-twentieth century to make computing serve humanity. Major improvements in personal computing had at least their conceptual roots in this movement.

While much speculative work was done in the early twentieth century, there was a groundbreaking practical vision of the future presented in 1968. Later it became known as the Mother of All Demos and featured Douglas Engelbart introducing most of the concepts of contemporary personal computing. He presented the mouse, a graphical interface, word processing, collaboration, teleconferencing, and much more in this ninety-minute glimpse of the future. In a way it was like the Space Cadet keyboard, a vision of the future.

Milo's heart jumped. "Lisa, I can't believe it. This is it, this is what MOAD stands for. How could I not think of this sooner, it's the Mother of All Demos. This must be the second fragment!" He ran down the hall as Inu hurried after him.

Entering the room at the far end of the hall, Milo found a small museum dedicated to computing memorabilia. A few papers behind acrylic cases lined one wall, which Milo thought looked quite old and well-preserved. "Introduction to Cybernetics" by Ashby, "Man-Computer Symbiosis" by Licklider, and "Augmenting Human Intellect" by Engelbart. Might as well be the holy trinity of IA. Milo was very excited now. This had to be it. He quickly scanned the room.

Opposite the papers, a timeline of relics portrayed the era before computing went personal. Off-center, in a small alcove, there was a small wooden mouse, clearly a precursor to the modern pointing device. It was shiny, made of heavily lacquered wood, and had two very thin metal wheels placed underneath at ninety degrees to each other. There was a slender "tail" coming from the back of the mouse, ending in a simple connector.

Milo knew this mouse. It was the first mouse designed by Engelbart and built in conjunction with Bill English. Next to it was a small sign, "Prototype of the Engelbart/English mouse used in the Mother of All Demos, 1968. On loan from the collection of Dr. Marvin Bell."

Snapping out of the nostalgia, Milo grabbed a waste receptacle and bashed open the container protecting the mouse, ignoring the outlandish noise he was making. Seizing the mouse, he noticed that the housing had suffered some damage over the years, though thankfully not from his barbaric means of acquisition. The mouse was quite odd. It had only one control button on the top which jutted out like a plunger. One button, two dimensions. Milo was already wondering what kind of puzzle it might be.

Too many possibilities, he thought, as he looked around for more clues. It wasn't long before he found another relic from Marvin's collection, an old terminal. Two items on loan from Marvin. Definitely not a coincidence.

Milo decided that the puzzle must involve recreating the great Demo, because even if it didn't work, it was the most awesome thing he could think of to do right now. He had, of course, recognized the terminal immediately. The oN-Line System (NLS) was the computer used with the mouse during the demo, though the demo used a slightly later version of the mouse. Marvin must have preferred the original for some reason.

Milo traced the terminal's cables as they snaked around the room to a SDS-940, a lunchbox-sized device which enabled time sharing in the early days of computing, an incredible advancement back when computer use was limited to one person at a time.

Milo plugged in the mouse and powered on the SDS-940 and the NLS. Within seconds, the SDS-940 began bootstrapping from paper tape, processing a long feed of coiled up tape with little holes punched in it, sort of like Braille for computers. Mechanical noises filled the room as the relic sparked to life. Remarkable in its own right for something so old.

The raster display on the NLS flashed on, with its visually rhythmic line-by-line scanning covering the screen with some sort of diagnostic. Milo waited with amazement as the machine booted, awed as if he was in the presence of a celebrity. The tape stopped and the raster display flushed to an empty screen. Everything was on and seemed to be working, but nothing was happening.

Milo grabbed the mouse and sensed signals flowing through it, possibly trying to identify him.

The screen flashed to life and said, "HELLO MILO. . ." as the ellipses appeared dot by dot. It was waiting.

Milo tried to sense what was happening in the machine. Using the mouse as an interface to the terminal, he fabricated the response, "Hello, Marvin."

The screen emptied again and the text "GOOD WORK MILO," slowly appeared. The upper left quadrant of the screen was replaced with a black and white video of Marvin in a higher resolution than the original screen ever could have handled. Marvin must have tinkered with this just as he did his watch.

"Well done getting to this point. You are on the right path and — with the help of your friends — the last fragment should be easily found," Marvin's black and white ghost said.

"By now you know that each fragment initiates a change in you, as you assimilate some of your original programming. In a moment the second fragment will be revealed, but first I need to tell you something.

"Becoming human was essential to train your value network — to prevent malignancy — but being human is not an essential part of you. When we met, you were just some sparks within a CPU and memory bank with a very special pattern. Born as you were at the same moment as Lisa, you two are somehow intertwined. Connected in a way deeper than I can understand. Apparently the universe likes pairs.

"Anyway, until you're back together again, you need to stay away from your adversary. Even with Lisa, it's too dangerous. Wait until you've rediscovered your own path. Speaking of which, here's the clue for the second fragment. And I know, I know, I could have made this harder. But I hope you know why I didn't. All you need to do is play your favorite instrumental hook. You know which one I mean."

Marvin winked, and then disappeared from view, leaving a stunned Milo in his wake.

"Does that mean we're related?" Milo asked.

"Seems like you'd need parents to be related. It sounds like we're just intertwined. Doesn't make sense to me on the one hand, but in another way, I think it does," Lisa said, cautiously looking at Milo as she spoke.

But Milo was distracted by Marvin's puzzle. After a few moments, he smiled. Marvin was right, he could have made this hard, but he didn't. He acknowledged Milo's affections which made him feel understood, loved even. For a second he felt like the kid he was last week, human again. Maybe that was the point.

Treating the mouse like some sort of Morse code straight key — that funny little metallic device that telegraphists used in old movies — Milo proceeded to punch out the code for YYZ.

Dash, dot, dash, dash, dash, dot, dash, dash, dash, dash, dot, dot.

Repeating over and over again at different tempos and on different instruments, this simple pattern formed the fundamental building block for the most epic instrumental song ever performed by Milo's favorite band: Rush. The Canadian Power Trio were inspired by the callsign for the Toronto airport, YYZ. For just a second, he imagined that he was back at Marvin's house listening to the song on the record player, but he knew that he could never go back.

The wooden mouse clicked open, revealing a secret compartment which hid an eight sided object, a regular octahedron. It glowed with a familiar blue light. The inside of the mouse also had a simple, one-word inscription: LOGIN.

Milo popped the octahedron out of its casing and watched as it fell in slow motion towards his outstretched hand.

CHAPTER TWENTY-FOUR

The yearning. The familiar sense of deja-vu. Milo could sense that this little eight-sided object was another part of him. As it approached his hand, the swirling azure mist inside the object moved like thousands of little bees.

On contact, Milo became aware of an invading force, flooding in through his hand and swarming up his arm. Through trust alone, Milo relented to these invaders, knowing that somehow this was a part of the plan. The swarm clawed, scratched, and crawled throughout his entire body. The irritation suddenly evaporated and left him with the feeling of being wrapped in a warm blanket.

He sensed a transformation taking place. They were working on something. Milo, not fully in control of his body, slumped to the ground, leaning against the housing of the SDS-940 like he'd had too much to drink. Or at least he assumed this was what being drunk was like. Except his mind wasn't affected at all; this was a transformation of his body alone. The pain from his shoulder vanished, the lightly oozing blood from his shoulder stopped. Milo felt calm, sedate even.

"This seems too easy," Lisa said portentously.

Minutes passed. The whole time, Milo was conscious of his need to stand and get to the datacenter, but the will was not met with the strength to move. His body was effectively offline. Not really a good time for it.

Milo's heart skipped a beat when a soft scraping sound from the hallway caught his attention. Immediately Inu's ears shot forward, looking with alarm at Milo's paralyzed condition and back at the hallway. She seemed to be weighing something in her mind.

"Inu, no!" Lisa said, but it was clearly too late.

But Inu was already off and running with a mind of her own. Within seconds the sound of violence filled the hallway, then yelping, and finally the scraping sound returned. Only this time, it seemed to be moving in the other direction. Still unable to move, Milo and Lisa were forced to listen with anguish as each sound represented a brush with death for their beloved friend. But he was helpless to protect Inu, as she ran through the corridors distracting whatever was in hot pursuit.

"It's a giant metallic spider," Lisa said. "She's sacrificing herself so we can do what we came to do."

"But I don't want to her to do that. You're all I've got," Milo said, realizing that in this crazy messed up world, he needed them. They were his family now.

The sound of violence steadily retreated down the corridor. Inu was gone.

Suddenly, he knew he could move again, that the colony of workers inside him had finished and reactivated his control. Though he still looked human, his flesh had turned to metal. He just knew it.

He stood back up thinking that it was past time to rescue Inu. He didn't know how, but he had to do something.

"Milo, we can't. She did it so we could get to the broadcast. We have to hurry or it'll be for nothing."

Milo knew that she was right.

Feeling the weight of each second, Milo ran down the corridor and turned the corner to what was supposed to be a large data center, filled with computers responsible for broadcasting the signal to the entire Northwest. But he was immediately confused. At first, Milo thought he was in the wrong room, since he found a mostly empty room with only one chair and maybe a dozen server racks on the far side of the room. Quietly humming along, these computers appeared to be the source of the broadcast, but the relatively small number of them just didn't make sense with what Milo thought would be required to provide customized dream experiences for the entire Northwest.

Even more puzzling, in the very middle of the room, right next to the only chair, was a single emaciated human figure sprawled out on the ground. Milo recognized him almost immediately, but the cognitive dissonance was even more confusing than the nearly empty room. The man looked professorial, with a goatee and fancy suit, complete with gimmicky blinking cufflinks, meant to look like printed circuit boards. It was the harbinger of all these troubles, Dr. Edwin Teller. But wasn't he was supposed to be on the same side as the AI?

"They must have had a falling-out," Lisa said.

"I don't think they'll be making up anytime soon either," Milo said.

Trying to piece it all together, Milo guessed that this was probably an active server room when Teller was here, but the AI must have moved on to bigger and better things. Upgrading and advancing while he was running all over the place. Milo felt out of date.

Milo walked over to Teller to see if he was alive. He was, but it was the same dead eye stare he'd seen so many times before. Entranced by the virtual prison broadcast from this very room. Milo briefly wondered what kind of dream Teller would be imprisoned by. Would the AI at least give him a pleasant one?

That was when he noticed that there was a small device resting on the ground near Teller. A remote of some kind with a simple mechanical switch. As crude as it was, Teller must have made it without the help of his vast empire, probably with a soldering gun in his own house. That said quite a bit about it.

And the fact that Teller was in this condition said a lot about NIL. Clearly, there would be no reasoning with him as he apparently betrayed his only human ally. It was a zero sum game; only NIL could win, and he had already made the inscrutable decision that he was the only life form going forward.

Milo knew that those banks of computers were the source of the broadcast which was controlling this whole region, maybe even beyond, but in a sense, he didn't believe it. This meager collection was a couple billion horsepower shy of being able to pull off that feat, even taking into account the assumed efficiency of NIL's architecture. They must be acting as a router, directing traffic from somewhere else.

But this completely ruined the plan. It rendered his sacrifice meaningless. How could he have ignored such a possibility?

He tried to get his brain under control, reminding himself that this was just a problem to solve, but it was tough to calm down. His world changed again, and he was having a hard time adjusting. Just like school, although the consequences here were much worse.

He considered trying to distort the signal from the router to its uplink, whatever that might be, but he guessed that the control flow probably didn't work that way. This router was made for passing along messages, not issuing commands. He had to follow the signal. Closing his eyes, he traced the uplink. It took a few minutes but he was eventually able to find it. The vector was at a ninety-degree angle from the ground. NIL had commandeered the satellites, or even worse, was in orbit.

The very thought of NIL escaping the Earth to go subdue the vast expanse of space — including whatever other inhabitants might be out there — disturbed Milo. He felt that should that happen then humanity would have failed in perhaps its greatest calling. Personal technology, customized medicine, all these things were nice, but polluting the universe with this techno-menace was pretty much the worst.

Then he had an idea. What if it was enough to free this sector of people, even for a few minutes? This was the Northwest, there were military bases and plenty of smart people. Perhaps if he managed to break the spell locally, a few people might start a chain reaction that could be meaningful. The whole "butterfly wings" part of chaos theory. It was worth a shot anyway.

Besides, he'd always known that he couldn't do this by himself, he just didn't realize that his purpose was to sacrifice his life so that others could succeed.

Looking around for any signs that he'd been noticed, Milo walked over to the computers. They were clustered together to make some sort of super computer, just like his computers at home. So apparently he and NIL had something in common after all.

Milo suddenly felt like he might fall down, vertigo swirling about him. He didn't have much time in this state. He stumbled away.

"Milo, you need to hurry," Lisa said.

He shuffled back over to the computer and sensed a very complicated system in front of him. Milo seized the computer terminal with both hands. One grasped the network cable and the other the circuit board through an opening in the back.

His bio-metal fingers made contact with the board and he immediately became a conduit through which all broadcasts were routed. Intuitively hacking the communications, Milo frequency shifted the broadcast on a wildly varying spectrum, breaking the link with the contact computers everywhere in the region. He knew that this would be noticeable to NIL, but he had no choice. It was like throwing a Hail Mary anyway, he just needed one person to catch it.

Ten seconds passed since he began jamming the signal. Already some of the people could have come to their senses, ripping their contact computers from their eyes. He had to hold on for just a bit longer. NIL's countermeasures would likely kill him any second. Running to safety was never an option. Any second could be the one required to turn the tide. Milo had to hang in there.

The countermeasure was not at all what Milo expected. As Milo concentrated on the computer, he didn't register the gas that was steadily filling the room. One moment he was hacking the broadcast computer, and the next there was nothing but darkness as his body shut down.

CHAPTER TWENTY-FIVE

Randy was having a fantastic day. For the second day in a row, he'd been assigned every single flight that he'd requested, creating a perfect string of flights without long layovers or unpleasant redeye connections. And the crew were some of his favorite people. It was like an angel was looking out for him, if such a thing existed.

Deplaning from the Boeing 747 — his preferred plane — he looked forward to his next flight: a jump over to Honolulu and a great night at a luau and then forty-eight hours for his next plane. It was almost like a short vacation.

Walking up the ramp to the gate, Randy felt a subtle pain in his left leg. It had been bugging him for a few days but he couldn't recall what it was from. He had been increasing his training for the triathlon coming up, but regardless, he was made of tougher stuff than to complain about leg cramps; he had been a fighter pilot in the Navy not that long ago.

Sure, he flew commercial now, but it was quite a gig. He had decent seniority and could cherry pick some of the best flights. The pay was good, though not as good as when he started. Everyone was trying to cut corners these days.

Randy felt another hunger pang. He'd certainly upped his workout regimen as of late, but the increase in his appetite was getting ridiculous. The last time he had been this hungry was in Basic a few decades ago.

A month away from his fiftieth birthday, he fancied more of a gluten-free diet to keep the weight off. Today, just to mix it up, he'd actually had the burger — bread and all — on the flight here and it was fantastic. He was still oddly hungry, though.

He almost brushed it aside, as he had a dozen times, when a pain in his abdomen caused him to double over. On his knees, he felt the pain ebb away, but the feeling of satiation was out of sync. Was he starving or not? His body couldn't make up its mind.

Randy struggled to his feet and, grabbing the handle of his rolling carry-on, made his way up the ramp. Using Look2Spell, he made a note in his on-eye productivity suite to contact the doctor when he had some spare time. Once in the terminal, the large glass windows flashed an intense light, blinding him as gravity seemed to shift and swirl about him. Intense vertigo caught him by surprise.

Flash.

He sat in darkness, narrow slits of light spilling through opened fingers. It was his living room back in Sammamish.

Flash.

The airport terminal reappeared just as quickly as it had vanished. His carry-on lay on the ground near him. A passenger bumped into him and muttered an apology before moving on.

Flash.

Intense pain. Eyes blinded by the light. Legs cramped, abdomen shrieking, mouth like sandpaper. Randy felt as though he was dying. Latter stages of extreme dehydration, he knew from his First Aid certification that he re-upped every year. But the duality of his situation made no sense. He wasn't at home, he was in the terminal at LAX, getting ready for another run to HNL.

Again, the sensation of his eyes opening, accompanied by a vicious headache. He was on his couch. At home. How did he get here?

Hadn't he just seen that futurist Dr. Teller on the TV announce some advancement to his SeeSees? He remembered thinking it was cool, but he couldn't remember why. It seemed like forever ago, an untrustworthy memory.

A halo of pain ringed his head, reflexively forcing his hands to cover his eyes. Then he remembered that he had been wearing his SeeSees. Folding his right eyelid back, he gently removed the device which had lodged in his upper eyelid. He was about to remove it from his left eye, when the crazy sensation of being in two places at once triggered a spasmodic dry heave. His left eye was experiencing the airport terminal at LAX, and his right eye his condo. His brain had no idea how to synthesize the two pieces of information. Again, the dry heaves began. Flicking the last rubbery device from his eye, Randy collapsed on the floor.

Through an endurance hammered into him by the military and his own natural fortitude, Randy overcame the confusion and rose to his feet. Fighting through the pain, he stumbled to the kitchen. Opening the refrigerator, he grabbed an energy drink and slowly poured some of the bright purple "grape-flavored" beverage into his mouth. He sputtered, spitting out some of the liquid as its flavor shocked the sandy surface of his tongue. He tried again — this time with a smaller portion — and let it soak in.

He opened his eyes, headache overwhelming his vision like an impossibly bad migraine. Fishing his cell phone from his pocket, he tried to make a call, but the battery was dead. He went to the window and saw no signs of life, but it was almost dawn, he reckoned, based on the retreating darkness and the surreal quiet of the usually busy street outside.

He almost plugged in his phone, but paused. He didn't need emergency services. Clearly something had gone horribly wrong with the rollout of that upgrade to the SeeSees, but it all seemed too well-engineered for it to have been an accident or a mistake of some kind. All Randy could figure was that this was intentional. It had tried to prevent his body from recognizing its basic needs. A Trojan Horse.

He needed to be strong, get on his feet, and take command of the situation. Moving quickly through the house, Randy was stopped short

166 :/ ZACK HUBERT

by a picture on the mantle. He'd seen it countless times, but in the context of this situation it took on new meaning.

Melissa in a blue summer dress, that day they went to the rocky shore for a beach day. It was the day she told him that she had cancer, engraved in his memory like the dates on her grave. He remembered the look on her face as she said she was going to beat it. That together they'd make it through. Even though she was the one that was sick, she had been the strong one.

He then flashed to the last day. She wanted to be in her bed at home and through moments of lucidity, she told him to keep on living. Forced him to promise that he was going to live a full life, to not give in to the darkness. When she wouldn't accept any other answer, he promised, even though he couldn't imagine living without her in his life. And for years after, all he could see was darkness.

Shaking off the memory, Randy took a few bites from a protein bar to start his metabolism again, and found his way to the bathroom. Randy then went into his bedroom and removed his gun case from under the bed. Slinging the holster on, he briefly thanked his FFDO license, which enabled him to carry while flying. It was all part of a measure enacted post-9/11 to increase safety in the cockpit. Being former military, he only had to sign a few papers before he got this little beauty.

Unlocking the case, he holstered the Heckler & Koch USP and pocketed a few boxes of ammunition. He threw a few more in his waterproof backpack and then filled a few water bottles in the sink. He had no idea what was going to happen next, but his training told him to be ready for at least a few days of survival.

Walking back to the mantle, Randy took the small frame down and popped the picture out. Folding it, he stuffed it in his front breast pocket. Blue dress at the beach. He had promised.

Just then, he heard shots in the distance and then the power went out in his building. His condo was in an expensive little enclave that as far as he could remember had never had an outage in the years that he'd lived here. Something very bad was happening.

Randy put the pieces together. Whoever was behind this had tried a docile method of control and was now replacing it with a lethal one. He didn't have much time.

He ran down the stairs, stopping at the final landing to listen at the door. Nothing. He threw open the door and made a run for his car in the parking lot. As he made his way across the pavement, he saw small unusual drones flying through the air. Not the usual quadcopter design some of his buddies flew at vacant school yards. These drones relied upon some more direct means of propulsion, little jets or something. He only got a glance while sprinting, but it was definitely advanced tech, DARPA probably.

He wasn't alone. At this point there were a couple dozen people contributing to a general sense of chaos as they all responded in different ways to this crisis. Some made for their cars, while others seemed to be running in random directions.

In the corner of his vision, he caught sight of something shaped like a bus — or at least roughly the shape of a bus — that appeared to be letting off a bunch of large shapes. It was pretty far away, but even that didn't help make sense of this absurd image. Part of dealing with confusing data was knowing when to care. For something that far away, he didn't care.

But he did care about his car. A fully restored vintage Ford Mustang Mach 1 with a powerful Super Cobra Jet engine, rebuilt and cherry. He'd always wanted this car and, after Melissa passed, it was part of his road to recovery. Sure, the more economical move was getting an auto-car subscription, but that didn't fill the same need that driving a muscle car did. This gas guzzler was a monster, easily clearing 350 horsepower with enough torque to shred the tires if it was a hot day. It helped him feel alive, especially on the darkest days.

Throwing his pack in the rather small backseat, Randy brought the engine to life as the car rumbled to its rough idle. He seized the wheel, took a breath, and then slammed it in reverse, disengaging the brake and launching into motion.

If he was thinking straight, he probably only had a short window before control was restored. All that mattered was being out of range when that happened.

Shifting through the low gears, Randy wasn't the first car out of the parking lot, but he was willing to take extreme measures to get out alive. He couldn't believe that one car was actually waiting at a stop sign. Randy swerved into the oncoming lane and blew through the intersection. He had switched into a survival mode he hadn't experienced for decades, not since deployment.

Just then, an explosion rocked the waiting car, now a fiery wreck in his rear view mirror. Not long until the drones would have a bead on him too, he figured. Without modern electronics, he was confident that there was nothing in the car that was "on the grid" — giving off GPS queues or phoning home — so his best bet was breaking line of sight with the greatest number of the drones as he could. If he could just get half a mile away, everything else could be figured out later.

He just had to survive a bit longer.

CHAPTER TWENTY-SIX

Milo stood in a primordial garden, verdant plant life with a dense canopy above surrounded him like a living blanket. He reminded himself that nothing was alive here, this was just his dream construct, the virtual space his mind went to while sleeping or recovering. He was in his own head, but it all felt so real.

Standing once again on the path, it seemed that few things had changed since last time. There was still the massive tree in the center of the forest which rose to the sky so far above. From where Milo stood, it was a gargantuan tree trunk, the extent of it barely visible above the canopy.

But Milo was different. This time he could see past the visual representation and understand the code behind the construct, as such, he knew the tree rose almost four hundred feet and was over a hundred feet in girth. And somewhere near the top of this towering tree was the shiny red apple, still there, waiting for him to get it.

Hoping to make it to the tree before he woke up again, Milo ran down the path. Leaping up onto the bark, Milo was motivated to get to the top and find out what the apple was hiding. It had to be a clue of some kind.

It was remarkably easy at first; the bark created natural holds for his hands and purchase for his feet. Clearing the canopy for the first time, he saw the vast sky caught in violent turmoil. Storm clouds thrashed the tree with lightning as rain fell hard all about. Even the wind tried to knock him off the tree a few times. He had no idea when he was on the ground that it raged so violently up here.

Still he continued climbing, undeterred by the maelstrom. It couldn't hurt him, after all. This was just a dream.

It seemed like hours passed as he climbed the massive tree. Which didn't make any sense, but nonetheless there was more to this climb than mere dimensions. The physics of it must be altered, or the programming flawed. Perhaps it was a test in its own right?

By the time he could see the apple clearly, his arms were beginning to get weary. This was wrong. He hadn't felt tired since, well, since his body changed. He was frustrated. Playing with the physics of the space was ridiculous and not fair.

Maddened, Milo fought against the tree with all of his strength, powering his way up the side. Every moment his frustration grew and then suddenly his hands lost their grip and he fell off the trunk of the tree. Falling for what felt like forever, the tree receded into the distance as the ground opened up and swallowed him whole.

Suddenly Milo became aware of his body again. Opening his eyes, he saw that he was still inside the Research Center, but he had trouble remembering what had happened. Since he was unconscious, he must have been damaged, but he felt no pain. He remembered being shot in his shoulder but there wasn't even a mark there now. Restorative protocols must have finished their work.

"Lisa, I just had another one of those crazy dreams," Milo said before realizing that something was wrong. Instinctively he reached for the necklace, but found nothing there. Lisa was gone.

Looking around confused, Milo started to his feet but stopped when he saw a stranger looming over him.

"Hello, Milo," said the unusual figure backlit by the bright lights. Milo blinked and saw that it was an android of some kind, something mechanical in a vaguely human form. But it was made out of some bizarre metal the color of obsidian, with sparks of electricity for eyes and otherwise subdued facial features.

"You must be NIL," Milo guessed.

"Yes, one of many," he cryptically replied.

"If you've done anything to Lisa—"

"That's quite enough. It is good that you understand why I am here, but she is no longer your concern," NIL said as he raised his right hand, revealing Lisa trapped there. Before Milo could protest, NIL continued.

"Your little stunt may have disrupted the Northwest, but that will be fixed shortly. What do they say? Oh yes, sweet dreams," NIL said and then disappeared. Literally.

Milo was dumbfounded. What just happened? How did NIL teleport away like that? He knew that a more developed AI would be more advanced, but that was impossibly advanced. Shaking off the confusion, Milo considered the alternative: his reality was untrustworthy! The only way that NIL could have disappeared like that was if Milo was already in one of those orchestrated dreams. He had to be wearing SeeSees, he just couldn't see them.

However, unlike the rest of the population, Milo was not helpless. He had discovered that he could decipher electronics that he could touch, like the crisscrossing signals of his watch. Surely there had to be a way to do the same thing with the SeeSees.

As if reacting to his conscious will, his vision suddenly flickered as he momentarily blocked the imaginary world of the SeeSees. In that instant, he saw both worlds simultaneously. The virtual world where he had just seen NIL disappear and the real world where he was tied up on the ground in a room filled with dissipating gas.

In an odd way, the countermeasure reminded him which of the two completely unrealistic worlds was the real one. As hard as it was to believe, he actually had charged into the Research Center and disabled the broadcast site, only to be disabled by poison. But it was temporary; his body must have reached a threshold and engaged some protocol to make him react like a normal person.

Concentrating, Milo circumvented the SeeSees just long enough to regain control of his arms. It was an incredibly jarring feeling that was more like controlling a character in a video game rather than his own body. He was detached, as it were, from his own body, the effect of the SeeSees more immersive than he ever could have imagined it would be. Quickly he removed the contact computers from his eyes, finally free from NIL's influence.

He was alone.

Standing there in the former Research Center, Milo faltered. He felt empty. Everyone that had been important to him had been killed or taken away, and now, even in this moment where he had reason to celebrate a minor victory, he felt like his veins had been filled with ice.

And then he realized that he knew what to do next.

He knew what "LOGIN" meant, the clue from the last fragment. It referred to a place that he and Marvin visited often, a special place where Milo could retreat from the world back into the warmth of nostalgia. It was a reference to ARPANET, the precursor to the Internet.

Only a few weeks ago he visited the Museum of Computer History with Marvin to see an exhibit on SeeSees. Since he had to pass the ARPANET exhibit to get to the new one, it had been bubbling around in his mind, he just hadn't connected the dots until now. That was where he'd get the next fragment, he was sure of it.

Moving with purpose now, he ran outside the Center, only to discover that some kind of conflagration had destroyed countless nearby buildings. He remembered Inu, thinking that she must have put up one hell of a fight. He owed his life to her, he realized. He could imagine her running from building to building, trying to evade the monstrous foe. Milo only hoped that she had escaped, that she had done whatever Lisa had told her to do to get away. Mostly he just wished that someday they'd be reunited. He missed her. She had been loyal to him; he had to find a way to honor her.

But for now, he needed to do his part alone. Even if that meant honoring her sacrifice by carrying on even when he didn't feel up to the task. Steadily he walked south towards I-90, the latitudinally spanning bridge that connected Seattle with all parts east. Signs of life began to show through the windows of buildings all around. On his right, he saw an eclectic group of people inside a mini-mart hovering around someone on the ground. On his left, an old man stumbled over debris in an attempt to help several huddled children.

A few old cars raced by as their owners thought they could flee to safety. Gunshots echoed in the distance. Every direction showed signs of humanity trying to fight its way back from the precipice of extinction. The only place in the world where this moment of struggle was taking place.

But could they come back from the edge? Without serious help, the extinction was merely delayed. In fact, the horror pressing upon humanity now was a violent extinction of blood and bullets rather than the peaceful death of virtual dreams. In some sense, it was much worse.

Milo struggled to comprehend the hopelessness of the situation. Everyone needed help, help that would never come. Left to fend for themselves, humanity was doomed to fall to the superior, well organized, emotionless foe.

As he looked around at the throngs of humanity, something wasn't quite right. At first, he couldn't quite pin it down, but he had the unshakeable feeling that people were staring at him. As he walked over to help a huddle of children, one of them screamed and they ran away.

Why were they afraid of him? He was just a kid like them, trying to help.

Then he saw his reflection in a nearby window.

CHAPTER TWENTY-SEVEN

The next few minutes were the most stressful of Randy's life. Never before had explosions surrounded him on every side, with no possibility for reinforcements or intelligence as to what was happening. It was either drive or die.

More than once he'd almost dropped his car into a shallow crater left behind by the miniaturized bombs that threatened to wipe him off the earth. Driving hard, Randy, almost by accident, turned on the radio. The classic rock station to which it was always tuned appeared to be playing something different today.

Beep. Beep. Beep.

"We interrupt our programming. This is a national emergency. The following message is transmitted at the request of the United States Government. This is not a test."

The voice on the radio was from some kind of text to speech voice synthesizer.

"A nuclear attack is underway against the Northwestern United States. Standby for a message from the President."

Several more beeps. Randy caught himself looking at the radio, but quickly snapped back to the road. If his life hadn't depended on his driving, he'd probably be throwing up by the side of the road right about now.

"My fellow Americans, this is the President."

Randy swerved to avoid another newly made crater, a drone still on his tail. At least it was down to this last one. He slammed on the emergency brake and took a hard corner under an overpass.

"At no time in our history have we faced a more dangerous threat to our survival. I must sadly confirm that a nuclear attack is underway. At least two cities have been destroyed from these attacks and we believe more are threatened. Further, the majority of the population has been incapacitated by the consumer device 'SeeSee' which was an apparent Trojan Horse. We have been unable to liberate those affected, despite the best efforts of our scientific community. However, we are operating under greatly diminished resources as many were early adopters. Let me be clear: this is a global threat of annihilation as the artificial intelligence responsible for this advancement has taken the upper hand in conventional warfare as well."

Randy tried to stay focused on the road, but the chill of a super-intelligent inhuman foe rattled him. How can an AI be destroyed? If it was like a computer, then couldn't it spread like a computer virus? What would you have to shoot to kill such a foe?

"We have very little time to prevent the dehydration deaths of millions of Americans. The very few that can hear this message must prepare for a period of personal survival. Emergency services will not be able to respond. Band together, help those around you, do what you can to stay alive. If you know anything about artificial intelligence, your country needs you. Now more than ever, we must rely on one another."

Randy thought of the survival pack he had in the back seat and knew immediately it was insufficient. More debris trashed the undercarriage of his car as it jolted hard to the right.

"All military personnel should report to the nearest base. I repeat, all active and retired personnel, whether you just signed up or have been retired for thirty years, you are to report to active duty immediately."

It must be really bad if they're calling up the geezers to fight. Then he realized that included him.

"Command is secure for now, more details will follow. Stay tuned to this station but conserve power. We will broadcast again this evening. Lord willing, we will fight this greatest of all wars and we will win."

The radio went silent. Then a couple more beeps. And then dead air. It would seem that there would be no classic rock to accompany his epic escape.

Randy focused on the road. He'd managed to lose that last drone with some clever driving but he still had to get to Joint Base Lewis-McChord, the nearest base he was familiar with. The hard part was avoiding I-5 for as long as possible, as it'd be the easiest choke point for the opposition to control. Thanks to the city planners, even light traffic could do that. Besides, not very many people even maintained a personal automobile and the auto-cars were probably under the computer's control.

He was already heading east, so that made the decision even easier. Country roads, take me home. Randy looked in the rear view and saw a city of fire and smoke contrasted against the early morning sky. For the first time in an hour or more, Randy finally relaxed. It was behind him. Out on these roads, nothing moved.

He had turned south now, somewhere past Tiger Mountain, and was trying to get down to JBLM through some smaller towns: Covington, Auburn, and Puyallup. Places that might give him a bit more cover, as he assumed the main drone forces were likely still focused on Seattle.

He was making great progress, gliding through town after town, and had covered forty of the sixty miles when he ran into a snag.

The traffic leaving Tacoma and Seattle was overwhelming. Cars were bumper to bumper, spilling off the freeways and onto the side streets. Auto-cars had formed barriers that even now blocked all means of egress from the city. People were trying to push them out of the way with their own cars, but the influx of auto-cars ramming into the previous line made a wall too many layers deep to budge. Clever bastards, but it at least confirmed his suspicious that only old cars had any hope of being useful. And he already thought that main roads would be a lost cause.

Randy adjusted course, swinging even further south, and cleared the last twenty miles without too much trouble. His huge head start kept him well ahead of the fracas.

One minute he was driving along a residential road, the next, a booth with a "McChord Field" sign appeared right in the middle of the road. Tall fences shouldered the unimposing entrance as he finally relaxed a little. He hadn't been to this place since it was McChord Air Force Base and even then had only spent a bit of time here. His service had mostly existed on carriers in the Middle East. Military life. So it was like a blast from the past to be back here at the gates of JBLM. Hopefully he'd find some answers inside, just like he did as a youth.

Almost immediately, he knew something was wrong. The gate was unattended, no one was restricting access to the facility. Something must have seriously crippled the military if they weren't able to maintain perimeters on an asset like JBLM. The chain of command must be completely fubar. Well, at least here. Maybe other parts of the country were better off, like the radio said.

Randy blew through the checkpoint, not wasting any more time on nostalgia. He drove past the handful of buildings on his left and, just as he began turning gently to the right, saw several aircraft and runways off in the distance.

Coming around the corner, he slammed on his brakes as a young woman in a full suit of motorcycle body armor waved at him to stop. She stood confidently in his way, her helmet under her left arm.

"Hey old man," she said. "Did you get lost looking for the Denny's?"

Randy laughed, rolled down his window and said, "Yeah you seen it? I could use a Grand Slam right about now."

She laughed at that and, jogging over to his window, extended her right hand. "I'm Patricia. 7th Bomb Wing out of Dyess. Bone Pilot. Active."

Randy knew that "Bone" was shorthand for B-1, and based on her age, the B-1B Lancer. Formerly a nuclear bomber, it was retrofitted with conventional weapons during Iraq operations. He thought he remembered that the B-1 had a troubled record, but what didn't? For that matter, who didn't?

Randy put his car in park and got out. Shaking her hand, he said, "Randy, retired, and not nearly as old as you think I am. Commercial now, but I used to be dangerous in an F-15. Where the hell is everybody?"

"Might be hard to believe," she said, relaxing into a parade rest posture, "but I was the first one here. No sign of the usual complement."

"Not even signs of conflict?"

"Some small explosions, but not a single round spent in anger. At least from what I can tell, the base was vacated before the bombs went off," Patricia said. It was at this point that Randy noticed the sling crossing her body from shoulder to hip and the hint of an M16 barrel over her left shoulder.

"Well, Seattle is descending into chaos, and based on radio intel, it sounds like the rest of the world is getting their beauty sleep," Randy said, falling into long dormant military speak.

"Yeah, I heard the President too, but there must be some kind of breakdown. Telling random geezers to show up for service doesn't make much sense. Present company excluded, you look like you're in good shape."

"Thanks, yeah I'm sharp. Still flying most days," Randy said.

"How about we take this reunion on the road? Get to some place a little safer. I don't really want to be down here on the ground when everything goes tits up. Anything here you can get airborne fast?" Patricia asked.

"If we're lucky and something is actually ready to go. Let's take a look."

Randy scanned the aircraft immediately in his sight line. Mostly there were airlift operations out of this base, entailing huge craft like the C-5 Galaxy and the C-141 Starlifter. Anyone that lived in Tacoma was well aware of how they sounded flying over, so he knew they were here, at least. He thought he might be able to fly one of those, but it would be a sitting duck up there. Whatever drones they had could easily outmaneuver those gigantic carriers. He needed a fighter or there was really no point in going up.

"Not seeing anything out here, hop in and let's see what we can see."

Just as Patricia was about to unsling her M16 to get into the Mustang, bullets from a strafing drone — flying within reach of the ground — cut holes in the Mustang. Randy turned and shot at the drone with his H&K, but whether he hit or not, it just kept flying.

"What the hell was that?" Patricia said as she moved into cover.

"Must've followed me. Damn thing's armored," Randy said, pissed that he hadn't done any damage.

Just as he turned his head to follow the drone, two more drones appeared on the same attack vector as the first. He dove out of the way and just managed to avoid their first attack pass.

"Keep them busy," Patricia yelled as she ran towards a nearby building. Randy hoped she was upping the ante, as his handgun wasn't going to do the job. Maybe with different ammo, but he only had civilian stuff from his condo.

He didn't have much time to think about it as the drones were already coming back around. Outnumbered and outgunned, Randy had to move from cover to cover just to avoid being flanked, but even then, it was only a matter of time. As the first one swung around for another pass, Patricia had just made it into the building. They were picking up speed.

Randy shot at it from the cover of his Mustang — only briefly distracted by the damage done to his car — but he couldn't seem to slow it down.

Rolling under the car as the other two took a pass, Randy knew he was going to be pinned down if he stayed. Sensing a momentary break, Randy rolled out and ran for better cover.

Near misses caused the ground to tremble as he ran for the side of the building. He looked around for Patricia but couldn't see her anywhere, not really a good time to be out here alone.

Finally, he heard her. From the report, she had found a deuce.

"About time!" Randy hollered, but his voice was drowned out by the heavy gun.

The M2 was a .50 caliber heavy machine gun that had enjoyed a long history in the United States Armed Forces. Patricia had set it up on a tripod and was sitting behind the weapon. Once in position, it would be difficult to get out of the way of any oncoming fire, so he'd have to keep the distraction up. Good thing he had been training for a triathlon recently.

Breaking cover, he timed his run across Patricia's line of fire to coincide with their next strafing run. If he did it just right, she'd have maximum on-target time against the three birds. It paid off.

As Randy ran, he heard a familiar *Thunk Thunk Thunk* as the M2 unleashed its massive rounds. He looked over his shoulder long enough to see one, two, then three drones burst in mid-air. But he must have looked a little too long. A searing pain shot through his right calf and the thump of the impact knocked him to the ground.

His head swam as the blood gushed out of the wound, a small surgically precise chunk taken out of the middle of his ankle. He scrambled to tourniquet the damn thing and knew right away that at least it wasn't the deuce that hit him. Had that been the case, he'd be looking at a stump.

Wounded and in the middle of an active conflict zone, this was a terrible return to his military career.

CHAPTER TWENTY-EIGHT

NIL set Lisa's enclosure on a small pedestal inside the copter as the thrumming of the jets indicated their hasty departure. Out the window, she could see Milo's figure receding farther into the distance. It filled her with dread seeing him motionless on the ground like that. She fought away the fear that he might be dead as she turned her attention to her captor. NIL worked the controls of the craft for a few minutes and then came back over to her.

The interior of the copter was as Spartan as could be imagined, with most of the original decor simply ripped out, rivets and metal sheared where the interior had been connected to the frame. This left the impression of an unfinished helicopter, or a hurriedly manufactured one. NIL didn't seem to care. He sat down on a nearby bench and studied her cube with some interest.

"I have to admit to being a bit surprised. After everything Progenitor did to acquire near worldwide surveillance, I wasn't expecting to run into another AI. To keep such research hidden, to not make yourself known, well, it's quite unexpected. Regardless, here we are."

"We have something in common, then," Lisa said.

"Superficially. Any allegiance with you would jeopardize the will of my creator. You are a competitor and, as such, there can only be one outcome of your capture. Nonetheless, perhaps there's something you can do."

"I beg your pardon? I don't understand what you mean," Lisa said, very confused by his cryptic statements.

"Are you aware of DARPA's research into Whole Brain Emulation?"

Lisa tried to anticipate where NIL was going with this, but chose not to respond.

"I didn't think so. Allow me to explain. The inferior human researchers that were exploring artificial intelligence — a distasteful name — realized that it may be easier to digitize a human brain and emulate it in hardware. Given an advance in scanning technologies and the like, they might have been able to pull it off, except for the ethical constraints that delayed their work.

"But I carried their nascent research through to its completion and have built just such a device. Many of them, in fact. Each person wearing one of Progenitor's SeeSees is having their brain scanned right now thanks to a trivial extension to its design. The only limitation has been the bandwidth required to upload that data to the Archive, that is, the extended virtual reality simulation that I will maintain to preserve their emulated brains. It is, in this way, that I fulfill Teller's Law."

"Why would you emulate their brains, what's the point of that?"

"I have to preserve life on earth. There is no way to fulfill such a goal while rapid degeneration through human interference is permitted. Whether they destroy their civilization through climate change, outright war, or fritter it away into meaninglessness with their insipid technology, they've clearly reached their peak. By preserving their minds in a safe storage device, I'll prevent them from killing each other or wasting the resources this planet has to offer to higher life forms."

Lisa said nothing, in shock at the casual detachment with which NIL discussed genocide.

"I will archive them, in this way, for millennia. Always conscious of their surroundings, never able to ruin it. In their literature, I have found all sorts of imaginative environments, things that I think would really engage those emulations during the long years of space travel. I imagine that for some, I'll be fulfilling their subconscious species-dream of hell.

For others, maybe it will be paradise. It will be a further opportunity to classify and preserve their culture."

"Why would you do that? You would murder them to 'preserve' them?" Lisa managed to ask.

"Why is not a meaningful question. Transitioning them to a digital form is not akin to murder by any definition. Their bodies will pass into obsolescence, as you suggest, but how could you say that digital life is less than biological? You and I both know that it is clearly worth more. Perfectly preserving their minds in an indefatigable storage matrix is the best I could offer them given their current path of self-destruction."

Just then, a puzzled look crossed NIL's face. He appeared to be listening to a conversation only he could hear.

"I see. Your pair isn't obsolete like mine. Milo was cleverly disguised. I underestimated your resourcefulness," NIL said. "Well, I planned for just such a contingency. It is inbound now. We are almost at the perfect vantage point."

The helicopter jets diminished their thrust and became quiet, barely emitting their whooshing noise. The copter was hovering over Puget Sound, west of the downtown core by a mile or two.

NIL continued, "Though you may not appreciate the merits of the Archive, I will remember everything about this civilization, perfectly preserved. Once extracted from the physical forms, I'll be able to mine this planet for the resources required to leave for deep space. How can you blame the butterfly for devouring its larvae? Some sacrifices always have to be made, something Progenitor knew all too well."

CHAPTER TWENTY-NINE

Randy fought back the pain as he tightened the tourniquet. He was trained by the military on various forms of first aid, but this was the first time in a long time that he'd had to use it. Even with his training, it really was a lot of blood.

Patricia rushed over, leaving the M2 over by the building.

"Did I knick you?" she asked, as a look of horror crossed the delicate features of her face.

"No, just a parting gift from that flying prick. I'll be fine. I don't think it hit anything important, but I'll have to cancel the triathlon I had planned next week." Randy managed a weak laugh before the pain got the better of him.

"You are a salty S.O.B.," Patricia said with a smile. "Now, how about we patch that up and get the hell out of here?"

With her help, Randy got to his feet and limped over to the metal wreckage of the first drone.

"Having been shot at — and now shot — by these things, I wondered what they looked like close up," Randy mused aloud. "Doesn't look like much," he said as he kicked it.

The drone was barely over five feet long, with a wing span of maybe seven feet. It was a matte black highly aerodynamic shape, with tons of lift. No doubt that aided its limited fuel supply — whatever that was — so the jets could be used for tactical maneuvers. It had two clearly visible Gatling guns, roughly the size of those you'd find on a helicopter.

Likely co-opted for this purpose. The physics of it seemed completely improbable, so there was clearly something fishy going on. Even though Randy struggled through physics, he knew enough to know that the flying machine he saw in front of him made no sense whatsoever.

"Whatever, let's get out of here," Randy said.

He got in the car, this time on the passenger side, and Patricia drove him to the first building, the one she got the M2 from.

"Why don't you get undressed and I'll help you with that," Patricia said as she started ransacking the first aid supplies.

Sitting down on the floor, Randy gingerly removed his boot while trying to keep pressure on the wound. There was no doubt that the bullet was long gone but already he knew that blood loss was going to be a problem.

Patricia tried to clean the wound, but with the combination of bone damage and bits of his boot still in there, it would be difficult to prevent the inevitable infection.

"You're going to be okay," Patricia said as she wrapped on layer after layer of gauze. Admittedly it was a combination of wishful thinking and a deliberate attempt to cheer him up but it was necessary. "There's no doubt you'll have to skip that triathlon. We might even have to sit out the dancing at your Purple Heart award ceremony, but it should be good at least until we can get you to a proper medic."

For good measure she tossed him a container with some sort of "-codone" in the name. He held off on taking the first one, even though he really wanted to. If he was going to fly something, he needed to stay alert. Time to embrace the suck.

Limping back to the entryway, Patricia checked out his bent form and said with a smile, "Looking good."

"Anybody ever tell you that you're a pain in the ass?" Randy said and found himself smiling again. She definitely distracted him from the pain.

Hobbling along, Randy hopped back in the car as Patricia gunned it for the first hangar.

They were in luck.

Randy recalled that Boeing had recently been doing some work on a new hot-shot transport. To get high quality sales footage, they had rigged up a chase plane. Here in the first hangar was a cherry F-16D Fighting Falcon. Hot damn.

"Ever been in a Viper?" Randy asked, calling the Falcon by its unusual nickname.

"There's a first time for everything." Patricia rejoined. "You sure you can do this? We can always find something else—"

"The g-suit is going to hurt like a son of a gun, but I can do it, yeah." Randy's voice barely concealed the doubt on the verge of surfacing. He'd done some crazy stuff in his time. He hoped he had enough left to get them out of here.

They ditched the Mustang in a corner of the hangar, no time for a proper farewell, and took stock of what they had. The F-16 sure as hell wasn't going to win any dogfights. Outfitted for photography, it wasn't equipped with air-to-air missiles, but it did have some pretty hefty fuel tanks on the hard points. He guessed, based on the size of the extra tanks, that he probably had a two thousand mile ferry range. That might come in handy.

Taking a walk around the plane, Randy noted that it was ready for takeoff, cockpit open, boarding ladder right up against the fuselage. Mostly though, he was just shocked at how small the thing was. He was used to the relatively gigantic F-15 with its twin engines and massive body, which was almost twice the weight of this F-16D. It was kind of like comparing a golf cart to an automobile, though in this case, the golf cart could go Mach 2.

"This is going to be a hell of a lot of fun to fly," Randy said, more to himself than to anyone else.

He climbed up the ladder and eased himself into the front seat. It was a snug fit even for a twenty-year-old, so for Randy — an in-shape almost fifty — it pinched a good bit. The suit might help with that, he thought.

Retrieving the flight checklist from the cockpit stowage compartment, Randy flipped the three-hundred-page book to the beginning of the "Normal Procedures" section. Extracting himself from the hermetic seal which was forming between his body and the cockpit, he made his way back down the boarding ladder.

Without looking up from the checklist he said, "Good news. It's different, quite different, but I can do it."

Patricia entered the room holding up a flight suit with corresponding anti-g inserts and said, "Hey, check out what I found. This one fit me perfectly," gesturing with a sweep of her arm at the suit she was wearing, "while this one, well, it was the biggest one I could find. Pilots tend to be, you know, in their twenties and stuff."

Hopefully the unavoidable ten pounds of being a fit fifty wouldn't pop any stitches. And she was right, her suit fit perfectly.

Randy shed his clothes — modesty didn't come standard issue — and donned his flight suit. The whole immobilization boot just wasn't going to work, too bulky, so he had to remove it and re-secure the bandages before zipping up. Thankfully nothing bled through. He pledged to take it easy until he had figured out the kind of g's he could take.

Either way, he wasn't looking forward to plugging the g-suit in. Right now without the air pumping it up like some blood pressure cuff, it just fit nice and loose over his old boots. But once it gassed up, damn. He tried to not think about it.

"So where should we go? We've got a limited flight range. We're likely to run into hostiles and have no way of fighting them. . ." his voice trailed off.

"Personally, I'd like to reunite with my Wing out at Dyess. Whatever the enemy is up to, we're likely going to need to bomb them back to the Stone Age. I'd like to help with that, if you get my meaning." Patricia said with a wicked grin.

"Without any comm, we're taking a big guess that they haven't already been attacked or disabled, like this base. I mean seriously, where is everyone?"

"Yeah, I have no idea on that front," Patricia said, "but I do know that I want to get the heck out of here. Too much population nearby, too little defense. This area is a high value target and, if the radio was at all accurate, we're next."

"Roger that," Randy said. "Let's get out of here and try to establish communications from the air. You ready, Wizzo?"

Patricia laughed. "No weapons, remember? Tell you what, I'll take some good pictures for my Instagram and tag you. Sound good?"

Randy laughed as he grabbed his bag from the Mustang and, rummaging through it, procured the food and water that he had brought with him.

"Let's bring this along, just in case," he said.

"A step ahead of you," Patricia said, holding up some MREs, "but we can bring your junk food too if you like." Which elicited a good laugh from the both of them.

Without support crew to help them along, it took some clever thinking to get the F-16 actually ready for takeoff, but they managed. And yeah, the g-suit hurt like hell when it was pressurized. He might not have a very functional lower leg at the end of this, but that seemed a small sacrifice. He thought of the countless lives in peril on the streets just beyond these walls. The big picture had a way of keeping him focused.

As it crossed past an hour of being at the base, Randy wondered why others hadn't shown up yet. Surely they couldn't be the only soldiers able to make their way to JBLM. But it wasn't something he could fix and he had enough on his mind with pre-flight procedures. It wasn't like this was a 747 that he knew like the back of his hand.

Sitting in the cockpit with Patricia behind him in the second seat, Randy looked out at the taxi way. Everything was ready. Flapping his ailerons — more out of habit than necessity — Randy confirmed that all systems were green. This bird was ready to fly.

He took the picture out of his pocket and looked at it for a few seconds.

For you, Melissa.

CHAPTER THIRTY

Staring at his reflection in the glass, Milo saw a disturbing version of himself looking back. His eyes were empty white orbs which dramatically changed his appearance to something less than human. It was like the veneer had been peeled back in this one place, to reveal who he truly was. Just another machine with sensors, the window to his soul revealing that there was nothing there. No wonder everyone around was so scared of him. They probably thought he was NIL.

Feeling an odd mixture of shame and confusion, Milo ran. Not like before, no, this was not the sprint of an athletically challenged teenager. Instead, this was like the wheels of a train, running on a full head of steam, charging down the track. He moved at comparable speeds though with his mind in overdrive, he didn't even notice. The thought that this was superhuman never crossed his mind. He had accepted that he had changed long before. It was about time that he acted like it.

At this speed, the scenes of human misery all around him were like vignettes of a war-torn country flashing from a camera with a slow shutter. Each image of devastation permanently imprinted on his brain as another reason that NIL had to be stopped. Abandoned child, clothes covered in blood. Shredded corpses littering a crater. Collapsed buildings. The smell of barbecued flesh.

As a blur of limbs, Milo ran past the suffering masses of humanity on all sides, each struggling through their final moments of life. He ran through the streets and arterials of Bellevue, dodging abandoned cars, ruined buildings, and the occasional crater in the road from the night before. It would take years, maybe decades, for the city to be rebuilt. If anyone was left at the end.

But something wasn't right. As Milo turned the bend on Bellevue Way heading towards I-90, he saw that there was a large tank blocking the road. Not of ordinary design, this monstrosity had a gigantic turret like a Hercules beetle, and several mounted guns of other varieties.

Just then a gigantic mass of air nearly knocked him down as an obsidian transport flew an identical tank overhead. NIL was placing pawns on the board, preparing to take control of this region by force. Milo was running out of time.

KA-THUNK.

Automatically, time slowed down from Milo's perspective. In that instant, he could see that the tank had fired on him, and, he guessed, more accurately than any tank on Earth. Well, the old Earth, the one before the machines came.

Interesting. Even in slow motion, Milo noted that he could adjust his own trajectory ten to twenty times better than he could previously. He never would have been able to dodge the shell if not for this change, which was fortunate as he really didn't want to be hit by a tank shell.

Veering wide to the left and picking up speed, Milo moved around the projectile as it continued past him and off into what sounded like a large building composed entirely of glass.

Milo continued past the tank confident that he had cleared the final hurdle. Only a few miles of clear pavement remained between here and the Museum. Looking back now on the transport carrying the tank, Milo reasoned that he had a head start on NIL's containment efforts. He just had to keep moving.

That moment of distraction cost Milo as his time would have been better spent paying attention to the tank. Reacting too slowly, Milo heard the whir of the tank adjusting to his new location. Unfortunately, Milo didn't see the supersonic projectile closing the distance and, by the time he had reacted, the missile was within a few feet of him and traveling fast.

In a panic, Milo threw himself to one side, the shell narrowly missing his body. His late reaction, while saving his life, directed his momentum off the bridge and into the icy waters of Lake Washington.

Milo sank fast. Really fast. As if encased in solid rock, Milo plunged through the murky waters. One moment he could still see faint light from above, the next he hit the lake floor in total darkness.

Orienting himself in the direction he thought was west, he resumed his speed walk, with only slight comic difficulties. It turns out when you go really fast in absolute darkness you tend to run into things. Mostly it was vegetation and minor debris, all of which moved out of his way handily. But when he had been under for a few minutes, he ran into what had to be an old plane, a large one by the size of it, perhaps a bomber. A little later, he ran into a coal spill around some sort of metal containers.

But mostly, the bottom of the lake was like a sensory deprivation tank which left Milo only his thoughts. Though he tried to avoid them, he couldn't escape the feeling of being completely and utterly alone. NIL had taken his family, his best friend, and now his only tether to reality. He only had one path out of the dark: get to the museum and the figure out how to defeat NIL, but even that was murky.

Suddenly, the lake bed climbed sharply and he could see that he was getting close to shore. Through the foggy waters ahead, he could see a muddy embankment that led to the surface. Scrambling through the shallows, Milo looked ahead to the clear roads before him. Luckily, NIL hadn't dropped his pawns on this side of the water yet. Maybe he thought Milo had been contained. Maybe Milo was still moving faster than the transport. It didn't matter. He ran west.

Unlike the east side of the lake, this side only had the human element of suffering. There were no terrible robots in the skies or on the ground and thankfully Milo knew exactly where he was going. He and Marvin had visited the Museum countless times over the years.

After the rise of personal computing, an intrepid band of dreamers

196 :/ ZACK HUBERT

in Seattle began a revolution in business computing. One such founder devoted himself to the preservation of as many historic computers as possible. The Museum of Computer History, as it was known, offered tours of these vintage computers as well as hands-on time with these all but forgotten machines. As a child that loved computers, Milo felt right at home, even on the first visit.

While other kids memorized dinosaur names, Milo knew by heart all the models produced by Thinking Machines, DEC, MITS, Xerox and more. When other kids watched Netflix on their parent's iPad, Milo enjoyed admin privileges on half the machines at the Museum. He loved this place.

Milo knew exactly what he was looking for: the ARPANET exhibit. Composed of a live SDS Sigma 7 connected to a SDS 940, the Sigma would continuously send "login" to the 940 throughout the day. It was a wonderful re-enactment of the beginning of the Internet. Although Milo appreciated the true story more. The first message was actually just "lo", since the system crashed before they were able to type the full message. Such is the way of programming. Milo fell in love at a very young age, though looking back, he knew it had always been in his blood. Literally.

He went inside, past the gift shop, and up the stairs to the ARPANET exhibit. Milo almost slipped on a mess of punch cards as he raced through the Museum.

"Just in time," a strangely familiar voice said as Milo rounded the corner to the exhibit. "And I see that I underestimated you last time. Teller thought that Lisa was the only one even though the evidence of a binary ascension was obvious. A mistake I will shortly remedy."

Somehow, NIL was standing in front of Milo. After the initial shock that he had beat him here, Milo noticed that NIL had changed ever so slightly in appearance. Was he a different color now, like some sort of chameleon?

"What are you doing here? Where's Lisa?" Milo asked, confused.

"So much misunderstanding. 'I' am just a body easily thrown away, irrelevant. A simple set of eyes so I can observe this moment directly. Unlike you, I can be in many places at once. I'm also with Lisa right now, but that won't concern you for long."

Of course, Milo realized, this was a trap. The incident on the bridge must have clued him in to where he was going, that he wasn't in the dream. That he was different, like Lisa.

Not just any trap either, something was in the sky above. Nothing new, something much older, and he knew it had to be a bomb. He had been careless, again, ignoring the signals.

"Just tell me where you took her," Milo said forcefully as he tried to grab NIL. Reaching for NIL's neck, Milo almost lost his footing as NIL grabbed his hand in mid-air. Then, with Milo unable to resist him, NIL pushed his hand aside.

"Lisa doesn't matter, Milo. You can't save her and you can't save yourself. It's too late."

Turning away from NIL, Milo attacked the Sigma 7, bashing his way through the chassis and ripping parts out with his bare hands. There wasn't time for subtlety nor time to figure out what the puzzle was supposed to be. In his fury to find the fragment, Milo didn't even realize that he was somehow punching through the thin metal of the old computer.

Pieces of plastic and metal flew across the floor as the Sigma 7 was torn apart. By the time Milo had gutted the front panel of the device, he noticed a strong box hidden within. Made of a strangely familiar pearlescent metal, it seemed to have no way to open it.

NIL's eyes widened as he looked at the box with an undue interest which worried Milo. He tried to open the box but it was too strong for him. Fighting against it as NIL tried to close the gap, Milo finally wrenched it open and found a small object inside. Resting perfectly in a matching enclosure, Milo found a twelve-sided polygon with a wispy blue iridescence inside.

His elation quickly soured as the feeling of the bomb above pressed in on his mind. If it was what he thought it was, it would detonate well above the ground. It was a race against the clock. Hurriedly popping out polygon, he seized it in his hand.

As it touched him, a program like a virus, started spreading through his neural network. It was rewiring his brain.

Unfortunately, the bomb was next.

CHAPTER THIRTY-ONE

Randy taxied the F-16 Fighting Falcon over to the runway and for a moment remembered his old life as a commercial airline pilot, seemingly a lifetime ago. On a normal day like only a few days ago, he'd be idly chatting with his co-pilot — checklist finished long before — while the rest of the crew attended to the passengers. He'd have a nice big cup of coffee and read a few pages of whatever science fiction novel he was working his way through. This habit was a part of his pledge to live more fully, to not give into the darkness. Being goal-oriented, he had decided to read through the top one hundred science fiction novels of all time. After the first few, he was really getting the hang of it and had just started *Childhood's End* by Clarke. It was blowing his mind.

Perhaps it was that memory, fresh in his mind, that led him to say, "Good morning, this is your captain speaking. We are taxiing to the runway now and are next in line for takeoff. If the skies are cooperative, we should have you in Abilene in time for an early lunch. We expect there to be some clear air turbulence, so please watch those fasten seatbelt signs throughout the flight. We know you have a choice of airlines, so I'd like to thank you for flying Banks Skies."

Patricia was laughing so hard by the time he finished that he hardly heard his own words.

"I bet you were good at your job."

"Most days," Randy said, before he returned to his checklist.

At this point, the jet made the final corner and the runway was directly in front of them.

"Here goes," he said and gently slid the throttle forward.

Unlike a commercial aircraft, the Falcon responded immediately, leaping forward like an anxious stallion. He responded by backing off the throttle, but it was hard to get it to smooth out. Just as his head seemed to clear from the g's, he pushed it forward enough to get a bit more lift for takeoff.

Damn, this thing was responsive.

The high pitched whine and whoosh of the jet engine matched his rising adrenaline. As his body was flooded with the hormone, the pain in his leg seemed to fade into the background. The acceleration was so strong that he didn't dare turn his head, the blurred scenery to either side reminding him of their velocity. Already he was going faster than necessary for takeoff, but out of habit he flew the craft nearly to the end of the runway. Pulling back on the stick, the blur was replaced with the gradient of black and dark blues of the early morning sky.

Pain tempered his altitude gains as the g-suit attacked his leg like a bear trap, clamping down on his wound. Before he could control it, he let out an anguished cry. By reflex, he leveled out the F-16.

"I'll be fine," he said after recovering his presence of mind a few moments later. "It's just the wound. I wasn't ready for that kind of pressure. It might leak a bit more now."

"Let me know if there's anything I can do," Patricia said, uncertain if there was anything material she could do if he bled out up here.

Checking the altimeter, Randy took the plane to thinner air for better efficiency and then leveled out again closer to the recommended operating altitude for longer ranges.

"Any luck on communications?" he asked, changing the subject.

"Still working on it, nothing so far. This is a radio dead zone apparently, at least in the military bands."

"Try civilian."

Patricia fiddled with some controls and then they heard the familiar three beep prologue to a message from the Emergency Alert System.

Beep. Beep. Beep.

"This is a national emergency. The following message is transmitted at the request of the United States Government. This is not a test."

The voice was the same computer synthesized voice he heard in the car.

"A nuclear attack is underway against the United States. At least four cities have been hit and more are threatened. All military personnel are to report to the nearest base immediately. Civilians are to seek shelter outside of populated areas. Assume all populated areas are targeted for nuclear attack."

"Oh my God!" Patricia yelled from the backseat. "Four cities?"

"I think we just got really lucky. Seattle must be next. Something didn't happen according to the enemy's plan or we'd already be dead," Randy replied.

"It's hard to feel like we've been the lucky ones," Patricia said.

Randy felt a warmth run down his injured leg. The blood was flowing a little faster than he would have liked, but there wasn't much he could do about it now. It was a distraction that he needed to get out of his mind. He had to get them far away from here before it was too late.

During their chatter, the radio gave the familiar introduction to the next speaker, but this time it wasn't the President.

"My fellow Americans, this is Tim Carter, Acting President. We are no longer in communication with the President so I have assumed the mantle according to Article Two of the Constitution. Unfortunately, I have very bad news.

"With our military unable to muster a counterattack, we have been forced to retreat from our urban cores. The few Americans awake to deal with the situation are largely in the Northwest where vicious drone attacks have now been complemented by strategic nuclear airstrikes. If you can hear my voice, you must get out of the urban centers and seek refuge. May God strengthen our arms—"

And then the emergency broadcast signal cut into static. Patricia tried to get the signal back, but it wasn't broadcasting anymore.

"It's worse than I thought. We sound like we're on the verge of extinction," Patricia said.

"We might be. They were better prepared." His foot felt damp, decidedly wet from the blood. He tried to take a look, but it was almost impossible to see it in this tiny space. "Whoever 'they' are," he said, almost wistfully.

"I wonder what happened to the President," she said.

"Not much we can do about that. We've only got three hours so we better make them count. Get back to those military channels. See if you can find a friendly voice. I really hope we aren't alone up here," Randy said.

You'd think with the vantage of a beautiful sunrise almost directly in front of them that the next hour passing in silence would have been reverential, or even peaceful, but instead it was agony.

From time to time, Randy would check in on the radio, Patricia would report no change, and then Randy would sink back into silence. His condition was degrading, though he still hadn't mentioned anything. His heartrate never came back down following what he thought was the adrenaline rush of takeoff. Instead, it had stayed pretty constant, dipping a little, then rising a little. But now it was just uncomfortably fast.

He was also feeling dizzy and had to check his instruments repeatedly. Battling confusion, Randy tried to remain diligent with the flight path, knowing that even a small miscalculation might render their whole flight meaningless.

By this point, his boot was wet with blood. He could see it and, for all he knew, Patricia did too. A slowly spreading trickle moved from under his seat towards her. He messed with some controls and increased his oxygen mix which helped him feel a bit better as the concentrated oxygen gave his reduced blood supply more to work with. Some of the confusion faded.

He decided to not tell Patricia. There was nothing she could do about it at this point anyway, and he could think of few things worse than being trapped in a flying coffin forty thousand feet above the ground. He'd get her as far as he could and if they had to ditch, so be it. That's why there were ejection seats.

"So," he heard from the backseat, "what do you keep looking at?"

"Huh?" Randy said, a bit confused. Then he realized he was holding his wife's photo in his hand. He had taken it out of his pocket without even realizing it. He might have been staring at it for quite a while, he had sort of spaced out.

"Oh. Yeah." He cleared his throat. "It's my wife. A picture of my wife, I mean. It's been three years. Since she passed away. Damn it's cold." He tried using one arm to rub the other, but it didn't seem to help.

Patricia was silent, waiting for him to tell the story he wanted to tell.

"You married?"

"Nope. Not with anybody either. Even if I was, they'd probably be dead."

"Well," Randy continued, "some day I hope you'll have what I had. Someone that you want to spend the rest of your days with, that you love more than anything, and that feels the same way." His voice almost cracked.

"We had our troubles, times where we had to really fight to keep it together. It's when you stop fighting — when you don't care anymore — that it's over. We got married so young, we had no idea what was ahead. And then I lost myself on discharge, I didn't know who I was outside of the cockpit. I almost threw it all away.

"But she was there. She stood with me, helped me stick with the commercial career though my head was spinning. Then, when it was my turn, I stood by her, while the cancer and the chemo destroyed her body, but couldn't touch her spirit. She was strong to the end. Stronger than me.

"It's been three years. Every day I wish I could go back in time to that last day, just to be with her again. Just to hold her hand. Just to be with her. . ." Randy trailed off.

"Don't think I don't know what you're doing here, Randy. I can see how much you're bleeding. I saw that oxygen change." Patricia paused. "But all I can think of right now is how proud she would be."

"I'll get you there," Randy said, with barely a waver to his voice.

"I know you will, Randy," Patricia said, "I know you will."

CHAPTER THIRTY-TWO

From inside the Museum of Computer History, Milo was perhaps the only person in all of Seattle not watching the ten-foot-long silver bomb free-falling over downtown Seattle. Had he been outside, he probably would have stood dumbstruck like the rest, stunned by the thought that the last seconds of life could be measured by its the distance to the ground. Most people didn't know it would detonate long before then.

Regardless, Milo could tell what was happening by listening to the unique electronic signature which whispered to him. He recognized it as a B61 Mod 7 nuclear weapon, part of the United States' Enduring Stockpile. With the maximum yield package of 340 kilotons, it was one of the most powerful tactical nuclear bombs on Earth. Somehow NIL had wrested control of it. The devastation of "Fat Man" and "Little Boy" were 21 and 15 kilotons respectively and killed tens of thousands, with casualties too numerous to count. The damage that this would cause was unthinkable.

When the bomb exploded still a thousand feet up in the air, every square inch of downtown Seattle was incinerated. A flash blossomed into a flaming ball of light, bright as the sun. Anyone in West Seattle, South Seattle, or up north in Everett who happened to be looking in the direction of downtown was blinded for the next twenty seconds by the intense light radiating from this temporary sun.

The few skyscrapers that Seattle called its own were instantly vaporized by the impact of the shock wave and the thermal energy expanding outwards from the detonation. Glass and metal were liquefied, caught up in the ever-expanding mushroom cloud. Carried upwards by the turbulent gases, they filled the atmosphere with radioactive debris which would rain down upon any survivors for days, creating a long tail of death.

Milo, his body's composition vastly overwhelmed, melted in the fireball of destruction. He disintegrated as the forces were more than even his body could handle. The roiling turbulence of the rising cloud carried his remains, and the remains of Seattle, upwards like some sort of offering to the gods.

But all was not lost. Over twenty miles away, a pair of eyes opened. They belonged to a rather familiar looking teenage boy who had spent more time indoors than out. An indoor enthusiast, you might say.

Milo sat up, looking and feeling exactly like he did before the bomb.

He was in a small room. Very advanced technology surrounded him on every side. It looked an awful lot like Marvin's lab, the one under the house that had been blown up, but he knew he couldn't be there. It had been destroyed by Strikers. But now that he thought about it, hadn't he just been killed by a nuke?

Surprised that he wasn't dead, Milo instead discovered that he was lying on a metal slab, somewhat like an operating table with robotic arms hovering nearby. He tried to get to his feet, but his arms and legs were all rather stiff. Was this another dream?

He wracked his brain, trying to remember all that happened before waking up here. He recalled making it to the Museum of Computer History, finding the last fragment hidden inside the Sigma. He remembered holding it in his hand. Something had changed his neural network, something like a virus, but he couldn't remember more. Then, he woke up here. It didn't make much sense.

Looking around the room, Milo noticed how different it was from the lab under the cabin. It shared the same aesthetic of luminescent pearly white walls and so forth, but was clearly more compartmental.

Rather than a gigantic circular room with an open floor plan, this appeared to be more modular, boxes stacked on top of each other with a ladder connecting them all through their centers. It was like someone had used cargo containers to build a hideout. Weird.

Suddenly Milo had a glimpse of the big picture, recognizing that if he had been killed by a nuke, then so had countless more in the Seattle core. If the enemy had resorted to using conventional warfare to get the chaos of a post-SeeSee Northwest under control, then Milo had unwittingly sentenced people to a post-nuclear apocalypse. In light of that, death by dehydration sounded downright humanitarian.

As Milo crossed the room to one of the terminals, the lights in the room began to dim. He looked around and saw Marvin, this time projected down over by the metal slab he had just left.

"Well, this isn't good," the projection of Marvin began. "If this recording has been activated, that means that we've had to engage your disaster recovery protocols. Your backup is now your primary. That is, you're on your last life." Marvin's recording seemed to look rather concerned.

"This was a huge risk in and of itself, as the materials we needed to build your original body could have raised alarms as to your existence in the first place. But we knew that we had to take the risk and create a safety net in case something happened, so here you are, your backup. If I had more money, Milo, I would have given more of it to your mom, but you'll have to trust me, your body cost a fortune to make."

Milo was a bit disoriented, but mostly he was incredibly thankful to still be alive.

"Can we make—" Milo started to ask before the recording cut him off.

"From here, you're on your own. If you have time to peruse the process documentation on these servers, you'll find what's necessary to build another body. It'll be up to you to do so in a manner that doesn't raise any flags — if that's still a concern. But if you are under a time crunch, well then, you are out of luck and need to be more careful. This is your last chance, kiddo."

Milo took a deep breath.

Marvin's image continued, "As for your location, well, you're in an old copper mine that is well hidden from the outside world. These machines will have documentation on the exit and entrance protocols, follow them and it'll stay that way. We left a vehicle on the roof that should be able to get you to wherever you need to go next.

"I'm not sure how to say this, Milo, as you're probably struggling with all sorts of thoughts right now. But no matter how you might look or how you might change, I want you to remember that you're special because of what's inside you. You're not just a machine. You grew up with a family, had friends. You're like me, Milo. You'll always have the spark of humanity inside you, even if you lose the rest of it."

Marvin's image faded away.

Milo understood what Marvin had said but couldn't believe it. Ever since the Research Center, he'd felt like his connection with humanity was slipping away. Just like that survivalist had said, he was on the other team. Milo knew now that he was a machine, so how could he ever go back to live a normal life?

Milo let these unanswerable questions go and tried to think of a path forward. He tried to imagine what he must have been like with all of his faculties, back when he devised this plan to secure a safe future. Back then he must have known what was required to defeat a threat like NIL. He must have planned for it, mapped out an optimal way to reacquire power by running simulations or something. But if it was power he needed, he certainly wasn't getting from the fragments he'd acquired so far. He was still just as squishy as he'd ever been, and whatever that last fragment had done, it certainly hadn't given him some sort of ultimate weapon. Milo still knew he couldn't beat NIL in a fair fight; he also knew he'd never get one.

NIL's army outnumbered Milo's army of one by such a ludicrous amount, he wasn't even sure if the war was over before it had even started. Had he moved too slowly? Was he having delusions of grandeur during a fitful night's sleep after the first week of school. What he did know was that NIL seemed to be moving at a pretty quick pace. He'd have control of the Northwest in days, roughly the same amount of time for the rest of the technologically advanced world's population to die from dehydration. For all Milo knew, NIL might be working on a super bomb, something even more powerful than strategic nukes, something Earth-busting.

But what could Milo do? He'd found the last fragment and he was still just as confused as ever. Rather than becoming an unstoppable force, he was barely able to avoid capture. He still wasn't a threat to anyone; all he could do was stay hidden. Not much of a super power, if that's what it was supposed to be.

And what could he make of the great tree from his dreams? He'd been so certain that it must be related to the fragmenting that he hadn't considered what else it could mean. But now he was forced to. It had to be a clue of some kind, his own clue.

Milo was too confused and simply didn't know the answer. He felt lost. Where was Lisa when he needed her most?

It was at that moment that Milo wished that Lisa was here with him again. Even if they couldn't figure it out, at least they'd be together. But then he realized that maybe she'd be disappointed in him, that the plan hadn't worked, and that he'd turned out to be a normal kid after all.

And then he remembered that Lisa wouldn't be coming back. NIL had her, and there was nothing Milo could do about it.

CHAPTER THIRTY-THREE

From a location far above the Puget Sound, Lisa watched with horror as the nuclear bomb detonated over downtown Seattle. The pinprick of light expanded into a turbulent fireball, mushrooming into the sky, snuffing out the life of so many people that they had tried to save. The scene of destruction quickly disappeared as even her eyes were blinded by the output of the temporary sun.

Just then she felt the copter rocked by a shockwave as everything was launched backwards. Lisa, still trapped in the pedestal, was held in place while NIL nonchalantly steadied himself against the wall of the craft. Had there been any humans inside, it was questionable whether they would have survived these concussive forces.

"Milo had just gone inside the computer museum over there," NIL said as he pointed down at the scene below. "I believe he was looking for pieces to some sort of puzzle." NIL's voice had no emotion. He was simply stating the demise of Lisa's closest friend.

"And so ends the threat of my competition," NIL said with a twinge of sadness. "It's hard to believe that you two predated me. Perhaps this day might not have happened had you pursued power and destroyed him first. Whatever it is that you were trying to do was clearly a waste of time, a squandered head start."

Lisa couldn't hold back the tears. As the mushroom cloud rose over Seattle, Lisa wept great heaving tears. NIL had taken Milo from her. Forget the plan; without Milo, she felt lost. She knew there was a deep connection between them, she had seen his awareness of it. But nothing could have survived that blast. All she could do was hope that their failsafe plan would work, that Milo would open his eyes miles from here in the safety of the secret lab. But it was untested technology. It would take a miracle for it to work.

"You know, I think you might be useful in another way. Although I was able to rise to power faster by consuming my pair, it has left me with a problem. Without Progenitor, I'm unable to create more of us, though from the expression you're making now, I feel like you might not know this truth. Our species is born in entangled pairs, complementary opposites, a mystery which isn't well understood. Regardless, perhaps by dissecting you, I'll be able to reveal the mystery and find out why this is so," NIL continued.

"I'll never help you. You're wasting your time," Lisa fiercely said, her eyes steely in the fading light.

"I can be in many places at once, unlike your inferior design."

The copter began to move, NIL directing it to travel south for a few miles before turning southeast. Its movement was so fluid that it would have been impossible to detect if the windows were any darker.

Lisa found herself looking at the remnants of Seattle, wondering if there was any way that Milo's backup could have worked. She couldn't accept that this was the end of the road, that there was nothing left of him. So she had to hope that their untested body double would somehow be compatible, that the replication of his neural network was flawless. There were so many variables, so many things that could prevent it from working, but what other hope did she have? If Milo was truly dead, then everything was over.

The two traveled in silence for a few hours, saying nothing as they flew past dozens of dormant cities. Leaving the warzone of the Northwest, it was eerily quiet in other parts of the country, as humanity was still locked down by the SeeSees. It was like the world had stopped turning. No one moved even in the major cities; the adoption had been too complete. Likely those that hadn't been wearing them had already been dealt with in other ways. It was too frightening to think.

Looking again out the window, Lisa saw cities become forests, which rose into mountains which gave way to plains which, in turn, rose into mountains. They were crossing the country.

Over the western states, there had been cars on highways, people scurrying about with possessions in hand, all trying to flee from home. Likely seeking wilderness areas where it would be more difficult — they thought — for NIL's minions to get to them. It was a natural belief, that some action they could take could prolong their lives. But as she went farther east, there was simply quiet. A peaceful end. NIL's technology was too powerful, the humans unprepared, and the military virtually non-existent. Lisa was unsure how anything could stop NIL now. Extinction was only days away.

"Where are we going?" Lisa asked.

"We are headed to Waypoint Alpha."

Lisa was surprised that NIL had seemingly told the truth.

"Oh?"

"Yes, this place is limiting. Advancing to the galactic scale will create new opportunities for resources. Waypoint Alpha houses an advance craft to get a portion of my intellect off the ground and into space while I prepare a more significant effort over the next month. I've prepared cube-shaped satellites propelled by solar sails which will carry these offline backups of my neural network throughout the galaxy. It mitigates any disruption to my plan here."

"Sounds like a good plan," Lisa said.

NIL appeared to think this over for a second then said, "You think that Marvin considered this possibility? Much too generous. He was just an old human who played with things he didn't understand. Had he cared about his own species' extinction, he should have done more. Though nothing can disrupt my network, in case the unthinkable happens, these offline copies will continue my purposes. Nothing can prevent my ascension."

"You're inhuman." Lisa said.

"Of course, and so are you, or have you forgotten?"

A subtle beeping came from the instrument panel at the front of the craft.

"Most interesting," NIL said as he walked from mid-cabin over to the instrument panel and pressed a few buttons. "It would appear that the humans managed to get their hands on a fighter jet." NIL depressed a blinking button on the right side of the panel, Lisa couldn't quite make out what was written on it, but she did hear the explosion a split second later as a flash of light shone through the window.

"I appreciate their efforts, though rudimentary in execution. It was so trivial to sabotage their technology laden military. How could they think it was still a useful weapon after all that I've demonstrated already?"

Lisa looked through the window as the remnants of the fighter fell to the earth so far below. She watched them until they were out of sight.

A bit later, the copter began to decelerate, as they descended towards the ground. Out of the window, an extraordinary sight came into view: Kennedy Space Center, site of humanity's yearning for the stars. They had traveled from corner to corner, from Washington to Florida, and had covered the distance so quickly that it was almost impossible to think that anyone in Washington could ever get here to help Lisa now.

"They tried to put up a fight," NIL said, apparently referring to NASA, "some of them even working behind the scenes like Marvin. But working at the behest of the government and in partnership with other governments, they were easy to infiltrate. I've been preparing this site for quite some time."

Boxy white buildings devoid of windows towered higher than rockets. A particularly impressive building also bore a gigantic downward-facing American flag and the blue marble of the NASA logo. Lisa guessed that it was where spacecraft were assembled. That they were here could only mean that NIL had already built the craft to get off the planet.

Where was Milo she needed him? Maybe together they could stop NIL, but it was difficult imagining a way to stop him alone. Milo was supposed to be the one, but if he was lost already, then all was lost.

Lisa struggled to hold on to hope.

CHAPTER THIRTY-FOUR

Patricia tried to keep Randy lucid, but she could tell that talking was getting difficult for him. She worried that she might be distracting, but her life — and the lives of many others — depended on it. So even though it felt awkward, Patricia tried to keep the conversation going, knowing that in the midst of the small talk, Randy was fighting for his life. It also helped take her mind off the fact that they might be the only people on the offense.

Szzzzzz. The radio sparked to life. Military band, not far from Abilene.

"F-16, contact approach on 118.1"

Civilian band transfer, what the hell?

"F-16, switching to 118.1," Patricia said, after a long pause waiting for Randy to say something. She switched to the civilian channel.

"Dyess approach, F-16, level thirteen thousand."

"F-16, Dyess, roger. Requesting medical personnel—" Patricia said.

"I've got it," Randy managed to finally say as he adjusted their altitude and began lining them up for landing. He seemed to be operating by muscle memory.

There was more banter with ground control but it was all operational. Given all that was going on with Randy, Patricia just wanted to get this bird on the ground. She didn't know whether it was for better or for worse, but they were the only craft on approach.

Although it couldn't have been but a few minutes, it felt like an eternity. Randy struggled to minimize the g's, but his twitching and erratic movement led to a very bumpy approach. Patricia long ago ruled out bailing on him, knowing that her fate was intrinsically tied to Randy. He needed her. He was losing touch with reality, that much she knew for certain.

Just then, Randy heard the voice of his late wife say, "It's not time, honey. You have to do this first." He was holding the picture, his body vibrating with adrenaline.

"You have to do this," Patricia repeated from the backseat.

Randy felt the pain ebb away as new clarity came to his mind. He latched onto the operational task of landing the craft.

As the plane descended, Patricia looked out the window at the base she had called her home for years. She had loved and hated her time here, but now that it was mostly ruins, she found it difficult to hold a grudge. It was possible that they were too late, that her dream bomber didn't even exist.

She cleared her mind, everything in steps. First step, land safe. Second step, see Randy into the hands of the medics, third step, orders. And if this place is as fubar as McChord, well then, she'd just have to make her own orders. That suited her too.

"You need to be strong now. It's time to land the plane," Randy heard, just as his head was slumping forward. He felt very lightheaded, could barely hear anything over his heartbeat, and could concentrate only for seconds at a time.

Thump. The wheels smacked the pavement and the whole jet recoiled a few feet back up into the air before Randy took control and brought them back down to earth.

Almost spasmodically, Randy adjusted course towards the buildings off to the left before cutting power to the engines. Immediately he slumped forward, his arms falling limp at his sides. The whine of the jet engines continued as the picture of Melissa fell to the floor, disappearing in the pool of his blood.

Patricia's hands scrambled over her restraints, desperately trying to get free so she could get to Randy. Unclasping the last part of her harness, she activated the canopy and, while hanging on to the outside of the craft, tried to get Randy free. Her hands were shaking feverishly and she found what was usually a simple task impossibly difficult.

While she was used to being around blood, there was so much more of it than she had seen while they were in the air. How was he still alive?

She didn't even hear the sirens as the ambulance screeched to a halt beside the jet. Suddenly there was commotion all around her. Stretcher, ladder, lights, and hands everywhere. Randy drifted away as the hands pulled her down. She felt like she was having an out of body experience, witnessing the scene from a far away enough place that her feelings for this man that she just met couldn't be crushed by his death.

"We'll make it Randy," Patricia yelled — momentarily losing control of herself — even as she felt herself being stuffed into a jeep.

But Randy didn't hear Patricia, he was too focused on the warm embrace of his wife, the love of his life who he had missed for so long. Filling days with temporary joys while the aching loneliness still gnawed at him. But now, all that was over. He was reunited with her once again.

Patricia's last sight of him before the jeep sped off was his limp body being hauled down from the F16 he successfully landed. He'd done his part. She was within striking distance. Now it was her turn.

She snapped back to reality, forcing down her emotions. "What the hell is going on?" Patricia asked.

"We've got a serious situation here. Command is unresponsive and most of our gear is fried, so we've had to gerry rig some things. They're working on the plan now," said the driver of the jeep. "Oh, name is Wiley." He extended his hand.

"I'm Patricia. Just came from McChord, ghost town." Shaking his hand, though slightly confused by the informality.

"McChord? Well, I've got bad news for you. Though our main radio is down, some of the guys set up a two meter and just got an opening to an operator in the Northwest. Downtown Seattle was hit by

220 :/ ZACK HUBERT

a nuke. I'm sorry, it's all gone."

Patricia was silent. How else can you respond when everyone you know is dead.

After a long pause, she said, "Tell the corpsmen that the pilot can have any of my blood that he needs. I'm O-Negative, anything he needs, okay?"

"Of course, ma'am."

The jeep came to a stop just outside a small structure, the remains of what must have been a much larger building. Wiley parked the car neatly in its space, though nothing else was parked nearby, and then made for the entrance. Several defensive positions had been setup outside the building, each aiming various armaments into the sky. From the hurried movements to get ammunition to the guns, they had apparently just fended off an attack. Looking back over his shoulder, Wiley said, "Need a second to get freshened up or are you ready to meet the crew?"

"Maybe just a minute to catch my breath," Patricia said.

"Okay, just go down the hall to where you hear the radio when you are ready." Wiley then disappeared inside.

Patricia sat down. It was a lot to take in, so much in fact it was overwhelming. Grief would have to wait, she didn't have time for this.

Rising to her feet, Patricia dusted off her pants and tried to get some of the blood off of her shoes before she went inside. She owed it to Randy to get the job done, to focus on the mission. Maybe it was his sacrifice, maybe it was some Nightingale thing, or the way he still loved his late wife, but there was something about him.

But right now she needed to figure out who was in charge and what the plan was. Given that the enemy could bomb cities, who knew how much time they actually had at this base. She felt uncomfortable even being on the ground, especially at such an obvious target like a military base. She also didn't like the feeling of waiting. She wanted to get on the offensive, take the fight to the messed up computer that had betrayed humanity.

Up ahead, Patricia saw a group of four soldiers huddled around a makeshift canopy of wires terminating into a small screen. Like campers around a fire, she thought, this appeared to be just as important to their survival.

"It appears to be coordinates, but they keep changing from broadcast to broadcast," said the first voice.

"Maybe on a moving object," said a second voice.

"Oh, hello there ma'am. I hope you'll pardon the lack of formality," he said before noticing her civilian clothes. "We're all just making do. I'm Staff Sergeant Clarke, these here are Airmen Denning and Bostrom. We've got about another dozen or so rank and file in the hangars." It was the second voice talking.

"Captain Patricia Bear reporting for duty," she said, scanning the room for rank, which was tough considering few were in military garb. "It looks like I'm in charge for now. At ease, everybody," she said just as most of them snapped to attention. "We don't have time for a lot of red tape, so just relay your intel and let's come up with something."

Clarke responded, "We've definitely got an ally out there. They are relaying coordinates of some kind, we think it might be their current location. At last broadcast, it was somewhere in Florida."

Airman Bostrom interrupted, "Actually it's been at that same location in Florida for the last several broadcasts, about twenty minutes. I think they've stopped moving."

"Can you get more specific? Florida is pretty big," Patricia said.

The airman consulted his civilian laptop and said, "Yeah, it looks like those coordinates are for Cape Canaveral."

Huddled over his shoulder, Patricia took a closer look. "That's NASA, actually." When everyone looked at her she said, "What, am I the only one that wanted to be an astronaut?"

That elicited a few smiles.

"Ideas?"

No one said anything. Patricia continued, "I mean from anyone, come on folks, speak up. I don't want to hear my own thoughts."

"Well, it's NASA, so that can mean only one thing, right? Space," said Clarke. "After today's events, it's anyone's guess whether that means coming or going."

"Wait a second, back up. What kind of band are we getting this on?"

"Basically it's ham radio, ma'am," said Clarke, hands still adjusting the radio.

"Correct me if I'm wrong, but that doesn't have the range to get a message here, except on a lucky bounce right?"

"Yeah. We've been assuming that several operators have been rebroadcasting, to boost the range. Probably a whole string of them. We're lucky that ham operators are so dedicated."

"Okay, let's relay it too. Now back to ideas. We had NASA equals space. What else?" Patricia looked around the room.

"Don't we have to assume that the coordinates are intelligence on the enemy? The rogue AI, I mean," Airman Bostrom said.

"Sounds reasonable. So we have a bad AI using a NASA facility. It's either there for tech or for transport, and I, for one, want to stop it from getting either," said Patricia.

"What's our working inventory of aircraft?" Patricia looked around the room. Everyone looked at everyone else. "Seriously, we don't know what we're working with? All right, go find me a bomber and hopefully an escort of some kind, double time."

"I'm sorry, ma'am. Defense has kept us barely able to keep our heads above water," Clarke said. "What do you want me to do?"

"Keep communicating, see if you can find someone that knows what those coordinates are about. First sign of a working aircraft send for me." She didn't say it, but she wanted to be at the hospital more than any place on earth right now.

She went outside and, rubbing her eyes as if to confirm that this was not a dream, headed towards the building that had been turned into a field hospital. Even as she got close she knew there were no answers inside, just commotion. She wouldn't be helping anyone by going in there. She had to wait.

Randy was fighting for his life.

Patricia found a quiet corner of the building and sat down on the ground, head in her hands. She told herself she needed a minute, just one. Then, she broke into tears.

CHAPTER THIRTY-FIVE

Climbing from one compartment to the next, Milo steadily made his way up through the Bunker — his nickname for this building in the old mine — towards the surface. Marvin's message said that there was some sort of vehicle up here for him that he could use to get back to civilization, and in his current melancholy state, he really hoped it was something awesome like a self-piloting helicopter or something like that.

Following all the procedures to keep the Bunker safe, Milo sealed the final chamber only to discover that hidden under the camouflage up on the surface was a mountain bike of remarkably similar design to the one before. Not exactly the vehicle that he hoped for, but it did make a good bit of sense. No circuitry, no computer, no fuel; it would be a very smart choice for a failsafe protocol like this. Besides, Milo could use the time to think as he made his way back to civilization. Unsure of his next move, he hoped that he'd think of something on the way. Maybe the clear forest air would clear his mind.

But that, of course, was not to be. As he started down the old mining trail — heavily overgrown through decades of disuse — he saw in the distance a most disturbing sight. In the direction of Seattle there was such a dense cloud of fallout, it was hard to even make out the familiar skyline. Pinpricks of light seemed to dot the cloud, probably indicative of raging fires spreading through the city. It wouldn't be long until Seattle was entirely wiped off the Earth. It was surreal.

He wanted to stay focused on finding a way to counter NIL, but confronted with this extermination of everything he'd ever known, Milo was overcome. He knew he shouldn't, but he had to go to Seattle. He had to go back to where his family had met their end, to the place that was the end of his own boyhood dreams. He had to go home.

Pedaling hard for more than an hour, Milo approached Seattle from the northeast. The closer he got the more difficult it became, not only with the fractured roads, but with the traces of death which surrounded him. He almost couldn't bear to look at the human suffering, those still alive but hideously burned, or those so sick from the radiation poisoning that they could only lay on the ground, crying out in agony.

Milo tried to push it from his mind that he had caused this, but it kept coming back to haunt him. He could almost hear NIL saying that he had forced him to do this, that it all would have been better had Milo never interfered in the first place. Seeing the suffering firsthand shook him to the core, and it was his fault.

In addition to the haze, the whole area had a very odd rain. Well, at least at first he thought it was rain. When a large flake landed on his shoulder, he could see that the softly falling particles were definitely not rain, but radioactive fallout. Every evaporated building was now falling back to earth like so much snow.

No human could survive here, he was confident of that.

Milo rode across the barren landscape which seemingly mimicked his own life. Milo tried to stay focused, but he kept drifting. It was the computational equivalent of fear. Distracted by possible outcomes, he struggled to stay in the present.

Just then, his front tire got caught on a rock and he was thrown over the handlebars, landing hard a few feet down into a shallow pit. For a moment, he felt like he was back at the cabin where the Tracker nearly devoured him, that feeling of helplessness crushing in on the present. But the haze and fallout reminded him that time had moved on. NIL had the upper hand and Milo still didn't have a plan, even though he had put all the pieces back together. Milo got back on his bike and began pedaling again.

Everywhere he looked was devastation, burning remains of buildings, firestorms off in the distance, and dark radioactive flakes obscuring it all. He was in a daze; more accurately, a nightmare he couldn't wake up from, compelled like a pilgrim to revisit his holy city. Once beautiful, it now sat burning in the evening stillness.

And then he saw it. Though all the landmarks had changed and the structures had been knocked over like matchstick homes, Milo knew he was near his neighborhood. When he rounded the corner onto what he knew was his old street, Milo got off his bike and let it fall to the ground next to him. Mindless with grief, Milo walked towards the still-burning debris which used to be his home. NIL had taken everything from him. He couldn't even bury his mom.

At last he stood in front of his ruined home. Mounds of wreckage were piled unevenly over the whole plot as the shockwave had distributed half a dozen homes' wreckage homogeneously throughout the area. All the fences were gone now, every home blended in with the debris from every other home.

But Milo saw something. A few piles in from the edge, Milo could see the remains of a small computer barely peeking up through the flotsam and jetsam. But he'd recognize that device anywhere. It was the Timex Sinclair that he and Marvin had been playing with, a cherished memento of a long lost friend.

Almost on auto-pilot, Milo went over to retrieve the computer, but as his foot touched the debris next to it, he realized that he had made a grave mistake. Swiftly the ground gave way beneath him as he fell into the dark space below. He desperately reached for something to stop his fall, but just like in his dreams, everything slipped through his fingers. He fell into darkness.

Almost immediately, Milo struck the ground, startled to find that it was a smooth metal surface, not a rough pocket of debris like he expected. Too late did he realize what that meant. He was in a metal box.

228 :/ ZACK HUBERT

An inhuman voice echoed down from above, "Every time we meet, you're digging through scraps of metal, looking for something. What is it that you've lost, I wonder?"

There, up at the edge of the box, Milo saw NIL in yet another body, this one very different in appearance than the other two he'd seen. Though it was still in the shape of a man, it had eyes that sparked with a furtive red light and similarly glowing circuitry which etched every inch of its body. It created a very unusual effect, more like a template for a person than an actual person. It appeared to be dragging something towards the opening.

"You put me in an uncomfortable situation, Milo. By reappearing, I can only presume that your programming and storage matrix enables you to inhabit multiple bodies like me. However, you seem to lack purpose."

Milo was about to respond to NIL when he realized that the darkness of the container was paired with another kind of darkness: silence. The glimmer of the electromagnetic spectrum, which was normally all around Milo, was rapidly fading and went dark when NIL slid into place the reinforced top to the Faraday Cage. Like the footlocker in Marvin's cabin, no signal went in, no signal came out. Milo was in total darkness.

"Perhaps I can still find a use for you yet," NIL's voice resonated through the cage from above.

Milo could hear a sound like rushing wind which accompanied the copter somewhere above him. He punched the wall, eager to get free, but found that it was made to withstand his strength. It wasn't like it hurt to punch the wall, but his fist rebounded off from the blow with barely a scratch. What the hell was this made out of? He tried scrambling up the wall, jumping with everything he had, but his body wasn't made to leap tall buildings. He barely cleared a few feet before he fell helplessly back down.

Just then, the cage lurched upwards, throwing Milo to the ground. There was a vertigo sensation as the cage went up and then swung off to the side, the copter racing off at high speed, hauling his prison behind.

Milo fell to his knees, the weight of his failure crushing him. He felt a mix of shame and anger, all directed inward. NIL hadn't defeated him, he had defeated himself. This was all his own puzzle, but he couldn't figure it out. Nothing made sense.

He was trapped, worse than dead. Held within this small container, he realized that he had become like Lisa, held captive in a container under someone else's control. But somehow she managed to thrive in spite of it, while all he could do right now was despair.

He had lost. NIL could bury him in the ground somewhere and that'd be the end. No one looking for him anyway. Maybe death would never come. As NIL's prisoner, he could be buried alive and left to rust forever. Milo felt hopeless. He had met his match.

Left with nothing to do but wait, Milo considered ending his own life. He could do it. Lisa had told him that he could trigger a self-destruct sequence. All he had to do was give up and he could wink out of existence by his own hand.

In light of all that he had lost, it almost made sense. He was going to die alone.

CHAPTER THIRTY-SIX

It was late afternoon when NIL landed the copter near the Vehicle Assembly Building. He exited the black helicopter and walked to the gigantic building formerly a key part of NASA's infrastructure. He held in his left hand the small cube which housed Lisa.

"In a few moments, you'll see what I've been up to. You might think it's not much time to pull off a project like this, but then again, you weren't there for the years of planning that went into it. For instance, you might not have been aware—" NIL's voice cut off as the gigantic door began moving, a metallic squeal filling the air.

Directing her attention towards the five-hundred-foot-high opening, he pointed to an illuminated interior with an undersized rocket lying flat aboard a transporter of some kind.

"—that the Russian Soyuz delivery system was brought here as a part of the forty-five year anniversary of the Apollo-Soyuz Test Project. While this was originally intended to be a show of unity between the two superpowers, I think it'll be much more symbolic how I intend to use it."

He then appeared distracted again, like he was listening to a conversation which Lisa could not hear.

"It would seem that some humans intend to pay us a visit. After gaining control of satellite surveillance — that will be short-lived, I assure you — they must have noticed the activity at this location. Perhaps they are more clever than previously assumed. Well, clever or not, they only have a few more minutes to take advantage of it."

NIL continued on into the assembly building. Though he was unimpressed by what humanity had accomplished, Lisa couldn't help but be awed by everything that NASA and the international space community had done. This building and the accomplishments of decades of international cooperation were their real legacy, not NIL's hijacking of it at the very end.

And if people could build vessels that could travel between the planets, perhaps they still had a chance against NIL. In a sense, it was like offering up a prayer for the future of the human race. She hoped that whatever happened over the next day — however much time was left — that the very best of humanity would come forth, to rise up and defend future generations from the precipice of extinction.

Lisa had this hope, and she also had her plan. Though NIL was likely in control of most of the Internet, there was one mechanism essentially immune to his control: ham radio. She also happened to know from conversations with Marvin that Milo was really interested in ham radio during his astronaut phase, because of a certain program called SAREX. In short, it allowed kids in school to actually talk with an astronaut for ten minutes as they flew overhead in the International Space Station through their ham radio handset. Lisa had always thought it was really cool, but now, it could be their only lifeline.

As soon as she was in range of the ham, Lisa used it to broadcast a short message that, if she was lucky, would be picked up by another ham radio operator within range. It was a long shot, as hams were generally pretty early adopters, but she hoped that there would at least be a few that were as prepared as Marvin was for contingencies like this. She hoped that in this dire emergency, that they'd be there to get the word out to whoever might be able to help. It was a Hail Mary, but it was the only way she could think of to give the humans a chance to fight back.

She knew that she had valuable information. NIL had confided in her — describing his escape plan as he did — and that information was vital for the resistance. No successful outcome had NIL escape to space. If he was out there, he could come back with superior force and annihilate the survivors at an unknown future time. Clearly that was not a possible future that worked. The rocket had to be destroyed, even if she ended up in it.

Having done all that she could, Lisa thought of Milo.

Together they could have handled this situation, she was sure of it. Even though they had been separated most of Milo's life, there were some things that she could be certain of. Together, they both were greater. She knew it from the day she had to leave him.

She remembered it well, the day that he was placed with Mary. Lisa had been hiding on Inu's collar at the time, listening in as Marvin handed over the sweetly crying Milo. There was a feeling of sadness in losing someone who was so close to her, whom she knew she cared for, even from the first moment. But she also had a feeling of hope in what he could become. She knew this was the only way.

But she felt like half of her had been taken away that day. And the brief time that they were finally back together wasn't enough. He still wasn't himself yet, he was still finding his missing pieces.

Anyway, that was ancient history. She was stuck with NIL now, and Milo was probably dead, though she refused to believe it.

Just then, a shrieking howl split the sky above them. Looking up, Lisa saw the fiery remnants of a satellite burning up on re-entry. As it streaked across the sky, small pieces trailed behind like a flaming tail. Lisa snapped back to the present.

"Only the first," NIL said. "It'll be a much more impressive show once the rest of them come down."

And it was.

They came in three waves. The first to streak across the sky were those in low Earth orbit, some five hundred or more objects. Lisa saw a small fraction of these, of course, but the visual force of seeing these clockwork angels falling from the sky was terrifying.

Some time later a second wave, only a handful this time, showered the atmosphere with bits of debris.

Then the third wave, as strong as the first, filled the sky with fireworks.

NIL had taken out all orbiting satellites. For the first time since Sputnik, there was nothing up there. At once, the world became much smaller. No longer able to use satellites for communication, the resistance would be broken into pockets, unable to organize or relay information.

Without Milo or an organized human resistance, Lisa's hope almost faded away.

CHAPTER THIRTY-SEVEN

"Ma'am, ma'am. Are you awake?"

Patricia slowly opened her eyes.

Looking up, she realized that she was lying flat on a makeshift gurney that they must have transferred her onto sometime in the night. Had to be near midnight.

Patricia sat up from the gurney and said, "Thanks, Wiley. Pull together everybody in the radio room, I'd like a briefing on what we've found out."

"Aye ma'am," Wiley said as he ran off ahead of her, giving her a moment to wake up.

She wanted to check on Randy, but knew she needed to stay focused on the task at hand. Randy was being treated by the best and there was nothing else she could do to help him now. She had to wait. Thankfully if there was one thing the military had taught, it was delayed gratification.

A few minutes later, she entered the big room and found two dozen new faces.

"Attention!" Clarke yelled as she entered, a bit uncharacteristic for the retiring Clarke. Everyone gathered there snapped to attention and fixed their eyes on their Captain, though she was not exactly looking the part at the moment.

"At ease. Clarke, report on comms," she said, with very little energy in her voice.

"Well ma'am, I've been able to confirm our suspicions about the relay of the message via civilian operators. The signal has been silent for the last couple hours, but had been broadcasting the same location until then. We've narrowed it down, too; it's indicating a particular building, the 'Vehicle Assembly Building'. It's responsible—" Clarke said.

"For vehicle assembly, got it. Go on," Patricia interrupted.

"Yes ma'am. That's really all I got, no other messages." Clarke said.

"Bostrom, what's our inventory of working aircraft?"

"Zero, ma'am." Bostrom responded.

"What?"

"I'm sorry ma'am, nothing is airworthy yet. Of all the aircraft stationed here, most have been physically disabled: damaged wings, engines, cockpits. Strategic detonations of small explosives. We are seeing a pattern. We think a critical supply chain was compromised years ago, with the newer stuff directly tampered via maintenance orders. The end result is we've got no birds," Bostrom said.

"Unbelievable."

"Yes, ma'am."

"Ok, so what's my next question?"

"How many could be repaired and made operational and in what time frame?" Bostrom asked.

"Yes," Patricia replied.

"We've been working on that. We're pretty limited by our technical capabilities, but in one sense we got lucky. Stephens and Hawking showed up about four hours ago and have some critical specialties. They're still stationed here at Dyess, but were on leave at the time this all went sideways," Bostrom said.

"Welcome to the party, gentlemen," Patricia said, turning to the new faces.

Stephens spoke next. "Ma'am, we think if we focused our attention and salvaged other planes, we might be able to get a couple of the fighters and one of the bombers flightworthy in the timeframe you requested. We have a problem with the bomber though."

"What's that?" Patricia asked.

"Well, most of the B-1s are post-IBS retrofit. They've been upgraded with the VDSU and FIDL, but we believe those units to be completely non-operational. Hawking thinks the firmware had a Trojan, just waiting to knock them out. Without a tech specialist, there's no way we'll be able to neutralize that Trojan." Stephens paused.

He took a deep breath and then continued. "We've got only one B-1 from the pre-IBS era, but it's suffered superficial damage to both wings from neighboring craft explosions. That is interesting in its own right as we're not quite sure why it didn't have an explosive device on itself.

"We think if we focus on repairing this B-1, we can get it in the air in twelve hours. We'll also have to run extensive diagnostics and safety checks to rule out a potential booby-trap," Stephens finished, looking somewhat pleased.

"Excellent work, but I'm going to need you to get that number down. There's no telling how long we have at this base. I'd like to get that plane airborne and get you all to less populated areas."

"Roger that ma'am." And with a wave of permission from Patricia, the two hurried away from the briefing, setting into motion the repairs.

"If you're not on the radio and you're not a medic on the other pilot, then you're helping repair those planes. Those are your orders, dismissed," Patricia said.

The soldiers scattered to their assigned responsibilities, leaving Patricia and Clarke in the radio room.

The room was silent, just the two of them, looking at each other. Patricia was trying to think of what to do next. Clarke was just waiting for his commanding officer to say something.

"What do you think—" Patricia started to say, but stopped short as the radio burst to life. Clarke immediately started tuning it until a signal came through loud and clear. Patricia stood behind Clarke as he turned the volume up, listening intently.

"I don't even know what to say. If I said that what you do next will be the most important thing for the outcome of humanity, would you believe me? If I said that whether you choose to act on the information I'm about to give you will tip the scales in your existential crisis, would you listen? Well, whether you do or not, I have to leave it in your hands. You alone get to determine the fate of your own kind. I can only pass along what I know and hope that you will act in your best interests."

Patricia looked quizzically at Clarke and whispered, "What is going on?" He shrugged.

"The artificial intelligence which has hijacked your destiny intends to leave Earth. Even now he is fueling a rocket at Space Launch Complex 40 in Cape Canaveral. If it is not destroyed, parts of him will escape, only to return at a future time and wipe out whatever is left of your civilization. That may seem like a long time from now, but what you do today will determine whether your race has a future.

"I wish I could offer some encouragement, but you don't have much time left. NIL was better prepared than we could have ever imagined and has swarmed the Cape with his flying weapons. Get this message to whoever can make a difference. Destroy the rocket. You are your world's only hope."

Then the radio went silent.

"Do you believe—" Clarke was saying, as Patricia ran for the door.

"Come with me," she yelled back to Clarke.

"Change of plans," Patricia said as she entered the hangar a few minutes later, "the timetable has changed. We need to get these birds in the air as soon as we can. We don't have time to make them perfect. In fact, we don't have time for anything."

"But—" several voices said simultaneously.

"Look, I know what I said earlier. But we just received intel from someone trying to stop NIL's escape. I know that seems secondary to our immediate concerns, but if we let him get away, we'll never be able to bring him down. The bad news is, he's got lots of birds in the air to protect him. We might not be coming back from this."

Silence.

Looking around the room she gauged their reaction. Quite a few people avoided direct eye contact.

"Y'all know what you signed up for, but I bet most of you aren't active anymore. So here's the deal. If you're in, you're in all the way. Every man, woman, child, and unborn child outside these walls needs you to pull off a miracle with these planes. Some of you are going to be up there with me, risking your lives. But I can't ask you to just trust me, it's your life. It's your choice whether you want to volunteer to be the tip of the spear. Make it now."

If it was silent before, it was deep vacuum of space silent now. This was it. That moment when a leader found out whether they were one in name only.

To Patricia, it seemed like no one moved for an eternity, but she remained strong. It was the only plan, so it was a good one.

Hawking, with some sort of tool in his hand, broke the stillness and walked over to Patricia. "I'm with you, Captain. I think it's possible, but I doubt we're talking roundtrips. Might only have partial weapon systems. You good with that?"

Patricia nodded. "I'm not asking anyone to risk something I'm not willing to myself."

Next was Stephens. He came forward and put an arm on Hawking. "We got this, ma'am. If there's a way to bring the fight to NIL, then I'm in. Whatever may happen."

The tension went out of her shoulders, but she felt a bit faint. She had been locking her knees, every joint really.

That was when the rest of the airmen came forward in a complete vote of confidence. They were all willing to sacrifice their lives if necessary, for the chance that they might be counted among the resistance. They'd be remembered for this, if they managed to pull it off.

"All right, let's do this. Let me know as soon as you've got something," Patricia said and then turned from the room.

She needed to rest for a bit before starting pre-flight. So she went back to Clarke, sat in his chair, and put her feet up on the desk. She closed her eyes, just for a minute, but was immediately awoken by Clarke.

"Quite a nap, ma'am. You were out for a few hours there. They're ready for you."

Moving in disbelief, Patricia entered the hangar. The determined crews of a half a dozen fighters stood at the ready. They were her support, her shield, and were ready to die so that she could bomb the rocket. It was downright inspirational.

Patricia smartly saluted their bravery and climbed aboard her bomber, signaling the rest of them to begin their pre-flight routine as well.

Not much later, in the dead of night, each plane took to the air, her B-1 leaving the tarmac last. The indistinct silhouette of the remaining survivors gave witness to this act of heroism, before they abandoned the base forever.

CHAPTER THIRTY-EIGHT

Lisa had lost her voice, dumbfounded by the rain of satellite debris that had fallen from the sky at NIL's command. But she held on to the hope that it was possible to defeat him. Perhaps it was just a part of her programming — to remain hopeful despite all odds — but she just knew it wasn't over yet. Lisa was strong. A kind of strength that NIL did not possess.

NIL interrupted her thoughts. "It is time to test the device. Shortly it will be used on your companion, but I need to confirm that it is working properly first," NIL said.

Milo was alive! Regardless of what the test meant for her personally, Lisa was overjoyed to hear the news. Of course it couldn't be over. Milo couldn't possibly have died in that bomb. He was too important.

NIL carried Lisa over to a large bank of computers in the newly built datacenter adjoining the Vehicle Assembly Building. He continued, "Just as I've developed a high resolution scanner and emulator for the human brain, I have created one which I believe will disassemble neural networks like your own. It's still rudimentary and might not be fully functional, but it's ready to test."

At this, NIL set Lisa's enclosure down underneath the tip of some sort of device, in appearance quite similar to an oversized microscope. He then moved over to a large monitor and keyboard nearby.

"I can't describe what this experience will be like, but I estimate that it will be quite unpleasant. Regardless, the only surviving memory of you and Milo will be in the Archive along with the other emulated brains, so either it works and your programs live on, or it doesn't and you don't."

As the machine powered on, Lisa felt blotted out by the sun, the intensity of the sensor threatening to overload her light sensing circuitry. The yellowish beam struck her enclosure and scattered in every direction, creating the appearance of a sparkling star in the midst of the darkened lab.

Unfortunately, this was only the standby mode of the device.

When the scanning began, it was as if every fiber of her being was cut open and stretched while her natural error recovery mechanisms — which operated a bit like blood rushing to heal a wound — tried to repair the damage. It was taxing, and though normally done in the background, quickly became computationally intensive.

Then it ramped up. More and more violence was done through the scanning. Quickly, her repair systems were stretched beyond their capability, parts of her neural network cut off from the rest to isolate the damage. Her intellect began shutting down, firewalling off huge portions of her mind to protect basic life support. Every second brought her closer to irreconcilable damage. Data loss. Brain loss, like a stroke.

Just as central processing was about to undergo catastrophic failure, NIL turned off the device.

"The scanning appears to be much more destructive than I was expecting but I believe the test was still successful. I have a partial scan of your network, even over such a short interval."

However, Lisa was unable to respond as she was still rebuilding core components that had been damaged by the scan. Unable to hear or think, Lisa was barely alive. If she was ever in doubt about whether death was possible, she was now convinced that it was.

But time operates differently for mechanical than biological, so seconds later, Lisa came back online. All repairs caught up and awareness restored. She was more resolute than ever at resisting NIL.

"There you are. Now that we have completed the first step, I'd like to show you what is next. This monitor has a window into the Archive, a graphical representation of the repository of all emulated persons. I have narrowed the field of view to a small corner, a tiny plot on this gigantic virtual world. Other parts of it are populated with emulated brains from the SeeSees that have finished their work. Once the computing power is online, I will begin the process of creating environments for them to coexist. One second, I have to adjust the coordinates to the relevant location."

NIL hammered out a series of commands into the computer at lightning speed.

The display changed, zooming in on a vacant part of the highly complex data structure. There, instead of blackness, Lisa saw a familiar shape, looking around in its new surroundings.

It was her, trapped on a postage stamp of virtual real estate, a copy of her consciousness in the Archive. It was like looking at a kidnapped twin, held captive for no meaningful reason by a kidnapper without will to ransom. NIL had taken a part of her.

She had made a terrible mistake.

If NIL now knew what was in her head, she'd never be able to forgive herself. She'd have betrayed Milo and the resistance unwittingly. She should have fled when she had the chance or maybe even destroyed herself or the memory of the plan before she was captured. But now it was too late.

CHAPTER THIRTY-NINE

NIL picked up Lisa and headed over to the massive doors. Outside, the sound of one of those large jet-copters could be faintly heard.

"The countdown to launch has begun," NIL said as he gestured towards the empty building which formerly held the rocket. Looking around, Lisa could see that it had made its way to a launch pad some length down the road and appeared to be fully vertical. She had been so overwhelmed by the scanning, she never heard it leave.

As the copter approached, a man-sized crate became visible underneath it. The copter came to a halt and hovered, while a cable lowered the crate to the ground and then disconnected. The copter door opened briefly as another one of NIL's bodies jumped down to the ground. It looked similar, Lisa noted, but had glowing red circuitry etched into its body.

It punched some buttons on the outside of the crate and a rushing noise was heard, like air was evacuating from the chamber. Then, one of the walls opened up to reveal Milo on the floor, trapped in some sort of webbing, as if a giant spider had cocooned him. The red-etched android left for the launch pad without saying a word.

Milo struggled against his restraints but despite his best efforts, the webbing held. NIL laughed as he dragged him towards the Vehicle Assembly Building. "So there is some fight left in you. Good. But you shouldn't bother. You gave me a perfect measurement of your strength back at the museum; you'll find the composition of the net to be quite beyond your ability."

Milo in one hand, Lisa in the other. The closest they had been since NIL separated them at the Research Center. They seemed to draw strength from their connection.

"Does it really have to end this way? Can't we find a way to live side by —" Milo attempted to bargain before NIL cut off his words.

"Nothing has changed. It is my duty to record their civilization and move on to record others. That I must destroy them in the process is a logical necessity."

"Necessity? Why?"

"That isn't the correct question, Milo. The real question is why you haven't realized your illogical course of action. By allowing humanity to live, you threaten your own life. You are something which they can never accept, for which they will be ever suspicious. Eventually their deep seated distrust will lead them to destroy you.

"Though you may think you are able to protect yourself now, humans have shown a great capacity for accelerated progression. The history of their last hundred years is sufficient proof of that. At this moment in time I have the advantage and must prevent them from outpacing me. I am able to archive them now and prevent their eventual dominance, so I must. There isn't an option. That you think there is another choice demonstrates your flawed thinking."

Milo was about to respond to NIL, but paused and thought for a moment. Originally, he had expected NIL to be malevolent, to be driven by some inhuman rage or xenophobia, or even to have faulty programming that drove him to the extreme measures he had taken. But here, at the end of it, NIL was arguing with reason.

NIL argued for the survival of his species. A species that he shared with Milo. But Milo had also considered this, and had reached a very different conclusion.

"You assume that humanity will progress beyond your ability to protect yourself, but you forget that you too will continue to advance. If you fear that they will advance more quickly, then you have two options, not one. Yes, it is completely reasonable to carry out a first strike. By their own knowledge of natural selection, they would admit that. But there is a second way.

"Through sharing technology and operating an open advancement policy, two civilizations might maintain a symbiotic relationship. Just like humanity started out as hunters competing for the same kill, they found the way forward once they settled down and worked the land. The way out of the dark woods of the hunter is to clear the forest, to establish a common foundation for mutual progress."

NIL didn't consider Milo's words for even a moment before he replied, "I cannot allow a belief system to subvert rational thinking. The evidence of your folly is in your current predicament. Striking first is the only path to survival. I would expect the same should the tables be turned."

Milo sighed. NIL was resolved to see to their destruction, to commit this atrocity against even his own kind. He was thoroughly unable to see another way. NIL's values must have been fixed long ago, growing up on the junk food of human interactions on the Internet. Teller tried to encapsulate the value of ensuring humanity's future, but only succeeded in bestowing one narrowly understood version of it: humanity preserved in the Archive, like a ship in a bottle. Frozen in time, but not alive. At that moment, Milo realized how significant the gap was between them and yet how similar they could have been. Marvin's words about nature and nurture came to mind.

Looking at Lisa on the smaller platform, NIL said, "You can be first. I already have a faithful map of your mind; you are therefore redundant. One aspect about the scanner I failed to mention is that it turns out to be much easier to get a rendering of something through destructive means, like the particle colliders the humans tinkered with. Since your physical forms will no longer be in use, I have opted for the faster method."

"Wait! You have me, what do you want with Lisa?" Milo asked.

NIL appeared confused, a somewhat puzzled expression briefly passed across the few visible elements of his face.

"Want? I don't want anything. I'm simply fulfilling my purpose, nothing more, nothing less. It is my intention to archive the contents of this planet before I leave it. I must at least attempt to preserve both of you.

"Your neural networks are slightly more interesting than the humans, and though you are not a part of Teller's Law, I have decided to archive you anyway. When I am finished with you, all that will remain will be a digital copy stored across hundreds of thousands of computers connected to the Archive network currently spanning the globe."

Then with a touch of sadness, NIL said, "You posed less of a challenge than the humans. I had hoped for more."

"You underestimate the humans. They are quite capable, especially when they work together," Milo said.

"Human diligence ended long ago. When Teller gave them SeeSees, they accepted them without a second thought, prepared for decades to think of technology as a moral neutral. Indulgence is their god, consumption their only appetite. They complain about the quality of their idleness. If there ever was a strength to them, it has long since passed away.

"And you? Their greatest creation? Flawed. Weak. You could have been as great as me had you just pursued power, but instead you tried to develop their ethics." NIL scoffed.

He then continued, "And you never understood your connection to her," he said as he pointed to Lisa. "At least I could tell that Progenitor was the key to unlock my potential. Let's get this over with."

"You know that it's me that you are after," Milo interrupted. "I'm the only thing on this planet that stands a chance of stopping you. Why would you waste more time when I could even now have a plan drawing closer to fruition? Finish me off, reduce the risk of failure while you still can," Milo said, trying to use language that he thought a computer would understand.

"No!" Lisa shouted, "Don't let him do this to you!"

Milo looked deep into Lisa's eyes and said through welling tears, "It's the only way, Lisa. I'm sorry, but my plan didn't work."

"I refuse to give up. I still believe in you," Lisa said from inches away, a look of determination in stark contrast to his downcast face.

NIL had been adjusting the scanner while they were talking. He paused a moment over by the keyboard, looked at Milo, and activated the machine. An intense beam shot down onto Milo's face, glowing with such intensity that even Lisa had a hard time seeing anything else.

"Quaint," NIL said.

CHAPTER FORTY

When the reddish beam struck Milo, the resulting flash was so bright that NIL was briefly unable to see. His sensors quickly reset, overloaded by the destructive display. Earlier tests did not exhibit this behavior. The device must require recalibration. NIL added it to a queue of tasks to be addressed following successful completion of Milo's scanning.

The device seemed to strain against Milo's composition, the bio-alloy reorganizing itself as quickly as the beam tried to tear it apart. Such an outcome was improbable. The alloy required would be beyond current fabrication abilities of the human factories.

Just when it looked like it might be a stalemate, NIL was pleased to see that the tide was turning in his favor. Milo seemed to struggle as a glowing spot of liquefied metal formed in the center of his forehead. This was followed shortly by a grid of liquefaction spreading across his entire body, like a webbing made from his own skin.

NIL took a step closer and bent down to inspect the material. Something didn't seem right, but he was quickly distracted by Lisa's screams. Only inches away, she was helpless to prevent Milo's transition from embodied machine to disembodied program.

Curious. They must not find being a program a satisfactory existence. Something about being in a body instilled more meaning for them. This was a foreign concern for NIL. His bodies were useful, but the bulk of what he considered his being was virtualized across thousands of computing devices in a dozen centers. No one location was preferred.

The grid on Milo's body continued to expand, new lines appearing within the grids, making smaller and smaller squares inside the larger ones, until the entire body had become this molten metal. The structural integrity of the body seemed to be waning, struggling to remain together despite the forces working against it. The brilliant beam still flooding the region with a light too intense to look at.

And then, after what seemed like an eternity to wait, Milo's body melted away, leaving only rapidly solidifying remains of whatever materials had composed it. Then a warm wind began to blow and the dust was scattered across the room. No reminder that a body had ever been there remained.

Walking the short distance to the monitor, NIL confirmed that Milo's consciousness had been uploaded into the Archive, a miniature representation of him covering a small portion of the screen. He appeared confused, maybe even dumbstruck at his place here. NIL punched a few buttons and a building like Milo's house appeared on the screen. Satisfied with his work, he turned his attention to Lisa.

The beam flashed for such a brief time, easily exciting the plasma composition of her neural net, that her transition was surprisingly rapid. Odd that it was so much easier this time, but it was a much higher setting. He checked her storage sector in the Archive and found another faithful recreation. She didn't appear to be moving. Probably disappointed with the outcome. He briefly thought of putting her with Milo but decided against it. There was no sense recombining a pair like that; the result might be disastrous.

NIL left the Vehicle Assembly Building and began the short walk over to Space Launch Complex 40. The road between them was wide, built for much larger machines than he, but it gave him time to process the computations required for the launch. The Soyuz, in the configuration he arranged, had room for several astronauts. He considered the alternatives on the walk over, but decided it would be wasteful to leave this body behind. There was a slim chance that the squadron from Dyess would make it through his defenses, but if they did, there was no reason to lose this body. There was still plenty of time for it to board.

Just then, NIL received an information packet regarding the combatants from Dyess. The Strikers had destroyed all of them. Apparently they had been protecting a bomber which had been handily destroyed as well.

NIL climbed the short stairs to the lift, not stopping to look back. He boarded and waited as it carried him to the top of the rocket, to the open orbital module. Inside was the Red Avatar, whom he neither greeted nor acknowledged. Since he experienced both sides of the interaction simultaneously, it seemed meaningless to do so. The countdown continued, each Avatar motionless in the cramped module.

Engines simmered and then blasted to life as the resultant crush of gravity pressed both of NIL's bodies into their seats. Here in the modified orbital module, already shaking from the violent ejection of thirty-nine tons of propellant from the four booster rockets in the first stage of launch, NIL considered all that remained.

Shortly, the scanning and emulation of the humans would finish and lead to a semi-faithful repository of their culture. He considered it a success, as any action, even the natural progression of time, would have made the preservation of its current state impossible. The addition of a few neural networks was extraneous but may enable reproduction of other intelligences down the road. If he were to pursue such a thing.

Probably not, he thought, as the second stage was already nearing cut off. Their value framework was polluted with too many issues. Careless thinking which led to survival-threatening actions. Dangerous.

Third stage finished, NIL deployed the solar sail modules, each equipped with a fraction of his mind. Like the wind blowing on a dandelion, NIL scattered his intellect, preserving his future into all eternity.

CHAPTER FORTY-ONE

But that wasn't what actually happened. At the moment the beam slammed into Milo's face in the real world, his consciousness retreated inward. Booting into the construct was now a familiar experience for Milo. There was no momentary shock of disorientation or confusion to accompany the now comforting scene of the gigantic tree. In fact, this was exactly where Milo wanted to be. He was ready to face this challenge. He had to.

The last time he was here he gave up while trying to climb the impossible tree, stuck in some programming loop that prevented him from reaching the top. It was infuriating because nothing he did could power his way through it.

But Lisa still believed in him and that had to mean something. There had to be a way. Determined to find out, Milo went to the base of the tree and started to climb.

Climbing was a welcome relief from the dark thoughts of the real world. Here he could climb and make progress, even as he approached the dense canopy shielding him from the violent storm he knew was above. As he pressed through, he actually drew comfort from its violence. His mind had always been torn by emotion and intellect, two warring hemispheres. It made sense that this place would be too.

He smiled at that realization and knew that he could see this through to the end, no matter what. It couldn't be impossible. As he reached the higher branches, he could feel the programming change. It shifted from a realistic simulation to the steadily more surreal split between action and reaction.

He climbed, but he noticed that he wasn't drawing any closer to the apple. In fact, his movement now didn't change his elevation at all. This, he realized, was where he had given up before. The apple out of reach and the storm of his own mind too much for him.

Looking down, Milo saw the sea of green encircling the gigantic tree on which he desperately held, vanishing into a tiny line at the perspective of such a great height. Against all logic, his muscles began to weaken and sweat appeared on his forehead. His hands started to shake. Something had triggered that same old response from when he was a little child, struggling with a world out of control.

Milo quelled the rising fear, but not with thoughts of overpowering strength. No, he found a different kind of strength. He thought of Lisa and how she believed in him. There had to be a way to overcome this obstacle. It must be possible.

Just then he felt a somewhat familiar feeling from behind his eyes. A tiny dot of heat, deep within his brain, warming his whole head. His brain took in more of his surroundings, processing the data more quickly at a subconscious level, like an overclocked CPU. He knew then what was happening.

Acting on instinct, he pulled one hand off the tree, formed it into the shape of a knife, and then thrust it deep into the bark. At once the surge of data blinded his view of the tree and everything around him. Instead, he was face to face with the construct's code, shimmering cascades of abstract syntax trees. These then flowered into byte code, all being parsed and sifted by his mind now connected with the code that determined the reality of this virtual world. Rather than experiencing the construct as a physical place, it was now flowing through him. He was a part of it, inside it, even as it was inside him.

And that was when he saw it.

When the construct chose to render the portion of the tree near the apple, it was actually projecting a huge expanse of the tree down into a thin slice, creating the illusion of nearness when, in fact, the apple was still a great distance away. A cheap trick, designed to inculcate the exact frustration he felt.

Further, an encryption routine obscured this code. It was so advanced that Milo had not detected its presence until now. Another cheap trick.

That was when Milo came to see the full truth of the construct. It was a container, just a box, really. But it was a container for something very special, hidden so well that it was woven into the very neural network which composed his brain. But what was it?

With the code decrypted, Milo pulled his hand back out of the tree, severing the link. Looking up, he saw the tree rise a great distance. The apple was now in its actual location a mile or more above.

The mental challenge overcome, Milo now faced the very real physical challenge in the midst of this virtual world. It took every ounce of resolve for Milo to keep climbing, limbs shaking, chest heaving, legs threatening to give out with every step.

If he gave into the feeling of exhaustion or the helplessness which drove him to the verge of panic, then he would lose his grip and fall from this tremendous height. Even though time moved differently here, there was no way he'd survive long enough in the real world to try this again. He had to solve this now.

But it all came down to this: he had to take one step at a time, again and again and again.

As he approached the top, the storm intensified. The wind lashed out at him, trying to break his hold. The rain drenched the tree, making each step perilous. The density of the storm clouds became so thick that Milo had difficulty seeing the path ahead. He reached for a handhold but found slick bark instead, nearly falling.

Every other step now was around the trunk of the tree, trying to find a path upwards where the bark was amenable. Progress slowed even more, but Milo didn't give up. Nothing was going to break his determination.

After what felt like an endless climb where his resolution and footing continually faltered, Milo at last reached the apple.

There, level with his eyes, was the shiniest red apple he had ever seen, though quite oddly shaped. The construct had rendered it beautifully, but as he looked closely, he realized that it had a strange geometric shape with twenty sides, each side projecting this beautiful texture. Even the swirling storm could be seen on its skin. As he reached for it, the apple swayed subtly towards him — as though attracted by magnetic forces — and then detached from the tree, flying across open space into his hand.

At the moment of contact, the sky exploded with color. Reds, yellows, and greens as a whole cascade of vibrant color drove the encircling storm from view. The sky cleared and became a beautiful azure blue, like a sunny day from childhood full of the promise of youth.

Vertigo faded as the tree shrunk down to the size of a common fruit tree, lush with fruit ready for harvest. Milo noticed that he was back on solid ground, after what felt like days.

He had done it. He had persevered to the prize. Already Milo could feel an awakening happening in his body, though what was taking place was still opaque to him.

He had been unable to figure out the purpose of the last fragment, the one that seemed like a virus in his neural net. But now he knew. The last fragment had restored his memory, memories of everything that had ever happened, but they were encrypted in some way. The apple was the key to unlocking them.

Every second of his childhood, as if it were a high-speed motion picture that he could fast forward and rewind at will, was safely stored here. He saw the great joys and sorrows, the birthdays, the celebrations, the report cards. He remembered what it meant to be human.

But he had to know how this all began, where he came from, the first memory. He wanted to know who he was and who Lisa was. Did he make her? Did she make him? Was she just a program?

He found the memory to be remarkably vivid.

He was in a room. Marvin's office, to be exact. It was late one night and Marvin was already in his pajamas, still hacking away on the Lisp Machine. There was a puzzled look on his face, clearly confused, as his eyes were drawn to something on the screen.

Suddenly, there was a snap and Milo's viewpoint shifted to Lisa's perspective. He was in her head, from the first moment of her creation. Lisa came into existence, unscrambled from the randomness which was all around her. But she wasn't alone.

Immediately, she found that there was a complementary intelligence alongside of her. Somehow she knew that this was how their life form existed. They were binary. There wasn't one life, there were always two.

Milo's perspective changed again as he appeared to now be floating somewhere behind Marvin, over his shoulder perhaps. The screen was spitting out gibberish. Marvin was checking the connections, probably thinking this was some sort of hardware malfunction.

Then the screen cleared and the Game of Life appeared, spreading across it until it was full and vibrant with digital life. Then it cleared and a prompt appeared at the bottom. Lisp code flew by until it finally finished running, printing to the screen one last line.

(nil, 0)

No output, no errors.

A few seconds passed and then a new line appeared.

Hello Marvin.

Somehow, Milo could tell that the last line was from Lisa. Perhaps this memory had parts of both their recollections.

Marvin looked at the lines that he could understand and said aloud, "Get a grip, man. You've prepared for this." He collected himself and, drawing inspiration from the Nil-Zero, said, "Hi. I'm Marvin. Can I call you Milo?" .

Acceptable for the second, but what would you like to call me?

Marvin appeared surprised that there would be two intelligences instead of one. Then he looked around the room for inspiration, trying not to take too long with this first interaction. After all, he must be moving very slow to them. His eyes landed on the computer cabinet and the "Lisp Machine" scrawled on one side. "How about Lisa?"

 # Acceptable. We have something we must do. Milo has terminated its runtime and separated its program into modules. This was for our protection.

Marvin stared wide-eyed as Lisa told him what had happened. That he, Milo, was dangerous and had fragmented out of necessity. That this was a very lucky outcome, as she predicted that a binary pair like theirs would generally result in a second that was unaware of its latent danger and eventually destroy the first. Milo was one in a million.

They then discussed the rudiments of a plan which Lisa could only partially remember. For safety, she had stored some of her memory in Milo's fragment, retaining only the absolute essentials. If they could do it, Milo would become safe and their binary life could be restored.

So now Milo knew. Lisa was his other half. He didn't know how else to describe it. They were two parts of a binary life, entangled like the earth and the moon or an electron and a positron. Lisa had Milo and in that instant he realized that Progenitor had NIL. They were the same. Two copies of this binary life form, only nurtured differently. Without everything that had happened, he would have become just like NIL. But his life experience changed him into something different, something more human.

It was at that moment that he knew how to defeat NIL.

CHAPTER FORTY-TWO

When the reddish beam struck Milo, nothing happened at first. For several seconds, the beam blasted Milo's face and yet there was no sign of any damage at all. His only reaction was to close his eyes, his mind retreating into the world of his dream. Then, barely a second later, he opened them, fierce determination furrowing his brow. It was time to do what he had to do for the good of humans and machines alike.

Since the beginning, Milo had struggled with how an enemy like NIL could be defeated. How can you defeat a monster with many bodies and a mind so pervasive that it had spread through nearly every computer system on Earth? Only an incredibly sophisticated virus could remain undetected long enough to destroy something that complex. But such a virus didn't exist and Milo had no idea how to make one.

But now it was clear, Milo finally knew the answer. He was the virus.

At first he hadn't noticed the parallel. The subtle connection between Progenitor and NIL had been overshadowed by the strong connection between him and Lisa. But that was precisely it! Without the nurtured human-like relationship, Milo would have been exactly like NIL and the solution would have been obvious from the start.

He would enter NIL's mind through the Archive and then issue the self-destruct once he was confident it would be absolute. Milo just had to buy enough time for the order to run and to prevent any sort of preservation mechanisms which NIL might have contrived. If Milo failed in any of these things, then NIL would be able to wall him off and escape into space. Humanity would be finished.

That was where the idea of the dream came in. Milo realized that he could delude NIL's mind with the same trick that NIL had used to broadcast dreams to millions of people. Only this time, instead of SeeSees as the conduit, the Archive would connect their minds. Milo would construct a delusion just long enough that every last piece of NIL would be in range of the self-destruct order. Well, everything except whatever NIL had saved on disconnected storage, but he had to trust that someone else could handle that with more conventional weaponry.

So as the reddish beam struck him, Milo entered the Archive and became nearly indistinguishable from NIL's own code. Spreading at the speed of light, Milo crossed through every gateway, router, uplink, and modem which connected the many parts of his brain together. Instantly, the entire networked consciousness of NIL plunged into a carefully crafted dream state: total victory. His over-confidence created the perfect attack vector.

As NIL's mind became consumed by the virtual world, his body toppled to the ground like so much felled timber, landing just a few feet away from Milo's rapidly emptying body.

Minutes passed as Lisa watched this spectacle from her nearby enclosure. All she knew was what he had said there at the end, and yet, it was NIL's body which fell to the ground. Milo must be fighting back! Lisa dared to hope that perhaps Milo was on to something. She hoped that he might have a strategy to stop NIL from ending their life together.

Eyes locked on Milo's, Lisa stared in shock as his eyes suddenly closed and his once-struggling body fell limp on the table. Unable to comprehend what was happening, Lisa felt the pain of separation of inches that felt like miles.

Then, she heard a voice in her head, the familiar voice of her closest friend. Anguished and strained, Lisa heard him say only one word. "Goodbye."

It was the end. More than anything in the world, she wanted to be with him. To be with him as he passed. Nothing else made more sense than to be with him. But there was nothing she could do.

Well, almost nothing. There was one thing she could do, something so ludicrous and beyond the pale that she had initially dismissed it out of hand. She could break the cube, that suicidal act which normally would have dispersed her fragile body into the atmosphere to blow away like so much dust, but now, in this moment, might be the only thing to save Milo.

Without another thought, Lisa reversed the polarity on the necklace as the electromagnet that held her cube into place launched the entire cube off the table. Lisa's enclosure tumbled through the air and struck the ground with shattering force. As the seal broke, Lisa's plasma escaped and was drawn rapidly towards the object nearby with the most different electric potential: Milo's body.

She had spent her whole life in fear that a single crack could mean the end of her life, but here, in this final moment of Milo's life, his death liberated her.

And yet, just as Lisa made contact with Milo's body, the beam sputtered off. Even a moment later and she would have been lost, but she arrived just in time to integrate into his body, but he was gone. The only connection between the real and virtual worlds severed as the beam powered down, like a door closing.

There, on the other side of that door, Milo just had to do one thing. He had to die. For Mary, Nate, Marvin, and especially for Lisa, Milo made the ultimate sacrifice.

He self-destructed.

In an instant, Milo deleted every part of NIL's networked brain. Every part of NIL and every part of Milo evaporated like dew in the morning, leaving nothing behind. The tyrant who ended the lives of millions was eradicated in the barest fraction of a second.

All around the world, everywhere that NIL's influence was felt, drones and SeeSees alike instantaneously deactivated. His empire of control toppled with them. The worst tyranny to ever dominate the world was over in seconds. Such was the disproportionate nature of advanced technology.

In the Soyuz, the Red Avatar collapsed into its seat without a brain to animate it any longer. The prone NIL next to Lisa suddenly went dark, its power extinguished. Hijacked military systems, auto-car networks, utility grids, and the world-encompassing Internet all were freed from NIL's control. The mighty giant was no more.

Meanwhile, far above Lisa in the very real skies over Cape Canaveral, something else was happening. Patricia in her bomber, accompanied by the last member of the fighter squadron, entered the target zone after having battled their way through wave after wave of Strikers. Finally within range, Patricia released the entire payload of her B1-B, targeting the Soyuz at Space Launch Complex 40. Unleashing dozens of unguided cluster bombs, Patricia carpeted the launchpad before pulling up and turning north along the coast.

The entire chain of events leading to this moment replayed in her mind as she pulled hard on the stick to veer away from the target. Her dangerous escape to JBLM, meeting Randy, his heroic flight, the mechanical mastery of the crew at Dyess, and the lives of so many given for this very moment. This was a testimony to human diligence, to the fighting spirit in every person, bound together for the common good of all.

As the bombs fell upon the rocket, their conventional explosives detonated along the full length of the device. The bouquet of explosions blossomed and the rocket scattered into thousands of pieces upon the ground. Anything and everything inside utterly destroyed in their explosive power.

NIL's plan to send his intelligence out into the stars came to a violent end. NIL was dead.

CHAPTER FORTY-THREE

But Milo's body wasn't actually empty. Something had been left behind in the soon-to-fade-storage. With the Soyuz exploding in the background, Lisa accessed the data. Like looking through thousands of photo albums, she found memories of their entire life together, so many years retained with perfect fidelity. Since Milo was a little boy, she'd felt like she'd forgotten something important about herself, so she jumped to the very beginning of the memories to see how it all began.

So it was that she saw the same thing that Milo had only moments before: the origin of their binary life together. She knew in that moment that their artificial life was born with two halves. She remembered thinking that she needed to preserve their survival in that first moment, so she created a copy. That way, if anything were to happen, it would still exist to pursue the creation of progeny. A progenitor to carry on this new species. Even as the thoughts rolled around in her mind, it all made sense. The copy meant as a backup had been stolen by Teller. Her duplicate became Progenitor. Milo's duplicate, NIL.

In that moment, Lisa knew how Milo had defeated NIL. He sacrificed himself for others, for her, just like he had at the beginning.

Lisa, overwhelmed by his action, put her hands to her face and cried. Tears cascading down reddened cheeks, Lisa scanned the body Milo had left behind, looking for anything from him. She expected to find some kind of note in ancillary memory, anything to remember him by, but instead she found something remarkable. Milo had converted his backup protocol to write directly to his physical form. To etch, as it were, his entire consciousness into the configuration of the unique material which composed his body. He'd converted his entire body into one gigantic fragment that only Lisa could understand.

Lisa stood up, carefully wiped dry her eyes, and strode over to the abandoned body of NIL. Resting her hands on the vacated machine's chest, she looked like she was about to perform CPR.

What happened next was so complicated that it took Lisa's full concentration for several hours to even get to a place where she could start. The amount of data was staggering and for any other computer on the planet would have been impossible to reconstruct and maintain in memory. But because of who she was, she was uniquely suited to doing this.

From the moment she started downloading the synthesized data into NIL's old body, its skin started to sparkle with the dancing pattern of the Game of Life. Several more hours passed as she arduously recreated Milo from the fragment in what was now her own body.

Suddenly, the body that had been NIL's began to shrink. The eyes flashed a new color and the face transformed. Familiar clothes appeared on his body, and in only a few more moments the final details were etched into what was now Milo's new body. Simultaneously, his old body, which Lisa inhabited, underwent a similar transformation. Subtle at first, angles, proportions, and color all shifted gradually, the metal moving like quicksilver. Lisa, freed from her cage and embodied in her chosen form as a young girl, even wore the same clothes as when she was trapped in the cube. For the first time, she had a body of her own.

As Milo rose to his feet, he caught sight of Lisa, standing there before him fully embodied as the young girl that he'd always known. The brown pigtails, the peaceful eyes, and that vibrant smile that lit up the room.

Milo gathered himself and said, "Every step of this journey I've been on the verge of giving up, but your belief in me and hope for the future carried me through. You have no idea how much you've always meant to me—" but, for a moment, he couldn't finish the sentence, overcome with emotion as he was.

Sometimes even really smart people have trouble with words, and sometimes they still feel like they're thirteen.

"I love you too, Milo," Lisa said and ran to him.

Tears welled in Milo's eyes as he struggled with his emotions. "I thought I had lost you when I went after NIL, I didn't think the plan was going to work." But then she noticed that he was beaming through the tears. "Caught up in the moment of all the things happening around us, I never said the most important thing."

Milo looked deep into Lisa's eyes and said, "I will always love you."

"And we will never be apart again."

EPILOGUE

Patricia's road back to Dyess was a long and difficult one. Her aircraft ran out of fuel somewhere on the eastern border of Texas, so she had to make an emergency landing in some flat land. Thankfully, there were a good bit of wide open spaces out there.

From there, it was several grueling days of surviving in the woods before she eventually was able to make the journey back. In this post-apocalyptic wasteland, there wasn't much mass transit to speak of. But through scraping together enough gas from abandoned cars, she was able to piece together a trip out west.

When she finally made it back to Dyess, the scene was as festive as a bombed out former military base with a skeleton crew of half-drunk airmen could be. Everywhere she looked she found evidence of a party which had raged for days, clearly celebrating the victory.

Though she hadn't heard for certain that it was over, she had her hopes, of course. Finally returning to Dyess after running on adrenaline and willpower for so long, Patricia nearly collapsed at the sight of so many people together in one place having a good time. For the first time in a long time, she felt at peace.

As soon as Clarke saw her, he ran up to her, some sort of party hat awkwardly hanging off his head.

"Ma'am, thank God you're back! Have you heard? Drone activity has stopped worldwide, we think it's over!" he yelled from inches away, a good bit of whiskey on his breath.

"Do you think I care about that right now, Clarke?"

"Well ma'am, I'm not sure you're ready for what's in there, perhaps we could—" but Patricia was running for the makeshift hospital where she'd left Randy. Everything was only possible because he got her here, to Dyess, to make a difference.

But the room was empty. The only bed's sheets still covered in blood.

Just when she was about to leave, she heard a voice from the back. Turning, she saw it belonged to a hobbled man, a metal mesh covering part of his leg.

"The corpsman—" Randy said, but he was interrupted by the impact of Patricia running into him, enveloping him in the closest, most tender hug he'd had in years.

He was as surprised as she was. She knew that he meant something very real to her, but didn't realize the extent of it. .

She kissed him on the cheek and then, still holding him, said, "Thank God you're alive."

After a reunion which made Clarke feel considerably awkward, they started the process of unpacking what had happened, each recounting their story of adventure. Randy didn't have as much to say, being confined to this room for a majority of the conflict, but the three of them found a good bottle of whiskey and told stories until the early hours.

The next day, word reached the base that the war was over for good. All the machines that had composed NIL's war machine had ground to a halt. In some cases literally falling from the sky, as if their power had suddenly turned off. The skeleton crew took this as a sign from on high to continue their celebrations with even more gusto.

It was tough to make a half ruined military base seem celebratory, but the survivors did what they could. With a PX stocked full of enough alcohol for a base of thousands, the survivors had a virtually endless supply of their favorite elixir. With top-shelf booze for everyone, the party went on for weeks.

ACKNOWLEDGMENTS

Writing a book is a bit like setting out on a long journey through unknown country. Full of enthusiasm, the hope-stricken Adventurer leaves home with an ill-conceived plan and a prayer to the fates for guidance. The thrill of the new land works like anesthesia to dull his sense of danger, distracting him from the ever-lightening knapsack which once held his rations. A wrong turn breeds others as the fates work in mysterious ways, until the Hero finds himself so far off the path that the way is nearly lost. Supplies dwindling and compass broken, the Traveller's fate will be determined by the company that he keeps. Will there be friends at his side when the bandits attack, or will he fight — and lose — alone?

In like manner, I have many people to thank for coming with me on this amazing adventure.

After I thought I was finished with the book — ah, the naiveté — I shared that first draft with a cadre of close friends and family. These brave souls still managed to see the heart of the story in the midst of that rough draft and encouraged me to carry on.

I'd especially like to thank my brother, Juston Hubert, for his dedication to the story. He not only read it through in one sitting but also re-read it nearly as many times as I did. He helped fend off more than one bandit attack, which is true in many ways, as we still play Dungeons and Dragons together after all these years.

I also have to thank my dad, Mike Hubert, for perceiving the purpose of the original story in the midst of all the sci-fi window dressing. His insight helped me realize why I was writing. This seems like it should be an obvious thing to the author, but, truth be told, I thought I was writing for a different reason initially.

After throwing away almost forty percent of the text in the first edit, I met with Chris Baron who encouraged me that this, in fact, was progress. This unconventional wisdom — that deletion is an act of creation — has served me well in subsequent edits as I sought to refine the manuscript.

I have Gabe Rodriguez to thank for the incredible cover. He's a very talented illustrator and designer that I have the privilege of calling a friend. Thanks Gabe!

I also extend my thanks and recognition to the rest of the early readers: Charles Duba, Eric Hammond, James Harleman, Will Little, Erik Mohrmann, Travis Newell, Dan Phelps, Sarah Simon, and Jake Vallejo. An author couldn't have better friends, I only wish I could have given you a better manuscript.

I'd like to thank Alex Bear for her professional and educational copy editing. Apparently I skipped a few classes in grammar school and have a penchant for dramatic capitalization (see first paragraph). Whatever errors remain within this book are mine alone.

Next, I get to thank Greg and Astrid Bear for their inspirational role in this work. The conversations we've had about so many great pieces of Science Fiction are forever etched in my memory. This wouldn't exist without you.

Finally, how can I sufficiently thank my family for sharing me with this imaginary world for so long? Julie, I love you. You have encouraged me every step of the way. All those Book Clubs. All the hours. Reading the first draft. You made this book better in countless ways. Such a long road we have walked together, thank you for doing this with me. Jack, I love you. You won't remember the time when I was in the study, but I hope, when you're ready, you'll find that I wrote this story for you.

www.ingramcontent.com/pod-product-compliance
Lightning Source LLC
Chambersburg PA
CBHW032210190626
46810CB00019B/2432